Sny X
Snyder, Keith
Trouble comes back : a
    Jason Keltner $ 23.95
    mystery

TROUBLE COMES BACK

Also by Keith Snyder

Coffin's Got the Dead Guy on the Inside

TROUBLE COMES BACK

A JASON KELTNER MYSTERY

Keith Snyder

WALKER & COMPANY
New York

First published in the United States of America in 1999 by Walker Publishing Company, Inc.

Published simultaneously in Canada by Fitzhenry and Whiteside Markham, Ontario L3R 4T8

"Flat Busted Heart"
Written by Dwight Cooper
Copyright © 1973 Dwight Cooper Music (ASCAP)
Used by permission. All rights reserved.

"Southbound Freight"
Written by Dwight Cooper
Copyright © 1976 Dwight Cooper Music (ASCAP)/Hurricane Warning Music (BMI)
Used by permission. All rights reserved.

Library of Congress Cataloging-in-Publication Data
Snyder, Keith, 1966–
Trouble comes back: a Jason Keltner mystery/Keith Snyder.
p. cm.
ISBN 0-8027-3338-7
I. Title.
PS3569.N892T7   1999
813'.54—DC21   99-26944
CIP

Series design by Mauna Eichner

Printed in the United States of America
2 4 6 8 10 9 7 5 3 1

For Kathleen, who can

make the sun seem

insufficiently orange

My sincere and not even remotely self-serving thanks to: Jason Arthur for the time of day; Paul Bishop for cop stuff; Marty Cutler and Jennifer Mitchell and Steve Arkin for the invite; Buck Dharma for the insider rock star stuff; all who are Fred: Lori Snyder, Dawn Fratini, Lee Coltman (also for the label), and Blake Arnold (also for the Buffalo Splits); Eric Goldman for phonings and faxings; Gwen Lauterbach for kid checking; Cyndy Mobley for the legal details; Michael Seidman for only picking on things that need it; and all the people at Walker & Company who make stories into real books with covers. Also to Doug Wyatt for thanking me in his album liner notes even though I didn't do anything.

I don't have an agent, so looking for one in the dedication won't work.

King Miles appears courtesy of Atomic Records.

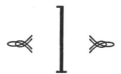

AN #2 was six-five and dark-haired and looked exactly like Robert Goldstein. He turned in the restaurant booth as the hourglass blonde exited, pointed at her, and said to MAN #1, "Now that, that's a tuchus."

The laugh track rolled and the picture faded to black. Sitting on the couch in Jason's front room, Robert Goldstein said, "Now that, that's not funny." A commercial started for dog snacks shaped like bacon.

"It's TV," Jason said. "You were good, though." He rewound it a little and played the same scene again.

"Now that," MAN #2 said, "that's a tuchus."

"Now that," Robert said, reaching forward and turning off the TV, "that's enough of that."

"How much did you make?"

"Enough for my half of the security deposit."

The phone rang and Jason got up from the couch. A system of black aluminum tubing loomed over his living room like a Tinkertoy monster, cradling electronics and synthesizer keyboards, its shoulders hunched against the ceiling. He felt through the papers on the gray work surface that integrated with the tubing and came up with the phone and an elastic band.

"This is Jason."

"Hey, boss, you busy?"

Jason turned from the handset. "It's Martin."

Robert waved. Jason pulled his hair back into the elastic band and said, "Robert says hi. How's the new job? How's Long Beach? How's your mom?"

"That's why I'm calling. You guys busy?"

"We were just watching Robert deliver a line on *Joanna*."

"What about you, you busy?"

"No, I just shipped my last tape of scary techno music for *Ghost House III* to Light Wizards. All I have left to do is invoice them."

"That's good. That's real good."

There was a pause. Jason said, "Um, something up?"

Robert's eyebrows rose.

"I could use some help, bro."

Jason said, "Hold on." To Robert he said, "You have any plans for the next few days?"

Robert shook his head.

Jason looked for a pen. "Give me directions."

he Manor was a huge turn-of-the-century boarding house. Or it had been, at the turn of the century. Now it was a leaking, drafty wreck. Jason, Robert, and Martin had lived in it for four years because rent was cheap, but their time was up; it had been sold, and the students and artists who lived there had to leave.

Martin had moved out almost immediately following the announcement, taking a job doing page layout for a small off-roading magazine in Long Beach, where his family was. Jason and Robert were supposedly looking for another place to live, but they weren't trying very hard.

Jason popped the back of the camper shell on his little brown pickup, tossed his backpack in, and leaned against the fender.

"Let's go!" he yelled at the Manor's second floor.

Robert's voice called, "Hold on!"

Jason drummed his fingers impatiently on the camper shell and looked at his old Plymouth. It had been sitting for a year on the dead grass between his flimsy back steps and the parking lot, and it had that soulless look that said it had made the transition from vehicle to geological formation. The Manor's residents had complained on and off for eight months. He really needed to do something about that.

Robert's door banged open and he came down the rickety back stairs with a bulging green backpack and slung it into the covered pickup bed. Jason closed and latched the back and they got in the cab and left for Long Beach, a forty-five-minute drive.

"What did he say, exactly," Robert asked when they were on the road. He was concentrating and tapping the dashboard with both hands, but he repeatedly fumbled and started over.

"You're still trying to think of it as one pattern," Jason said. "It's two. Three even beats with your left hand during the same period of time as two even beats with your right."

"Shut up."

"They're separate. Sort of."

"Shut up. What did Martin say was wrong?"

"He didn't say exactly."

"You didn't ask?"

"Were we going to help him either way?"

"Of course."

Jason gestured *so* with one hand. He pushed a cassette in and the old Cuban men of the Buena Vista Social Club accompanied them beautifully out of L.A. County on guitars and pianos, with Robert guest artist on dashboard.

The tape was in its third encore when Jason parked in front of a charmless apartment building distinguishable on a street of charmless apartment buildings only by address and trim color. He let "Pueblo Nuevo" finish before he killed the ignition, so as not to be disrespectful to Rubén Gonzáles.

He woke Robert and they went upstairs and knocked on number 20. A boy of about twelve, wearing shorts and a Bud Man T-shirt, opened the door and said, "Are you Jason?"

"Yes." He offered his hand.

The boy shook it. "I'm Leon."

Robert stuck his hand out and said, "I'm Sonic the Hedgehog."

Leon said, "You are not."

"I'm his brother Phonic. Phonic the Phedgephog."

Jason said, "Can we come in?"

"Okay. Martin's in the bathroom." Leon left the door open and walked away. They followed him in. The apartment was neither comfortable nor uncomfortable; it was rented space with objects in it: couch, carpet, dinette, dishes, shelves, TV.

Martin came out of the hallway, looked happy to see them, and said, "Yo baby, yo baby, yo."

Robert grinned lopsidedly. "Hi, Martin!"

Leon said, "He said he was Sonic's brother."

"Le, buddy," Martin said, touching Leon's shoulder, "I really wish you'd wear a different shirt. How about that one I bought you with those surfing gophers or weasels or whatever they are?"

Leon mumbled something.

"For me?"

Leon flicked a gaze at Robert and Jason, but he moped off into the other room.

Robert said, "Grownups suck."

"No," Martin said, "I suck, for treating him like a child in front of his peers."

Jason said to Robert, "That would be you."

Robert said, "Only emotionally. I am his intellectual superior."

"So," Martin said. "You guys eat?"

Robert shook his head violently.

Martin looked at his watch. "The best place is also the closest one. You mind a gay bar?"

Robert shook his head violently again and almost fell over. Jason said, "Is it bar food or real food?"

"No, they have a kitchen. It's good."

THE MUSIC WAS loud and thumpy. The plates were black and octagonal and the napkins were yellow. The '90s were scheduled to arrive in Long Beach after the millennium.

They sat outside under unlit patio heaters, away from the dance floor. Their waiter, neat and Midwestern with bad skin, said, "Good evening, gentlemen. Can I get you some drinks?"

Jason and Martin ordered soft drinks. After waiting for Robert to study the menu, the waiter finally said, "And you, sir?"

In a moment, Robert looked up and said, "I would like the blood of a freshly killed gazelle."

"Very good," the waiter said, and left.

Jason looked amusedly at Robert. "The funny part is now you have to drink whatever he brings you."

"I trust him."

Jason said, "So, Martin, what's your trouble?"

"It's a long story. Let's just chat and get relaxed a little and I'll tell you after the drinks come. So, Robert, I hear you were on TV."

Robert described his day on the *Joanna* set and how the other actors had been, and Jason talked about the computer game music he'd just finished for Light Wizards. The waiter brought their drinks.

"Two colas," he said. "One gazelle blood." He bowed efficiently. "I'll be back to take your food orders." He pounded his chest with one fist. "*Salud*, strong hunters."

He left. Robert's drink was something red in a snifter with a flexy straw and a leafy celery stalk with a blue paper umbrella stuck into it. He made a show of getting his lips past the celery and took a large gulp.

Jason said, "So?"

"'Ninety-eight," Robert said. "Summer." He made smacking noises. "The Sahara, I believe. Springy, but robust. Graceful." He swirled it under his nose. "O-positive." He nodded. "Excellent legs."

"Speaking of Light Wizards," Martin said, "have you heard from Platt or Paul recently?"

Jason said, "The last time I saw Platt was when he introduced me around at Light Wizards, maybe a year and a half ago."

"And Paul?"

"Not a word."

Martin looked at Robert, who shook his head.

Their waiter returned. "Are you ready to order?"

"Grilled cheese," Jason said.

Martin said, "Chef salad."

Robert said, "Filet of wildebeest."

The waiter wrote on his pad. "How would you like your wildebeest?"

"Medium charred."

"Dark meat or light meat?"

Robert said, "Uh . . ."

The waiter said, "The light meat is less gamy."

"Good. Dark meat."

"Very good choice, sir." The waiter looked Robert over. "I'm partial to light meat, myself." He scooped up their menus and left.

"I do believe," Jason said, "that you have just been cruised."

Robert acknowledged with a lift of his eyebrows and sipped past his celery.

"So," Jason said. "What's your trouble, Martin?"

Martin leaned forward on the table. "My trouble is my brother."

"Leon?"

"Actually, Ed is my trouble, Mom's boyfriend. Leon thinks he's great. He's starting to act like him."

Robert said something unintelligible around the foliage of his celery.

Jason said, "Drink or talk. Don't do both."

Robert emerged from his celery and repeated, "But you don't think Ed is great."

"Ed abuses," Martin said. "Ed uses. Ed deals, Ed steals, Ed lies, Ed swindles. No, I gotta say I do not think Ed is great."

Jason said, "What can we do?"

"Two things," Martin said. "First, I'm hoping that if Leon sees some men around who are cool and don't do all that stuff, he'll have a healthier outlet for those role model feelings."

Robert said, "The current term for cool is 'da bomb.' "

Jason said, "It was, anyway. What about you?"

Martin said, "Me? No, I can't be da bomb. I'm da mom."

"Why isn't your mom da mom?"

"She's too busy trying to get her life straight. Mom's not a great judge of character. You know? Her taste in boyfriends pretty well sucks. Ed's a real winner. You'll get the drift in about four seconds when you meet him. Here's the other thing: Ed put his hands on my mom the day before yesterday, in front of Leon, while I wasn't there. I was hoping you'd kind of back me up when I bring it to a head and maybe hang around for a few days and be like a strong male presence."

Robert said, "Put his hands on as in fondling, or put his hands on as in hitting?"

"As in gripping, and shaking."

Jason said, "Does 'strong male presence' translate as 'deterrent force'?"

"That's a pretty good translation."

Jason and Robert exchanged a glance, each to confirm that the other was okay with it.

Martin said, "I'll feed you."

"Okay."

When their waiter came with their food, Robert complained that his wildebeest wasn't hairy enough. The waiter offered to exchange it for the hyena plate, which he promised was excellent and should be suitably hirsute, but Robert said he would make do and ordered another gazelle blood. The waiter gave Robert his phone number on their way out. Robert stuck it in his back pocket and apologized for being straight. The waiter said that wasn't a problem for him.

THE WINNER BOYFRIEND wasn't there when they got back.

"Mom's shopping," Martin said, plopping onto the couch. "She'll be back in time to make us dinner."

Jason pulled a chair around from the dinette and sat on it backward. "It'll be nice to see her again."

Leaning against the wall, Robert stopped tapping his hands awkwardly on his thighs long enough to say, "It'll be nice to meet her, finally."

Jason looked at Robert's hands and said, "You should isolate the two patterns."

"Shut up."

Martin said, "She goes for the wrong guys. There ain't a dang thing I can do about it, and I accept that. But Leon's a different story. I been here three weeks, just watching and seeing. Well, now I'm done watching and seeing. I'm the breadwinner in this house and I say he's out of here. I just don't want to stand up to him by myself because frankly, he's bigger than me."

Robert gave up tapping and sat down. "What about the cops?"

"Mom'd never press charges."

"You're paying the rent, right?"

"Yeah, but it's her name on the lease."

"How did it happen the day before yesterday, when he put his hands on her?"

"I don't know, man. She's not talking, and Leon won't give me any details."

Robert said, "They're afraid you'll do something."

Jason stretched his legs out. "Which you will."

"Damn skippy."

"If nobody's talking, how do you know he put his hands on her?"

"At first it was just a vibe? Then yesterday I saw bruises on her upper arms, like thumb and finger bruises, like a grip. She tried to hide them but then when she saw me looking, she said she bumped into the car door."

"Eight times," Robert said, "then twice the other way."

"Against that fingerlike protrusion all car doors have at bicep level," Jason said. "When do you want to confront him?"

"Tonight. We have to stay for supper first, though, or Mom will be upset."

"We doing it here?"

"No, I don't want to do it in front of Leon, and I don't want Mom interfering. Also, I don't know if he'll be here. If he is, we'll hook up with him later in the evening. If he's not, we'll go to him right after supper."

Robert said, "You think she'd interfere?"

"Who knows? For all I know, she let me see the bruises so I'd ride to her rescue. But that doesn't mean she wouldn't stand by him while I did."

"Too complicated," Jason said. "Jase protect tribe. Bad men come, Jase make many head knocks, knock-knock."

Robert grunted, "Who there?"

Martin supplied: "Fuckwit."

Robert said, "Fuckwit who?"

"Fuckwit my family, and you go down, Jack."

"Martin make joke," Jason said. "Joke funny."

inner was chicken, microwaved cauliflower, Minute rice, and tension.

Martin's mother said it was a pleasure to finally meet Robert, and exclaimed that Jason had really grown up and gotten fine since she'd last seen him, which was when he and Martin and Robert were in high school. She looked more worn than the intervening years should have warranted, but she was still a pretty woman. Leon offered up a note from his teacher and said, "It was an accident." His mom read it tiredly and postponed discussion until after dinner. When she went to get more cauliflower, Martin picked it up from the table and read it. He showed it to Robert, who showed it to Jason. Leon had knocked a girl down.

After coffee and *dulce de leche* ice cream, Martin kissed his mother and said, "We're going out for a while, Mom. Don't wait up," and they went out into the evening.

Walking to Jason's pickup, Robert said, "This might be a good time to mention that I brought that gun I took from Ian Hibbit, and some ammunition."

Its mention recast the situation. They stopped at the pickup and looked at each other.

Jason said, "I didn't know you still had that."

"We didn't know what kind of trouble Martin was in, so I brought it."

Martin said, "I wouldn't put it past Ed to be armed."

"If he brought out a gun," Jason said, "would our having one be dissuasive, or would it escalate things?"

"Probably escalate things."

"Let's not escalate things."

Robert nodded. "I'll leave it in the backpack."

ON ANOTHER STREET of apartment buildings, past a Buick with a little girl in the passenger's seat, down a yellow hallway, was a door that bore a security company sticker and two deadbolt locks. Jason and Robert stood out of peephole range while Martin knocked. The peephole darkened briefly and then the deadbolts slid back and the door opened a few inches. A man Jason couldn't see said, "I got no time for you right now. You gotta call me before you come over."

"I need to talk to you, Ed." Martin gestured to his left. "I have a couple of friends with me."

Ed peeked around the doorframe. He was dark-haired and about Jason's height. The shoulder that showed around the doorframe was hairless and barbell-muscular in a tank top.

He took Jason's measure.

"I don't sell pot," he said.

Jason shrugged.

"Ed," Martin said. "Just let us in."

Ed looked at Jason some more and then opened the door.

A weight bench and weights claimed most of the gloomy

living room, with a few clothes and dishes scavenging the remaining space. When Ed closed the door, the only light was
from the kitchenette. The bedroom door was closed.

Martin said, "We didn't come here to buy drugs. We came
to talk."

"Yeah, about what, Marty?"

"Okay, straight up: I want you to leave my mom alone and
find someplace else to hang around."

"Fuck you."

"Ed, I've asked you many times to change your—"

"Look at you, just like a man."

"—to change your ways. But when you put your hands on
my mom—"

"What happens between your mom and me is none of your
goddamned business."

A drugged male voice behind the closed bedroom door
slurred, "Hey, man . . ."

"You hear that," Ed said. "You're disturbing my customers."
He opened the front door and glared at Martin.

A man in his late forties was standing outside the door with
his hands in his denim jacket. He leaned back a little as the door
opened. He had sandy-blonde hair that curled past his jacket
collar and a pink, lined face and watery blue eyes. Jason had seen
him somewhere before.

Ed was still glaring at Martin, with his back to the doorway.
"Now get the fuck out," Ed said. "All three of you."

The man said, "I'm here for Dwight."

Ed lurched around. "Who the fuck are—"

"I'm here for Dwight. Would you please bring him out?"

"Who the fuck are you to—"

"I've asked you politely and I'm not asking you again. Bring
out Dwight or I'll come in and get him myself."

"Who the fuck do you think you—"

The man slid a heavy pearl-gripped pistol from his jacket pocket and clonked the end of the barrel straight into Ed's forehead. Ed fell down.

The man pointed the pistol at him. "Stay," he said. He pointed the gun briefly toward Jason, Martin, and Robert. "You want some of this too?"

"Hell, no," Jason said. "We don't like him either."

Ed said to Martin, "You set me up, you dumb mother."

Jason said, "You're an idiot, Ed."

The man stepped around Ed and tried the bedroom door. It was locked.

"Dwight," he said loudly. There was no answer. The man turned to Ed. "You got the key?"

"Fuck you."

As the doorframe splintered, Ed said, "Aw, fuck." Another wavering "Hey, man . . ." issued from the bedroom. The sandy-haired man shook his head at what he saw inside and disappeared into the bedroom.

Ed said to Martin, "I'm gonna make you pay for this. You are gonna pay so bad for this." His face lightened as he got a new idea. He said, "Or maybe I'll make your mom pay."

Martin said, "Say that again."

"Maybe," Ed said, victorious, "I'll make your mom pay."

Martin nodded slowly, longer than a nod would usually last. "Uh *huh*," he said. He paused a moment, still nodding, and then kicked Ed viciously in the balls.

The sandy-haired man came out and said, "Listen, I don't— What happened to him?"

Jason said, "He fucked with Martin Altamirano's family."

The man looked at Martin. "That's you?"

"Yup."

"Guess I'll remember that. Look, I don't know you guys, but you want some free tickets to the Dwight Cooper concert to-night?"

The man's familiarity clicked. Jason pointed at him. "John Ray Hoffer."

"Yeah, that's me. You guys Dwight fans? You want some free tickets? Backstage passes? I can probably score you some tour jackets." He sized Robert up. "You might be too big."

Robert said, "That's okay."

Ed decided it might be time to get up. Hoffer pointed the pistol at him and said, "You stay down," and Ed got back down. There was a round, pink mark on his forehead where Hoffer had clonked him with the pearl-gripped pistol, and his forearm was clamped between his thighs.

Jason said, "What do you need?"

Hoffer angled his head toward the bedroom. "Help me with Dwight."

artin went ahead with Hoffer's keys and opened the back door of a black Chrysler limousine with mirrored windows that was double-parked with its flashers going, blocking the Buick they'd seen on their way in. Dwight Cooper's feet dragged on the ground between Hoffer and Jason and his long blonde hair fell forward off his lolling head. Robert walked in front to thwart paparazzi, but the paparazzi were off bothering someone else. Robert was extra-vigilant anyway.

They bent Dwight through the open car door with help from Martin and he unfolded onto the leather bench seat and lay flat. Hoffer flipped his feet in and closed the door.

Jason said, "Well."

"The pressure just got to him. Tonight's the pre-tour run-through gig with the new band."

"Will he be okay?"

"He'll make the gig."

"I suppose that's one definition of 'okay.' "

"I've been playing with Dwight for twenty years. He's a trooper. He'll be fine once he's onstage. What's your last name?"

"Keltner."

"I'll put you on the guest list tonight. Get some girls and come to the Jetty. It'll be under your name. It's not part of the official tour, so there's no lasers and explosions tonight, but the music'll be kicking."

"Thanks."

"You got it." Hoffer shook Jason's hand. "Dwight and Donna appreciate the help."

"Donna?"

Robert, standing in front of the limousine, pointed into it. "That's Donna."

Jason went around to the front. The blonde little girl they'd seen in the Buick was staring up at Robert's height through the limo windshield, hugging a Raggedy Ann doll, her eyes wide and her jaw dropped. Martin came around to see. He stopped and shook his head.

Donna's amazement grew, her eyes never wavering from Robert.

"Looks like you've got yourself a fan, there," Hoffer said.

Robert hunkered a little so he wouldn't look as tall, waved and said, "Hi, Donna." The little girl's amazement lingered, but she waved hesitantly back at him through the windshield. Robert smiled at her. Instantly, she stopped being hesitant and beamed at him.

"She's a little heartbreaker, all right," Hoffer said. He got behind the wheel and Donna and Robert waved at each other. She kept waving as the limousine drove away.

They stood in the street, looking at each other, and could think of no cogent commentary on little girls who were left in parked cars while their daddies shot up.

When Martin said, "What a prick," it didn't dispel the moment. Finally, Jason said, "We're not finished with Ed."

. . .

ED WAS EITHER gone or not answering his door, so they didn't get to finish with him.

"I don't like leaving it unresolved," Jason said in the hallway. "We'd better get back to Leon and your mom."

Martin said, "Yeah, maybe it's a nice night to take them to a concert."

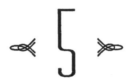

artin's mom found her old Dwight Cooper Band concert T-shirt. The stylized DCB logo swelled tight across her breasts, and the words "1979—North America" and "Flat Busted Hearts Tour" rolled around it in a semicircle. She was excited about the concert, and each time she was exuberant in her gesticulation, "flat busted" seemed less accurate. Jason was conscious of this as he waited with her in her living room.

"What was the last concert you went to?" she quizzed him. At her request, Martin and Robert were dropping Leon off with a woman who watched him sometimes. "You must go all the time, living in L.A. and being a musician and all. I think that's just so great."

Jason thought. "The three of us went to the African Marketplace a few months ago and watched the bands."

"How cool!"

"At one of the shows, Robert was the only American dancing, so they pulled him up on stage." He felt himself smiling. A life that included the memory of Robert Goldstein flailing like a happy tower among a lot of short black Djembe dancers was a life not entirely wasted.

"Well, I like that good ol' rock and roll," Martin's mom said. "I always loved Dwight ..." She shook her head in nostalgia and sang:

"If I say the right words, it'll all be all right,
If I sing the right songs then you'll stay here tonight.
But the words are just dust and the songs are untrue,
So this flat busted heart hits the road back from you."

Jason came in singing the Southern-flavored guitar riff that succeeded the verse.

She laughed happily. "You know it!"

"That one still gets airplay, Mrs. Altamirano. It's hard to avoid."

She leaned forward and smiled. "You shouldn't call me Mrs. Altamirano. You should call me Grace."

He became careful not to call her either. "Martin and Robert seem to be taking an awful long time."

She pushed up and arched back over the couch to see the clock. Jason looked away. She smiled when he looked at her again. "They'll be back soon. I saw the Dwight Cooper Band in a little place in New Orleans in seventy-three with Martin's father, and then at the L.A. Coliseum in seventy-nine with Will. No, with Henry." She raised her arms in display. "Still fits. Not bad for an old broad, huh?"

Jason smiled despite himself.

"Martin didn't like Henry," she remembered.

"Henry?"

"I just told you about him." She sighed. "Martin has never liked like any of my boyfriends. He's always had such a hard time with the men in my life."

It seemed to be Jason's turn to talk. He experimented with nodding and looking attentive.

"Do you have a girlfriend, Jason?"

"Uh, not right now, no."

"You should! You're a nice-looking guy. Anyone special?"

"Not, uh, not . . ."

"You're not dating? Why not?"

"I figure they're all intimidated by my chiseled jaw and manly good looks."

He was kidding, but she nodded in a way that made the deflective joke feel like a misstep.

A key slid into the lock and the door opened. Martin stood in the doorway, still holding the knob. "Y'all ready to boogie?" He gestured toward the hallway. "Let's go!"

Jason said, "Like, awright, dude."

"Heavy," Martin sang, "duty . . ." and he and Jason looked at each other and sang, "heavy duty . . . rock and ro-o-oll," and grimaced like guitarists.

"Party hearty," Martin said, displaying two two-fingered devil's heads.

Jason pulled his hair out of its ponytail, said, "Bang your head!" and rocked his head violently to make his hair fly around.

Martin's mom laughed. "Right *on*," she exclaimed. She offered her hand and Jason pulled her off the couch. "My god," she said. "You do have a lot of hair, don't you? Girls love that. It's very sexy."

Jason had a headache. He said, "Shall we?" and they went out to Martin's car.

Martin had traded in his twenty-year-old blue Honda for a ten-year-old gold Honda. Robert was standing next to it, stretching his back. "Robert, you get shotgun," Martin said. "I can't stand seeing him folded backways and sideward in the rearview."

Jason and Martin's mom sat in the back. Martin's mom touched his knee as she talked on the way there.

THE JETTY WAS a higher class of club than Jason had generally been to. It had two levels, each of which contained both auditorium-style seating and dining tables. The house P.A. was playing the Silver Bullet Band, and pretty waitresses zoomed through the pre-show din, parting the flurry before them with focused ire. Men in their forties shared booths with knockout girls in their twenties, and a coterie of unshaven white people who dressed like bikers had tables near the stage.

The rest of the audience was without obvious clique. In the front row of the upper level, a young man and his date sat next to a family of four, who sat next to a gay couple in their fifties, who sat next to an older woman and a younger one, probably mother and daughter. Most of the audience was white, but Jason was mildly surprised at the number of black and Hispanic people. He had expected the bikers and the plastic men with their vapid beauties, but he hadn't considered that Dwight would draw anyone else. Jason's own prejudices always fascinated him. He amended his notion of Dwight's audience.

The Silver Bullet Band faded and the house P.A. started playing a Lynyrd Skynyrd song. Jason leading, the four of them worked slowly to the side of the stage, where a huge man in sunglasses and a T-shirt that said "SECURITY" put up five bat-sized fingers to halt them and looked at their backstage passes.

"Who you here for?" he yelled when he'd carefully examined each pass, his hand still up to stay them.

Jason shouted, "John Hoffer."

The man raised a walkie-talkie with his other hand and yelled into it, "This is Gilbert at the south end. Is 'Cane there? I need him for a backstage ID."

The walkie-talkie squawked and sputtered, and Gilbert told it, "Ten-four," and yelled, "He'll come and get you."

Jason nodded. Something tapped him on the shoulder. When he looked back, Robert pointed. All the bikers were singing "Sweet Home Alabama" along with Skynyrd, except for one who was trying to talk on a cellular phone with his finger in his other ear. Jason looked at Robert and they both grinned.

Martin had his mom on his arm. "This is great!" she said excitedly over the noise. "This is so great! It's been so long since I've been out like this."

Robert shouted politely, "Ed doesn't take you out?"

"Oh, Ed," she said with a dismissive wave.

John Ray Hoffer came out the door next to the stage. As Gilbert took a step to talk to him, Hoffer spotted Jason and waved them over. "They're okay," he yelled. Gilbert nodded respectfully and rocked back into position.

The solid door shut behind them and the din cut down as though a valve had sealed. Hoffer said, "Glad you could make it. Come on up and hang until the show."

They mounted a flight of wooden stairs to a large area with folding tables and chairs. Styrofoam coolers held ice and canned drinks, and partial sets and flats from other productions leaned face-in to the walls. An empty blue flight case the size of a refrigerator stood on the far side.

Hoffer said, "Have a seat. What can I get you? Coors, Mountain Dew?"

Martin's mom said, "I would love a Coors."

They sat at a table with some other people. "Dwight should be out soon," Hoffer said.

"How's he doing?" Jason asked.

"He's fine. He'll be fine. Thanks for asking."

A woman wearing a CREW tag came up the stairs and put a stack of black denim on the table in front of Hoffer. He stood and touched her shoulder and said something to her, and she looked at Martin's mom, nodded, and left. Hoffer pulled the first tour jacket from the top of the stack and looked at its collar. "X-Large, that's you," he said to Robert, and then gave the other two to Jason and Martin, by which time the woman was back with one for Martin's mom. They were better made than anything Jason owned except for the jacket and slacks he'd bought for client meetings. The DCB logo, streamlined during the 1980s, was back in all its fat, swoopy 1970s airbrushed glory, red and yellow with star-shaped glimmers on the edges. Retro wasn't retro if it was the original goods. The tour name curved over a scrolling ribbon at the bottom: Trouble Comes Back.

Thanks were offered, but Hoffer rejected them. "You helped me out with Dwight," he said. "I appreciated it. I owe you one."

Martin's mom said, "Now that's a gentleman."

A minor commotion drew their attention across the room. Dwight Cooper had just entered, and he was nodding and not quite acknowledging the dozen people who had already stuck to him like jellyfish.

"Excuse me," Hoffer said. He got up and went toward Dwight. In a few minutes, he'd steered Dwight through the room and was giving him a chair at their table.

It became Dwight's table, and he looked around his table. The gaze was unsettling: Dwight's eyes were brown and clear between the blonde mask of his close beard and his ponytail, but the clarity was from the eyes, not the mind.

He had been seated next to a small, dark-eyed man in an ecru tennis visor. The man said politely, "Dwight, I just want to say

I've been a big fan of yours for years and I feel privileged to hear you tonight. Best of luck on your tour."

Dwight nodded distractedly, the eyes passing from one space to another.

Hoffer said to Dwight, "This is Dave Schuyler. He drums with Joe Damien's band."

Joe Damien was a good-looking TV star who had a band, and the name registered with Dwight.

"Joe Damien," he rasped. His voice was a trashed baritone. "Joe Damien's fuckin' band." He turned to Dave Schuyler. "You ever hear that fuckin' band?"

Schuyler began to say he played with them. Dwight said, "Fuckin' Joe Damien's band. You ever hear that fuckin' band?" Dwight paused as though for a punch line. He looked craftily at Schuyler. "Can't find the fuckin' four."

Embarrassment jolted through Jason's chest. Schuyler said something weak and inaudible and his smile got thin and hurt. Dwight's gaze banged around the table and found Jason at random. "You ever hear that fuckin' band?"

Jason shook his head.

"Can't find the fuckin' four," Dwight repeated with a derisive snort. "Can't find the fuckin' four." He laughed, finding friendly concurrence around the table where there was none. "Fuckin' Joe Damien's band. Can't find the fuckin' four."

"Dwight," Hoffer said, "Let me get you something. What do you want to drink?"

"Drink?" Dwight repeated, looking around the circle of people at the table, performing for his audience, "What do I want to drink?" He lurched to his feet and headed across the room. Hoffer obstructed his exit without seeming to, but was pulled along. The club noise flared and cut with the opening and closing of the door.

Jason couldn't look at Dave Schuyler. Robert gave the guy a sympathetic look, and Schuyler got up and went across the room to root intently through one of the more distant drink coolers.

"HOW CAN YOU miss something like that?" Martin said. They were seated together in front row center, ten feet from the stage, Jason and Martin on one side of Martin's mom and Robert on the other. The P.A. had worked its way up to Dwight Cooper Band songs. "How can she be so completely oblivious?"

Martin's mom had apparently missed the entire Dave Schuyler episode.

Martin shook his head.

Jason shrugged. "Maybe it's a survival technique."

The lights went out. At the tables, in the seating rows, and standing near bars and in the aisles, the capacity crowd put down its drinks and cheered and applauded. The waitresses continued along their flight paths, independent of the group mind.

A spotlight hit the left side of the stage and two men in collar-length hair and two-day stubble came out. The crowd cranked its cheering and stomping up a notch.

"Good evening, Long Beach!" said the shorter man. "We're Rick and Craig from ninety-six point eight FM, The Rock. I'm Rick."

"And I'm Craig."

"It's our great pleasure to introduce one of the true legends of rock and roll, Uncle Trouble himself, Mr. Dwight Cooper and the Dwight Cooper band!"

The crowd screamed and hooted. A chant went up: "Trouble! Trou-ble!"

Craig shouted. *"Are you ready to rock, Long Beach?"*

YES!

"Are you ready to rock?"
YES!
"I said, Are you ready to rock?"
YES!
"Well then let's rock!"

The electric guitar fingerpicking filled the club: Everybody knew it; it was the opening changes of "Goin' Back to Austin," and the crowd went nuts.

Rick and Craig stumbled down the stage steps as the curtain drew up. John Ray "Hurricane" Hoffer was right where he belonged in the pink and blue light, fingerpicking behind Dwight, who stood front and center behind a mike stand, a guitar strapped to him. A younger, good-looking guitarist with a flashy red guitar was off behind Dwight on the other side, watching Hoffer pick. The bearded keyboardist was playing a big Hammond B-3 through a Leslie speaker: the only real rock organ, too often simulated with electronics that weren't so heavy they required a road crew. The properness of the wooden monstrosity onstage made Jason smile to see it.

"That's a B-3 with a Leslie," he yelled at Martin. He made little propellor spins with a forefinger. "The speaker horn actually spins around inside the cabinet."

Martin looked politely interested.

As Hoffer neared the end of the four-bar fingerpicking intro, he twisted around to lock eyes with the drummer and jumped up in the air and came down on the one-beat and the cymbals and bass and B-3 crashed right down into the pocket of the groove with him and set off on a sweet, loping backbeat. The crowd loved it. The bikers danced with each other and the plastic men in the booths pretended to be into the music, moving in awkward mating attempts that were wasted because their dates were watching the cute young guitarist, who was now playing lines over Hoffer's and showboating on his red guitar to show how hard it was and how good he was to accomplish it.

As the keyboardist and Hoffer and the bass player traded glances and half-smiles, Dwight stood motionless behind his mike stand in denim and leather, the guitar hanging off him. A spotlight swept over Dwight's face, illuminating it. Jason's happiness in the B-3 and his enjoyment of the well-played music died. From front row center, the view was chilling. Behind Dwight's eyes, there was no Dwight. He was a coma balanced upright behind a microphone, his brown eyes dark as drains.

In a few beats, Dwight was supposed to start singing this song that everyone in the club knew by heart, but there was no sign that he was aware of it. Against the sickening moment, Jason's muscles tensed and his breath ceased.

The downbeat of the new section came.

Instantly, a relay somewhere in the back of Dwight's brain received voltage and clunked over; his eyes focused, and in his rasping baritone, he sang the verse about the woman in Denver. When the verse ended, the relay lost voltage and clunked back into its interrupt position. Dwight switched off. The crowd cheered.

Through the rest of the song, it snatched Dwight out of stasis for each singing part and then, when the part was over, snapped him back into it. When "Goin' Back to Austin" ended, Jason had the skin crawls because the toggling was so pronounced that he had begun to hear the clunk.

"I'm going to get some air," he shouted. Martin's mom tried to pull him into an impromptu dance, but he smiled without commitment and shook his head.

The club was a fluorescing smear of people and noise as he hiked up the aisle to the lobby, Dwight Cooper's dead gone stare still with him. Behind him, the drummer started a ticka-tacka train rhythm on the high-hat, and Hoffer's bottleneck guitar and the organ eased into "Southbound Freight."

Outside, he didn't feel like leaning against a lamppost or making eye contact with the people on the sidewalk, so he walked slowly past a row of closed shops. He felt insulated, the subject of an imaginary painting: man walking from nightclub. The Dwight Cooper Band was a remote and incoherent pulse and thump that reverberated against the dark storefronts opposite the club door and scattered dully along the street.

A few doors down, he sat on the curb and tried to reconnect with the cool air. Rock stars and heroin and loud music and little blonde children lived somewhere besides Earth, along with Humpty Dumpty and Satan and the Kennedys. He didn't want to be around it. He wanted to get in his pickup truck and drive back to Pasadena.

Instead, he found a twig on the sidewalk and bent it in progressive halves and quarters and thought about asymptotes. When it broke, he got up and brushed off his jeans and walked slowly back toward the club.

The club door opened and emitted a blast of warm air, an indistinct male vocal and a lot of bass, and Martin, rubbing his ears. He spotted Jason and walked over.

"Man," he said, "how come they always make the music so loud?"

"Because the sound engineer is deaf."

Martin wiggled a forefinger in each ear canal. "Oh, so he's just sharing? That's nice of him. You going back in?"

"I don't think so."

"Too loud?"

"Too freakshow."

"You mean Dwight? Yeah, man, he's gone. And I mean" — Martin cut the air with one flat hand—"gone."

"How can people let that happen to themselves?"

"Hey, it's easy. It's easier than not letting it happen."

Jason gestured down the street. "You want to walk?"

"Yeah."

A few doors down, Jason said, "You said it's easier to stay on drugs, but you got off them."

"I took a hard look at myself."

"So why wouldn't he?"

"You serious? That's *Dwight Cooper*!"

Half a block later, Jason was still trying to get it. Martin said, "Look: What's the junkie's biggest problem?"

"Uh . . . lack of self-respect, I dunno."

"Money."

"You mean not being able to afford treatment?"

"No, man, I mean not being able to afford the *fix*. That's the junkie's biggest problem. He gets up in the morning and he needs a certain amount of the happy sauce or a certain number of presto pills to keep him chuggin' along. He's got to pay for it. Where's that gonna come from? How's he gonna get it? That's the junkie's biggest problem. What's he gotta steal? Dwight Cooper doesn't have that problem. There's a whole bunch of things Dwight Cooper doesn't need to worry about because he's Dwight Cooper. Does he need to worry about money? No. And if he does need to worry about money, does he need to worry about where to get his fix? No, there's a hundred people in that nightclub right now would love to get Dwight Cooper high because he's Dwight Cooper. Does he need to worry about what people think about him? No, he's Dwight Cooper, get real, he's a rock star. Do you see that he would have anyone around him who'd tell him he needs help?"

A few doors later, Jason said, "No. He'd have a lot of people around him whose livelihood would depend on doing whatever's necessary to make the show happen."

"Now you're catching on. Can he look at his life and say, 'I'm going nowhere?' No, he's *Dwight Cooper*. He's *there*. Does he have any reason whatsoever to take a long, hard look at himself and say 'dude, you're fucking up?' "

"Yes."

Martin looked at him. Then he shook his head. "But obviously she's not enough of a reason."

"She should be."

Martin nodded. "Very true. Very true." They reached a corner beyond which was nothing worth walking toward, so they turned back.

"What did . . . uh . . ." He got stuck.

"Don't worry about asking. You can ask. What's your question?"

"Well, what did you get out of it?"

"I think escape."

"You mean like escape from yourself, or what?"

"Yeah, partly that, partly just pure escape into the groovy movie show: Hey, look, I can hear the orange. Far out, man. Make no mistake: Drugs is fun. At first."

"What was the hardest part about giving them up?"

"When you go on drugs . . . Whatever your emotional age was, stop the clock. Say you start using when you're fourteen, and you stop when you're twenty. You get to start the clock again right where you stopped it. It was eight-thirteen in the morning when you stopped the clock? Well guess what, bud, it's eight-thirteen now. Everybody else you know, they had that time to grow up, but while they were making progress and doing the work, you were off in a little suspended animation cocoon called 'I'm getting high' for seven years."

"Did you ever go to AA, or whatever the equivalent is?"

"Narcotics Anonymous. No, I never did. I don't know why."

"Do you ever miss it?"

"No. No. I don't think you miss wasting your life."

"Do you ever feel like you're still catching up?"

Martin stopped and looked at him in amazement. "All the time, man. All the time. With you and Robert around? You kidding?"

That hung for a second and then they started walking again.

"I'm glad you got clean."

"I'm glad I didn't get dead."

WHEN IT WAS late, they decided to go back into the club. Jason remembered that there might be some foam earplugs in his glove box, so they went to his pickup truck and found five.

"Robert can go deaf in one ear," Martin said as they inserted four.

Inside, Dwight and Hoffer—the only two onstage—were playing the ritard at the end of "Katie's Song." Dwight was on organ. Worshipful applause began as the last note faded. As Hoffer removed his guitar and gave it to a stagehand, Dwight sat bowed at the keyboard, staring at the keys, untouched by the applause.

The stage lights and house lights went out. The audience roared. Hoffer's silhouette stepped up and said, "Thank you, good night, drive safe," and the curtain fell.

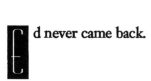 d never came back.

THUG #1 was tall and dark-haired. He glowered at hunky
Detective Sanchez, his eyes narrowing. The people who
were crowded into the walnut-paneled living room of Jason
and Robert's new groovy beach pad burst into wild applause. The
TV was set up so that it blocked the doorway to Jason's bedroom,
in which his music equipment crowded his futon. On the other
side of the small back house was the door to Robert's room and
the single bathroom. Between the two was the doorway to the
kitchenette. All the walls were clad in various hues of aging
paneling.

They'd moved the jointly purchased blue couch and an old
stuffed chair abandoned by a previous renter into the middle of
the living room. Martin's mom was sitting on the arm of the chair,
holding a cigarette and a beer in one hand. She flung the other
hand toward the screen. "Show it again!"

Jason rewound and played it a third time. The crowd in the
living room hushed. THUG #1 glowered and his eyes narrowed
at Detective Sanchez. Everyone applauded again.

"Speech!" Martin called, and the cry went round the room.

Robert stood, looked dramatically thoughtful for a beat, and sat down.

"Good speech," Jason said.

The phone rang. Jason wove through the crowd.

"Apartment-warming and thug party," he said. "Where do you need directions from?"

A female voice said, "I'm calling for a Mr. Keltner, please."

"Speaking."

"Is this the same Mr. Keltner who attended a Dwight Cooper concert last month?"

"Uh, yes?"

Relief in the voice. "Oh, good. I'm glad I found you. I was looking in Long Beach and Pasadena."

"What can I do for you?"

"My name is Celia Weather. John Hoffer asked that I call you. We have an odd situation, and we're hoping you can help."

A gig? The bearded keyboardist had quit? Did he want to play with Dwight Cooper? He didn't really play that kind of music. In fact, he sucked at it. He embarrassed himself when he tried. Forget it. He'd have to turn it down.

He moved out of the living room into Robert's bedroom, paneled in three hues of walnut, none of which appeared in the rest of the house. A mattress lay on the carpet, surrounded by boxes of books. On the wall by the bathroom door was a clock shaped like a banana, its white electrical cord trailing down the paneling to a socket.

The ceiling hook that was screwed into the far corner had inspired Robert to go searching for a fern the day after they'd moved in. He'd returned from the retro-hip shops on Abbott Kinney with the gaudiest used rain lamp ever crafted in the secret workshop of the kitsch elves. The upper and lower spires of the cylinder spanned three feet from tip to tip, painted gold. A gold reproduction Pietá stood inside, surrounded by plastic foliage, as though in a gazebo. A rigid tube, gold, rose out of its head, limned by a 30-watt bulb inside the upper spire. In honor of the party, the built-in pump was grinding, forcing glycerin "rain" up the tube to slide in sparkling beads down taut lengths of monofilament.

Only Robert.

"What kind of help do you need?"

"Would it be possible for us to meet?"

"Sure." Jason stuck his head back through the door and looked across the house into the open door of his bedroom. He couldn't see his calendar, just the black jungle gym of the music equipment support system that loomed over his futon, but he knew the calendar didn't have anything written on it anyway. "How's tomorrow lunch? Where are you located?"

"I was hoping you could meet now."

He looked into the living room. "Uh, now's a little—"

Martin's mom smiled at him.

"I've been authorized to pay you for your time. I would need to meet both with you and with two other people who were at the concert. One is a very tall man with dark hair, and the other is short and dark-skinned."

Not a gig, then. Jason watched Robert accept compliments across the room. "What is this about?"

"I'd much rather discuss it in person."

Martin's mom smiled and gestured that he should join the party.

Celia Weather said, "We'd like to employ you."

Jason considered how much he cared whether he met this person, and said, "Our joint rate for being rousted on a weekend during our own party with no details forthcoming is six hundred dollars, up front."

A long pause. "That's acceptable. You will bring the other two?"

She'd accepted the get-lost rate, so he was stuck. "Where shall we meet?"

"I'll send a car."

"I'd rather meet. Do you know where Washington hits the beach, in Venice?"

"I can find it."

"There's a place called The Cow's End. We'll meet you there in forty-five minutes."

"How will I know you?"

"We'll be overdressed and one of us will be very tall."

THE NEW GROOVY beach pad wasn't actually at the beach. It was across the street from a row of narrow houses and apartments that backed against the Venice canals, which were fed by an inlet from the Pacific Ocean. The canals were cut at right angles, and the houses along them were a jumble of architectural styles crammed up against each other as though personifying the architects themselves, crushed together in a row, all dressed differently and all clashing, but each convinced he was fitting in generally while making a new statement with his unique hat.

The people who lived there paid several hundred dollars more per month than Jason and Robert did because they could see the canals without crossing the street. But this was a mere skirmish in the war for status. The real winners lived half a mile away, on Ocean Front Walk. When not obstructed by vendors, 'bladers, bicyclists, gangbangers, police officers, film crews, oil platforms, drunks, tanker ships, bums, bulldozers, berms, lifeguard towers, fraternity boys, and tourists, their view of the ocean was beautiful, and rental of a small single cost three times as much as the mortgage on a stately pleasure dome in Xanadu.

They walked past Jason's favorite window, a big wooden arch. Robert said, "You didn't ask what she wanted us for?"

Jason shook his head. "I should have, sorry."

Martin said, "I'm more than a little curious, tell you the truth."

Winding through the canals, slowing only for waddlefooted squadrons of ducks that hurried down the sidewalks in front of them, they came out on Washington, a wide street that hesitated abruptly at the beach and then shot out over the ocean as the Venice Fishing Pier.

The Cow's End was across Washington from the canals, a coffeehouse that displaced the first two stories of a wooden, salt-worn three-story building. At night, the clientele was mostly regulars. Unhygienic dweebs with laptop computers pecked and scratched. Screenwriters. Robert greeted a few on the way in, accepted a few complimentary gestures directed at his red sport coat, and went to stand in line for coffee.

Martin behind him, Jason mounted the open interior stair-way until his eyes were at shoe-level of the second floor. A trim woman in a smart blue business outfit and thin gold necklace looked at him from a red velour armchair. Beyond her was the closed door to the windowed billiards room, where cigar smoking was encouraged.

He looked down at Robert and indicated the upstairs. Robert nodded. Jason went up, Martin following. The woman watched them.

"Ms. Weather?"

She stood. "Yes. You're Jason Keltner?"

"Yes. This is Martin Altamirano."

Her gaze went behind them. "Did you bring the tall man?"

"He's getting coffee."

She looked as though she were considering going to see for herself. Jason offered his hand. "Nice to meet you."

"And you." She shook his hand and Martin's.

He sat on the orange couch across a scarred coffee table from her. Martin pulled up a faded green hassock.

They waited awkwardly for Robert.

Jason said, "Did you have any trouble finding the place?"

"No, not at all. I take it you live nearby."

"Yes, we walked here."

"I see."

She smiled impatiently. The moment dragged. He considered telling her about the ducks, just to have something to say.

They continued to wait for Robert.

"Lots of ducks in the canals, on the way over," Jason said.

"That must have been very nice."

He nodded. She looked at Martin. He smiled at her.

Robert came upstairs very slowly, each step of his too-careful tread amplifying a standing wave in his oversized mug. Whipped cream and chocolate goo sloshed over opposite sides in alternation and splatted on the thin carpet. Beyond him, on a ledge over the front door, was a life-sized plastic cow.

Jason stood. "Robert Goldstein, Celia Weather."

"Hi," Robert said, sitting on the couch next to Jason.

"Hello," Celia Weather said, studying him. Robert let a moment of this pass and then gave her a goofy smile.

"I'm sorry," she said. "I didn't mean to stare. I've just been curious what you really looked like."

"How strange, I have too," Robert said.

Jason said, "So."

"Yes," she said. "So." She smoothed her skirt and got businessy. "As I told you on the phone, I'm an associate of John Hoffer and Dwight Cooper."

"Associate?" Robert said. He had a whipped cream mustache. Martin pointed at his own lip and Robert wiped his mouth.

"Yes. I'm a private security consultant in the employ of Mr. Cooper."

Robert nodded seriously and slurped his mocha.

"There is a threat to his daughter's safety. I've been hired to protect her, and I think you can help."

Robert nodded cooperatively.

Jason said, "How?"

"Donna is a very high-strung little girl. I need someone watching her twenty-four hours a day, and she doesn't like it. I can't tell you how many men I've been through, trying to find one she won't scream her head off at. After exhausting my roster, I sat down with her and her therapist, and we talked about it. At the end, her only concession was that she would let three people stay with her: The Giant and his two helpers."

Robert said, "The Giant?"

Jason said, "You."

"I'm The Giant?"

Martin said, "I'm a helper. Want to trade?"

She nodded. "Yes, you're The Giant. Apparently, you made quite an impression on her. You've been her hero for some time. The Giant comes and saves little children."

Jason said, "So you only contacted me to get to Robert."

"That was my original thought, yes. Yours was the only name Mr. Hoffer could remember. But then as a matter of course, I checked up on you. The names Norton Platt and Carl Swofford came up."

"I like Platt."

"I couldn't reach Platt. Swofford said you were 'a pain in the ass but competent for small jobs.' "

"Swofford's a pain in the ass too, so I guess he'd know."

"He recommended that I bring you on."

"Doing what?"

"Not letting Donna be alone."

"Uh, look . . ." He paused. "I've done a couple of things, but I'm not professional. I don't have a background or any schooling. None of us is a security person."

"You wouldn't need to be. I'll have security people around the perimeters. What I need is someone to walk next to Donna and keep his eyes open."

"How seriously do you take the threats?"

"Seriously enough that I want someone around her at all times. Not seriously enough that I think she needs to be taken out of school and given an armed escort."

"Do you know who the threat is from?"

"Yes, but I will not discuss that without a non-disclosure agreement in place. But I can tell you that besides the actual potential for kidnap, we believe the person is not dangerous."

"What do we do if there's an attempt on her safety?"

"The idea is that your presence deters that."

"But if there is?"

She shook her head. "It's not that kind of job. Your role is to discourage, not to defend."

"But if there is?"

She looked impatient. "If there were, the regular security people would move in. But there shouldn't be."

He nodded.

"This job is about the child not being alone, not about heroics. You two are both big men, and all three of you look like you could be dangerous. Just keep alert and that should be enough."

"Gosh, ma'am, you probably say that to all the big, dangerous men."

She looked at him for a moment. "Mr. Keltner, I'd rather you didn't flirt with me."

"I wasn't flirting with you. I was soft-pedaling the compliment."

"I see." She didn't seem convinced.

Martin said, "He thinks being called dangerous-looking is a compliment."

"Do we live on site or something?"

"Mr. Goldstein would. The other two have the option. There's room for you in Mr. Cooper's house while he's on tour with his band. Donna needs to be taken to school at eight and picked up at two. She goes to sleep around seven, at which time one of the security people will enter the house and stay the night, leaving before she's up in the morning."

"The Giant," Robert said, trying it out. Martin glanced at Jason.

"I'll pay the standard rate of seven-fifty a week for you, and nine hundred for Mr. Goldstein. The higher rate is for the live-in. It's a Monday-through-Sunday week for the duration of the tour, which is four months; or until the threat is neutralized; or until the client decides he doesn't need our services. I pay the following Friday."

"Who can vouch for you?"

She seemed a little startled. "Ah, some law enforcement people, some lawyers." She nodded. "I can put together some references."

"I haven't seen a license."

She produced one from her bag.

"All right. Would you give us a moment, please?"

She stood. "I'll give you two." She went downstairs.

Jason said, "What do you think?"

"I don't know what to think. What do you think?"

Martin said, "It's a little unusual, but it could be on the up-and-up."

"You have anything going on, Mr. Giant, sir?"

"No, you?"

"No."

Robert said to Martin, "You've got that day job."

Martin shifted. "I could make a change."

"You want to do that?"

Martin thought for a minute.

"Yeah," he said. "I hate that job."

Jason coveted Robert's mocha covertly. "Rent's due in three weeks."

Robert said, "I have my half."

"Me too."

Robert slurped his mocha. Martin shifted on the hassock. Jason looked at the young people shooting pool. People in their mid-twenties seeming young was a relatively new thing for him. He sort of liked it. It made him feel less stupid.

"Let's just take it," Robert said. He put his empty mug on the coffee table.

"Martin?"

Martin nodded and smiled sheepishly.

"What," Jason asked.

"Oh, nothing." He shrugged. "I just kinda missed you guys."

Robert grinned at him.

"Okay," Jason said. He clapped his hands onto the knees of his jeans in finality. "We'll say yes. But not for the 'standard rate,' I don't think."

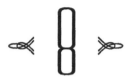

elia Weather had spent her time downstairs putting together a list of references. Jason told her he'd call her as soon as he'd checked them, and they left with the list and a check for six hundred dollars from Bellweather Security Consultation.

He flapped the yellow check at Robert as they walked back on the sidewalks through the dark canals. "Want to go to Rio?"

"My baby hasn't smiled at me," Robert said regretfully. "Oh, my oh me-oh."

"You don't have a baby."

"Then it would follow, wouldn't it?"

A little while later, Robert said, "The Giant." Martin looked at Jason.

The groovy beach pad was a small back house behind a smaller front house, and its entrance faced the back house next door. They went up the short staircase and into the living room. No one was there anymore.

There were six former clients on the list of references. It was too late to call them, but he left a message on Norton Platt's voice mail, saying hello and asking if he'd heard of Celia

Weather or Bellweather Security. He almost asked after Paul Reno.

They looked at the disorderly party remnants in the living room and went to sleep instead of cleaning. The phone rang at eight-thirty in the morning. It was Carl Swofford.

"I'm fielding Norton's messages for him. I don't know Bellweather Security, but I hear they're legit."

"Thanks. What's up with Platt; is he okay?"

"Yeah, he's fine. Just busy. You still got that crappy old Plymouth?"

"Why, your piece of shit minivan need a tow?"

Swofford cackled and hung up.

Robert was standing barefoot in the paneled kitchenette, weighing the benefits of three flavors of ground coffee beans in three little red bags.

"I don't know where I learned this macho banter thing," Jason told him. "I really don't enjoy it."

"It isn't something you learn." Robert put one of the bags back in the freezer. He tore open the other two and dumped them into the coffeemaker. "When you're in utero, a certain amount of testosterone gets trapped in your brain, and then when you reach puberty, it starts having your conversations for you."

Martin, wandering in from the bathroom, still brushing his teeth, said, "What does, your dick?" He pretended his crotch was talking in a falsetto. " 'Hey, c'mere! Hey you, c'mere!' "

"The level of sophistication in this house," Jason said, "is truly astounding."

" 'Of course I love you, baby,' " Martin's crotch promised.

They drank vanilla hazelnut chocolate raspberry truffle coffee and then went for Sunday brunch at a funky beach joint on Main, sat among funky beach hipsters, and ate too many servings of blueberry french toast.

Back at the groovy beach pad, Jason started calling the people on Celia Weather's reference list.

The first was a lawyer who said Bellweather had been honest, efficient, and effective. The second was a novelist who'd received death threats after she published a novel about a pope who converted to Islam. She said if she were ever threatened with execution again, she'd call Celia, unless it was the government threatening to execute her, and then she'd call Johnnie Cochrane. Jason went down the list. Everyone spoke well of Bellweather Security.

He phoned Celia Weather and said they'd take the job. When he named three thousand dollars a week, she said she could get four people for the price Jason was demanding for three, and Jason said yes, she could. She said she was over a barrel, and hired them. He felt guilty upping the price, but reminded himself that she would likely mark it up on her own invoice to Dwight, and that if they hadn't been worth it, she wouldn't have accepted. And that he wasn't interested in living on the financial precipice so much anymore if he didn't have to.

Her office was on a gleaming sixth floor in Westwood. They signed non-disclosure agreements and tax forms on her oak desk, and she photocopied their driver's licenses. She gave them each a large manila envelope and told them to look at the contents.

The first photograph was a black-and-white head shot of a cheekboned model whose name Jason didn't know, but whom he recognized from magazine covers. The name and telephone number of her agency in New York were printed on it.

"I'm sure you recognize Lissa Court," Celia Weather said, as though any man would.

"Hoboy," Martin confirmed.

"Is that her name," Jason said. He was still looking at the photo. She was visually compelling, but in an overperfect supermodel way that didn't attract him. But she certainly riveted the eyes. He slipped the head shot behind and looked at the second photo. It was of an attractive woman.

"Oh," he said, when after a few seconds, he recognized Lissa Court without her supermodel makeup.

Robert said, "She was involved with Dwight Cooper, I think, right?"

"More than involved," Celia Weather said. "She's Donna's mother."

"Yeah," Martin said. "You can see it in the mouth and the bridge of the nose."

Jason searched for signs of Donna in Lissa Court's face. He didn't find them, but he wasn't sure he could quite remember what Donna looked like.

"Miss Court is the source of the threat against Donna's safety. There should be a photocopy of a letter there as well."

There was. It showed a single line of handwriting. The rest of the page of a letter had been masked with tape or paper during photocopying, truncating the ascending and descending parts of the letterforms on the lines below and above:

underestimate me, Dwight. I'll do what I have to. Donna belongs

He turned it over. Nothing on the other side.

"Sort of maybe a threat," he said.

Martin said, "Yeah."

Robert looked at Celia Weather. "What do you think of it?"

"It could very possibly be a threat against Donna's safety. I'm paid to assume the worst. And now, so are you."

Jason said, "What's the rest of the letter say?"

"I am not privy to that information."

"I see."

She rose. They rose with her, still clutching photos and papers. "Study the rest of the packet, and memorize the photo of Lissa Court without makeup. If you have any questions, call me." She gave them a businesslike smile. "I'll meet you tomorrow afternoon at two o'clock, at Mr. Cooper's residence. Casual dress is fine as long as it's professional looking. The address is in the information packet."

She nodded. Everyone nodded. Jason nodded an extra time just because it was fun. She showed them out.

hat do you think of her?"

They were sitting in the front room of the groovy beach pad in the afternoon with the door open. A warm coastal breeze flowed in, carrying the sounds of people talking as they passed on the sidewalk and cars cruising the street for parking. The rain lamp in Robert's room was silent.

Jason looked up. "Celia Weather? Seems professional."

Robert nodded. Jason went back to studying his packet. "Why, what do you think of her?"

Robert contemplated.

"Nice legs."

"I hadn't noticed."

He looked up. Robert was looking at him one-eyed.

"Well, okay, yeah," he admitted.

"Too short," Martin said.

Robert looked back down at his papers. "Hey," he said suddenly.

Jason looked up. "What?"

"I didn't know that was Dwight in *Beach Monster Horror Party*. He was The Rock Star."

"There's a stretch."

"Did you see him on *Saturday Night Live*?"

"No. How was he?"

"Not funny."

"So he fit right in."

"Pretty much."

Jason said, "Says here Dwight dated Lissa Court for three years. Before that, she was in a two-year affair with Bernardo Rossini and Dwight was with . . . let's see . . ." He flipped through a couple of pages. "Emma Walsh, Kitty Wilson, Claudine Baskin, Yvette Lazar . . . Olivia di Bennetto, and . . . Audrey Swenson."

"And before that," Robert said, "I believe Lissa was tracking red shifting in the cosmic background radiation."

"Right, and Dwight had that think tank on the distal repellent force."

"Olivia di Bennetto's hot."

Jason waited.

"Grace Kelly was hot," Robert concluded.

Jason grinned. "Dorothy L'Amour," he countered.

Martin said, "Ann-Margret."

Robert nodded. Jason said, "You win."

They pondered Ann-Margret for a few moments and then went back to reading.

"Pop quiz," Jason said. He showed Robert the picture of Lissa Court. "Who's this?"

"Ann-Margret," Robert said.

"And this?" The blank side of the stapled paper packet.

"Ann-Margret."

"This?" The other picture of Lissa Court.

"Two jackalopes eating blue carrots in a purple meadow."

"Your accuracy is astonishing."

"Yeah. Let me see the one of Ann-Margret again."

"Celia Weather has nice legs," Jason said, "but I want to really blow her away tomorrow. I want us to know everything in these packets by the next time we see her."

Martin nodded. "Cool by me."

THEY WERE IN Celia Weather's silver, mirror-windowed Lincoln, parked.

Robert said, "He attended but did not graduate from high school. By that time, he was already playing in clubs in the Dallas/Forth Worth area even though he was under age."

Jason said, "Noticed by Glen Allen at a Battle of the Bands. Backed the Glen Allen Trio on acoustic guitar until Allen's death in 1972. Recorded three albums with them: *Meet the Glen Allen Trio*, *The Glen Allen Trio: Ban the Bum!*, and *An Evening with the Glen Allen Trio*."

"You've been studying," she said. "That's very good. Now if you can just recognize Lissa Court without her makeup, we're covered."

"Lissa Court?" Jason asked Robert.

Robert shook his head. "Lissa Court? Who's that?"

Martin said, "Isn't she that model?"

The Lincoln was stopped in a sloping, car-sized inset to the iron perimeter fence. The gate was one carlength down a driveway that fell off the edge of the narrow hill road and sank until it was swallowed by gloom and vegetation. They got out and walked over fallen carob fruit and bottlebrush to the gate. She gave them each a slip of paper. "This is the security code. Try it."

Robert punched the code in and it didn't work. She reset it

and he tried again, and the gate hummed and swung open. They got back in the Lincoln and she drove down onto twisting, crumble-edged asphalt.

The house came into sight around the first curve, two stories tall, its brown shingles thirty feet below the Lincoln and the hillside driveway. The same dry plant matter that littered the sidewalk and driveway was scattered across the peaked rooftop. Squirrels darted through the moving branches of tall black walnut trees that dappled the house and grounds in shadow.

The driveway descended and traversed a four-foot bridge that spanned a natural drainage culvert reiterated with concrete. She parked in front of the house, and they walked to the door in the mild wind. An invisible squirrel chittered, and a walnut dropped onto the stone walk, staccato against the rustle of trees.

Cora Smith was sixtyish and very nice, and it bothered Jason to meet her. She was an older black woman who worked in a domestic capacity for a rich white man. Jason didn't like stereotypes. But he liked Cora. He also liked her coffee. But he got uncomfortable with the little coffee service she set up on a tray. Robert, too, seemed unusually polite, and Jason interpreted this as unease. Martin was always exceptionally polite around women anyway, so it was hard to tell there.

Celia Weather had made introductions and then gone to pick up Donna, leaving them sitting on barstools around the island in Dwight Cooper's kitchen—really Cora Smith's kitchen . . . but not really—selecting sugar cubes with small silver tongs. The kitchen was open to the dining room and to the front entryway. Around through the entryway was the living room, where French doors looked out on a short back yard from which the hill climbed back.

"Dollop?" Jason asked Robert.

"Six."

Jason poured a lot of cream into Robert's mug from a creamer that matched it. Martin sipped his black.

Cora Smith got a copper colander from a cabinet. "Would you like something to eat?"

Jason was hungry, but he didn't want her to make anything for him, so he said, "No, I'm fine, thanks."

"No thank you," Robert agreed.

Martin said, "What you got?"

"I can make you some sandwiches."

Martin slid off his stool. "Don't trouble yourself, we can get it."

"All right," she said. "If you can't find something, you let me know. There's cold chicken in the refrigerator." She reached into a plastic grocery bag on the counter, pulled a small handful of pea pods out of it, put them on the counter, and began cutting their stems off and placing them in the colander. Martin found a sourdough loaf in the breadbox and looked through the refrigerator.

Jason said, "Does Donna eat at school?"

"She eats lunch at school," Cora Smith said. "I cook her breakfast and make her dinner."

"Is she hard to cook for?"

"No, not especially hard. The child has her likes and dislikes, though, I'll say that."

"What won't she eat?"

"Let me see now." She pulled a new supply of pea pods out of the bag, put them on the counter, and began cutting again. "Macaroni and cheese is her favorite. She will not eat beets, will not eat *green* olives, and she abhors cooked apples. She loves ice cream—only the smooth kind, mind you—but does not like custard. Mayo's in the door, Martin."

"Uh . . . Ah! Thanks."

Robert said, "What are you making tonight?"

"Tonight is pot roast, pea pods, brown bread and butter, and her favorite dessert. Sweet potato pie."

Martin's head popped back from behind the refrigerator, where he was working at the counter. "Somebody say sweet potato pie?"

"Donna calls it swee'tato pie." She turned briefly to glance at them. "There's plenty."

"Call it whatever you want," Martin said. "Ah'm *there*, Jack."

Jason's desire not to be served warred with his sweet potato pie lust. "Sweet potato pie," he said to Robert. Robert shrugged.

Pressing top slices onto cold chicken sandwiches—three of them, Jason noted—Martin said, "Robert, you never had sweet potato pie?"

"I don't think so."

Without turning toward them, Cora Smith said, "I make good sweet potato pie. You'll think you're back home."

Robert said, "Your sweet potato pie will remind me of Sunland-Tujunga?"

She turned and smiled. "My home, honey. Not yours."

Martin opened a drawer, closed it, and opened another.

"Second drawer over," Cora Smith said.

Martin found a knife in that drawer. "Sunland-Tujunga soul food," he snorted, slicing sandwiches on a diagonal. "Yeah, microwave burrito, maybe."

A clock somewhere in the house chimed two-thirty. Jason said, "Do you mind if we look around?"

"Help yourself. Why don't you look through the record collection and put some music on? It's over there by the TV."

Martin stayed in the kitchen and chatted with her. Jason and Robert took their sandwiches into the living room. Dwight had a dozen CDs in a little wooden rack on an entertainment center that held a forty-inch television, but it was dwarfed by two walls of floor-to-ceiling shelves filled with record jackets. Browsing head-sideways through the jacket spines, they recognized few of the names. Finally, Jason pulled out two at random and gave Robert the choice.

"Jukey Chapman," he said, holding up the first one, "or King Miles." Both covers were creased and aged, their cover photos depicting scruffy, long-haired, youngish men in open silk shirts with pointy collars. Jason wondered how they all looked now, and how many of them had survived the passing of their brief careers and how many had died of overdose.

Robert studied them. "King Miles has better hair."

When the first bass solo came around, Jason took it back off the turntable.

"You didn't like that?"

He put it back in its sleeve and jacket and on the shelf. "I can't handle any song with both an Alice in Wonderland reference and a bass solo. What CDs does he have?"

Robert looked through the little rack. "He's got John Tesh."

"You're kidding me."

"Maybe Donna likes it." Robert pulled one out. "Here's one. Eric Clapton?"

Jason looked through the records some more.

"Aha," he said. He pulled out a Staple Singers record and put it on the turntable. As it started, he opened the French doors and went into the back yard. The lot was sunken into the hills and the back yard was gray and cool under the harboring canopy of trees. From the French doors to the cut slope of the hillside was about fifteen feet, ten covered by low, weathered redwood decking. The other five feet and the hillside were bare dirt through which roots surfaced partially for a few feet of air and then disappeared. Higher, the hillside was leaf-strewn under black walnut and eucalyptus trees. The plant fragrance on the breeze was specifically Hollywood Hills, specifically money. You didn't get it in Hollywood proper, six minutes down the ludicrously narrow and winding streets. It smelled sad and faint, like the memory of summer camp.

The Staple Singers sang "Respect Yourself."

Robert came out. "It's weird," he said, standing next to Jason.

"You mean how normal it is?"

"Yeah."

"Yeah. Somebody must manage Dwight's money for him."

"No books, did you notice?"

"You're right. Just records."

Above them, the gate motor jolted and the gate began to crank open.

"Donna's home," Jason said. "How you feeling about this, Mr. Giant?"

"Fee fi fo fum. I feel weird."

"Me too. This is a strange gig."

They went in. Martin stood and said, "Showtime," and joined them in the living room. Through the kitchen window, they saw the silver Lincoln make the last turn around the entry drive and park in front of the house. Celia Weather got out. The passenger's door with its mirrored glass opened halfway and two little black shoes dangled behind it before jumping the few inches to the ground.

The key in the front lock turned and Donna blasted into the living room like a junior tornado.

"Cora, Cora, Cora!" She flew through the hall, a hurricane of little girl clothes and clutched papers, and disappeared into the kitchen. Mobile homes in Redding lost their roofs and submarine fleets were recalled from the North Atlantic. Celia Weather came in behind her and closed the door.

"Somebody got an A on something?" Jason asked.

She shrugged. "She didn't say a word to me about it."

They went to the archway between the living room and kitchen. Donna was up on one of the barstools, and Cora Smith was looking at what was laid out on the counter and drying her hands on a kitchen towel.

"This one is a *paramecium*," Donna was saying. She was careful with the pronunciation, and got it right. Jason came in a few steps behind her to look at the paper. It had crayon drawings of several blobby things with hairs sticking out of them. "And you know what they call these, like, hairs? They're called Celia! Isn't that weird?"

Cora Smith said, "Are you sure about that, baby?"

"Yup, they're called Celia. The teacher said."

Jason said, "I think they're actually called *cilia*."

She turned and looked at him, and then at Martin, but only for a split second, and then she saw Robert.

Celia Weather said, "Donna, I have a surprise for you."

Donna seemed frozen, her face tilted up and her eyes on Robert's face, unmoving. It was a tableau: Donna on her knees on the barstool, looking up at Robert with her mouth open; Cora Smith and Celia Weather looking at Donna; Robert with a friendly expression on his face. Jason glanced from Donna to Robert. The moment could go either way.

Robert said, "I like your picture. What are the other things called? Is that one an amoeba? I like amoebas. They're really squiggly. Did you see all these today? I had a microscope, but my brother broke it. Which one's the paramecium?"

"This one."

"Do you like those best? I do."

"Yes."

The moment drew out in silence. Nobody moved.

Donna turned to consider her artwork seriously.

She said, "I like the meebas, too. Yesterday we saw sugar? It was like little squares? That's why they call it sugar cubes."

Celia Weather said, "Do you remember The Giant, Donna?"

Donna nodded.

"He's really big, isn't he? Remember we talked about him keeping you company for a while?" She nodded at Donna, prompting a yes answer. Donna looked at her.

Robert said, "I think they call it sugar cubes because they make the sugar into cubes, not because the sugar grains are square."

"I don't think so," Donna said reasonably, considering his opinion but rejecting it. "Parameciums live in swamp water."

Robert said, "Cool, do you have any games?"

Cora Smith said, "Oh, she has more games than any three children."

"Our Nintendo's broken. I have Uno and Chinese checkers and snakes and ladders and Hungry Hungry Hippos and 'nopoly." She cocked her head on one hand and pondered. "Now, let me think." She tapped her cheek with two fingers. "What other games do I have?"

"You want to play one?" Robert said.

This was deemed acceptable. "Okay. What game should we play?"

"You choose."

"How about, um . . . how about . . . how about Crazy Eights?"

"Okay, but you'll have to teach me."

Jason said, "Can we play?"

She looked at him and at Martin and jumped down off the barstool. "Okay, come this way." She went off down the hallway, past a dark, tall grandfather clock. They followed.

"Dinner at five," Cora Smith said behind them.

Every other day:

Up at seven-fifteen and sit on the futon, discogent, drink a cup of tea because it doesn't lobby for a nap at four in the afternoon like coffee does, arrive at Dwight Cooper's house at eight-thirty to relieve the Bellweather security guy who did the night shift, pick up Robert and Donna, drop Donna at Wonderland Elementary School at five to nine, watch her go in through the teachers' parking lot and onto the yard, keep watching until she reaches Mrs. Kinsella, the teacher's aide who works the yard and watches out for Donna, say good morning to Robert on the way back, arrive at Denny's at nine-fifteen, arrive at the Cooper residence at ten-fifteen, hang out with Robert and read. Out again at two, watch Donna come out through the teachers' parking lot carrying more things than when she'd arrived, drive her home, hang around until she falls asleep, drive home, skip a day because it's Martin's turn.

She answered questions about school. After a few days, the answers got less perfunctory. At the end of the first week, there were actual conversations in the car:

"Our class is going to the zervatory," she announced as she climbed into the pickup beside Jason. Robert squeezed in after her.

"The Griffith Park Zervatory?" Jason asked, watching in his side-view mirror for a chance to get onto the street. Until this week, he hadn't known that parents picking their kids up from school lost all their driving skills and became stupider than a Hanson song. Another thing learned in the grand pageant that is life.

Donna nodded. "Mrs. Banks says they have a big telescope."

Jason got into traffic and they headed down the hill and toward Mulholland.

Robert said, "I like going to the *observatory*."

"Me too!" Donna said. "The zervatory's cool!"

"Have you been there before?"

"Nope."

"What are you going to do there?"

"Mrs. Banks said we're going to look at Saturn."

"I remember doing that when I was a kid," Jason said. "They have a big pendulum there, too, that knocks over pins as the earth rotates."

"What's a pendulum?"

"It's . . . uh . . . " What *was* a pendulum? "It's, uh . . . do you like going on the swings?"

"Yes."

"It's anything that swings back and forth like that."

She looked askance at him, suspicious that the adult was taking advantage of her, which he was, since his explanation was oversimple. She looked up at Robert to see what The Giant thought.

Robert said, "Why don't you look tomorrow on the playground?"

"Only the little kids have swings."

"You can still go look, right?"

She shrugged agreeably. "I guess."

Jason turned onto Mulholland, the street that capped the ridge of the hills. "You have a pendulum at your house. Did you know that?"

She looked guarded again. "No . . ."

"You do," Jason said. "I wonder if you can find it."

SHE LINGERED ON her way to the front door, looking uncertainly at the front of the house.

"I'll give you a hint," Jason said. "It's inside."

"Which floor?"

He smiled and sealed his lips pointedly.

"I don't like you," she giggled.

"I haven't liked you since nineteen forty-two," he said.

"I haven't liked you since nineteen forty-three!" she countered through her giggles.

"Good in intent," Jason said. "Weak in execution."

"I haven't liked you since nineteen forty-four!" she said.

"Okay, you win. Let's go inside."

She went in first. Robert said, "It's interesting watching you with a six-year-old. You treat them like adults."

"No, I just don't treat them like idiots."

Robert reflected. "That's true," he said. "The only people you treat like idiots are adults."

"The only people who are idiots are adults."

"That's an interesting philosophy."

"What's yours?"

"I think it's very important to always be honest with children."

"Well," Jason said. "Never having had children, I can't say."

"I think it's very important," Robert said definitely.

Inside, Donna, waiting, pounced. "I haven't liked you since nineteen fifty hundred gazillion!"

"Donna!" Cora Smith said from the kitchen, surprised.

"It's okay," Jason called. "We're just playing a game." To Donna, he said, "But we better stop, huh."

Her eyes sparkled with barely contained humor.

"Tell you what," he said. "You see if you can find that pendulum."

"What do I get?"

"The satisfaction of having expanded your nascent intellect."

She chortled. She clearly had no idea what he'd just said, but she found him very funny.

"Tell me a story."

"All right, then, you find it, I'll tell you a story."

She ran off into the living room.

"Clock?" Robert murmured as they watched her lift the sofa cushions. Jason nodded and went into the kitchen, called Celia Weather, and told her about the field trip. She said she probably wouldn't need them to accompany Donna, but she'd get back to him about it.

Donna was looking behind the big-screen TV when he got off the phone. She didn't find the pendulum that powered the grandfather clock until given a series of increasingly bald-faced hints that prompted her into the hallway. After dinner, to honor his part of the bargain, Jason told her the story of The Little Clam That Liked to Dance Even Though It Had No Feet. Robert did an interpretive clam dance. The critics were unanimous in their acclaim.

• • •

THE LITTLE CLAM THAT LIKED TO DANCE
EVEN THOUGH IT HAD NO FEET

Once there was a little clam named . . .

—Harold.

Okay, he was named Harold. Harold was—

—No, Herbert.

Herbert or Harold?

—Hhhhhh . . .

His name was Herbertharold.

—That's a stupid name.

How funny! That's what all his friends said. "Herbertharold," they said, "you have a stupid name." Do you already
know this story?

—No!

Are you sure? Because if you already know it, I won't tell it
again.

—I don't know it.

Okay. You're sure.

—Yes.

You're positive.

—Yes.

Because if you're not, I won't tell it.

—I told you I'm sure.

Okay.

All Herbertharold's friends said to him, "Herbertharold," they said, "you have a stupid name."

Herbertharold was very sad about this, because all his friends had excellent clam names like . . .

—Sally

And . . .

Burboosa.

Did I ask you?

Sorry.

What was the other clam friend's name?

—Um . . . Baboosa.

Fine.

One day, Herbertharold, Sally, and Baboosa were—

Burboosa.

. . .were walking to the—

Burboosa or Baboosa?

Do you hear me saying "Baboosa"?

No, that's why I was—

—It's Baboosa.

It's Baboosa. Were walking home after school, and they saw a flyer for an after-school dance class. Do you know what a flyer is?

—No.

It's a piece of paper with useful information on it. So they saw this flyer that told them that there was going to be a dance class after school.

"Oh boy!" Herbertharold said. "A dance class!"

Sally said, "Don't be stupid, Herbertharold. We're clams. We don't have feet, so we can't dance."

If they don't have feet, how are they walking home from—

Herbertharold said, "I don't care if I'm a clam! I like to dance!"

"Don't be stupid, Herbertharold," Baboosa said. "How are you supposed to go to a dance class if you have no feet?"

"I don't know," Herbertharold said. "But I'm going to that dance class."

When the day of the dance class came, Herbertharold was all excited. After school, he went to the auditorium to sign up with all the other students. When he got to the front of the line, the sign-up person said, "Why are *you* here, little clam?"

"I'm here for the dance class," said Herbertharold.

The person said, "But you're a *clam*. Clams can't dance; they don't have feet!"

"Oh yeah?" Herbertharold said. "I can too dance. Watch this." And he sucked in his clam gut—

Hrmp!

. . . just like that, and he limbered up his clam shell—just like that—and right in front of everybody, he did a little clam dance.

Just like that.

Then he finished and he looked at the sign-up person and said, "See? I can dance."

See?

And he stuck out his little clam tongue.

Bleah.

The sign-up person, whose name was . . .

—Mr. Blumpylumpy.

. . . whose name was Mr. Blumpylumpy, said, "That's the stupidest dance I ever saw. Go away, you clam."

Herbertharold was very sad. He left the auditorium and walk . . . uh, went home.

He was sad all day and all night. He was sad the next day and the day after that. He was sad at school and he was sad at soccer practice. Poor Herbertharold.

—Poor Herbaharaa.

You realize soccer has the same problem as—

One day, he woke up for school—

Sorry.

. . . and he said to himself, "I just won't do their stupid dances. I'll do my own."

Is she . . .

Um . . .

I think so.

'Night, sweetheart.

Sleep tight.

onna was always asleep when the Bellweather night guy showed up. Jason and Robert greeted him, got into the pickup, and wove its headlight beams through a dark macramé of hill roads that unraveled into the San Fernando Valley, ending at a booth in a deli in a large corner shopping complex.

After they ordered, Jason said, "It's been a couple weeks. How do you like it?"

Robert shrugged. "It's all right." He glanced across the restaurant.

"Just all right?"

"It's fine," Robert said, glancing again. Jason looked. The booth Robert was looking at contained two young women. One of them looked up and Jason's gaze flicked back to Robert.

"Look, look," Jason said. "Robert see girl."

"Let's go meet them."

"You go ahead."

"There's two of them."

"You're very tall. It'll be fine."

Robert gave him a look.

Jason said, "Look, drag me over there if you want, but—"

"Okay, let's go." Robert slid out of the booth.

They walked across the restaurant. The young women were both attractive. One was dark-haired, the other blonde. Both had nice figures.

"Hi there," Robert said. The women looked up. "I'm Robert, this is Jason."

"I'm Natalia," said the brunette. "This is Julie."

Julie said, "Hi."

Robert said, "Would you mind if we joined you?"

"Okay," Natalia said. She slipped around to Julie's side, and Jason slid in and made room for Robert.

Robert said, "We were just sitting over there and saw you, so we thought we'd say hello."

"Hello," Jason concurred.

Julie said, "Hi."

"Cool," Natalia said. "So, what do you do?"

Robert said, "I'm an actor." He raised a hand. "I know, another actor."

"No, I think that's cool," Natalia said. "Julie's an actress. I'm an executive assistant for a law office."

Julie said to Robert, "Are you working?"

"I just had a walk-on on *Robbery/Homicide*, and I had a line on *Joanna* a couple of months ago."

"That's cool," Julie said. "I'm still getting started." Both women turned to Jason. Julie said, "And what do you do?" and gave him an encouraging smile.

Jason said, "I'm a grape seeder. I take the seeds out of seedless grapes. Most people think seedless grapes just grow that way, but they don't, of course, because how would they reproduce?"

He smiled.

The women bore expressions that weren't puzzled, but which evidenced a lack of computation, as though after careful comparison of what Jason had said to anything stored in memory, a small yellow flag had popped up bearing the words ILLEGAL OPERATION : RETRY/ABORT.

Natalia turned to Robert. "Did you get to meet Joanna?"

Robert answered, but Jason wasn't paying attention anymore. His gaze was ranging about the restaurant, looking at other people, the decor, the bakery case, anything. He was aware that Robert was not pleased with him, but his disinterest in picking up these women was so pronounced that it would probably show up on a CAT scan.

The women and Robert were both looking at him.

"What?" he said.

Robert said, "How's a movie sound to you?"

"Not me," Jason said. "I need to be up early. Grapes are early bloomers."

Julie said, "I think you're making that up about grapes."

BACK IN THEIR booth, Jason said, "Sorry."

Robert dismissed the apology with a flutter of the fingers. "But you could have at least *tried* not to be yourself."

"Next time, I'll wax rhapsodic about my favorite Spice Girl."

"Natalia liked you."

"No, Natalia liked attention."

"She's cute."

"No click."

Robert raised a forefinger. "Hillel says 'He who waits for the click ends up dateless.' "

"Who's Hillel?"

"He's like Confucius, only for Jews."

"Did he say anything about thrusting friends into the lairs of wily shiksas?"

"No, Hillel is strangely silent on that subject."

"Did Hillel have any other useful dating advice?"

"Yes. He said, 'You're being difficult.' "

"I am not being difficult. I am simply not interested in Natalia and Julie."

"You didn't really give them a chance, did you? You made a snap judgment. How would you know you're not interested?"

"Some things are better intuited than deduced."

Their food came. Jason put Bermuda onion on his bagel and lox and said, "And anyway, my snap judgments are pretty good."

Robert was pouring syrup on his matzoh brei. "Not perfect, though. Your snap judgment of me in high school was that I was a drama geek."

"You were a drama geek." He chased down each little green caper that had rolled off the bagel and stuck it back on, tining it into the cream cheese so it wouldn't roll again. "I was a music geek, you were a drama geek."

"Was Martin an art geek?"

Jason felt back through adult interpretations layered on high school perceptions. "No, I think he was an artist."

"I thought he was good."

"He was. I didn't know you could put syrup on matzoh brei."

"I'm Reform."

"Which means?"

"I'm circumcised, but I like Latin girls and I put syrup on my matzoh brei."

"Oy vay."

Robert started to say something but ate instead. When he

started and stopped again, Jason said, "What."

After another false start, Robert said, "I was thinking of maybe getting bar mitzvahed."

"You weren't? Before, I mean?"

Robert shook his head.

"Don't you have to be thirteen?"

"No, you can do it later. What do you think of that?"

"I don't know that I think anything. You've been mulling it for a while?"

"A little while. I got a Hebrew primer last week and learned the letters. I've just been feeling sort of disconnected from, you know, my, uh, you know, heritage." He looked uncertain. "What do you think?"

"Beats me whether it would connect you with your heritage, but it sounds like a good challenge."

Robert nodded. The waitress brought the check. They requested dessert menus.

When they were considering the menus, Jason said, "Marisa called last week. She's getting married."

"Ah . . ." Robert nodded thoughtfully. He took a thoughtful drink of water, and then said in a thoughtful voice, "How do you feel about that?"

"I don't know." Jason turned the dessert menu over. Eclairs. He hadn't had an eclair in a long time. "I know I feel something, but I don't know how to identify the feeling. I wouldn't have thought it would affect me, because I barely think about her anymore. But it, ah, got in amongst me."

Robert caught the attention of the waitress and they ordered. Then he said, "So what do you think about it?"

"I don't know. Maybe it means I'm still unresolved with something. Or maybe 'unresolved' is pop psychology crap and I just need to give it a couple more days and it'll go away by itself.

Maybe I still love her somewhere. I don't think so, though. Maybe I feel unmanly for failing to stay married." He shrugged. "Maybe I'm having exactly the reaction she wanted; maybe there was something less friendly going on than 'Hi, Jason, I just wanted to let you know.' "

"I think that last part is likely."

"To be honest, me too, but why? What would she get out of making my stomach hurt?"

"The knowledge that she can still make your stomach hurt."

The waitress brought an eclair and a bowl of tapioca pudding and left a revised check.

Jason said, "But why would that matter? We're apart. She should be caring about how her fiancé feels, not about how I feel. I don't understand that."

Robert studied him for a long few moments.

"You're a very insightful man," he said. "It surprises me where your perceptions go blank."

Jason snorted. " 'You know, Jase, for a smart guy, you're awfully dense.' "

"Close, but not quite." Robert dug into his tapioca. "If it were you getting married, you'd give your fiancée all your concern and thought, without ever considering whether you could use the fact of your affiancing to hurt Marisa."

"Right."

"And that is a way that makes sense for you."

"It makes sense period, not just for me."

"I think you already know that just because something works for you, that doesn't mean it works for everyone."

"And I think you already know that some things are just the way they are, despite intellectual parlor tricks that show all philosophies to be of equal value. All philosophies are not of equal value. It's like art: What works is of greater value than what doesn't. Giving your attention to your current person in a positive way works better than giving it to your previous person in a negative way."

"For you."

"No, not for me, for anyone."

"You seem very sure of this."

"Yes, I'm very sure of this. How can anyone not be sure of this?"

"A lot of people aren't."

"A lot of people don't think very much." Jason bit off most of his eclair.

Robert said, "You do know your position is illogical."

"Lobic ifilobical."

"What?"

He swallowed impatiently. "Logic is illogical. Re-read Gödel."

Robert said, "Hm," and looked at Jason through narrowed eyes.

"You give me a system of logic that doesn't contain its own fatal paradox, and I'll show you where it says you shouldn't make your oversensitive ex-husband feel lousy when you remarry."

"You show me a guy who doesn't make any effort to get to know the women he meets," Robert countered, "and I'll show you a guy who's going home alone tonight, tomorrow night, next Tuesday night, and every night next year."

Jason said, "Hm."

Eclairs looked better than they tasted. He considered ordering another one.

"Maybe I'll just avoid her in the future," he said, and waved down the waitress.

arisa was at the doorstep of the groovy beach pad when he got home. She said, "Hi," as she stood, and smoothed her skirt. It was tan, and went perfectly with a cream-colored, ridged sweater that set off her dark skin and eyes. A flat gold necklace hung over the sweater. She looked excellent.

Because he couldn't think of anything better, Jason said, "Hello," and stood and looked at her.

After a few moments, she laughed. "So . . . can I come in?"

"Sure."

"It's a bachelor pad, all right," she pronounced, standing in the living room. She peeked into his bedroom. "Your music system looks bigger. There's no room for your bed."

"I came into a little bit of money last year. Can't make music without money."

"And that's Robert's room." She came back and they sat on the couch. "How is Robert?"

"He's fine."

"I saw him on *Joanna* and I said to Jack, 'I know him! That's

Robert Goldstein!' We watch *Joanna* all the time. And Martin, how is he?"

"Also fine."

She was wearing her makeup in a beautiful way that she'd not done when they were together. It worked well in the treacherous moonlight that came through the window, made it hard for Jason to remember anything. She shifted a little and from within the sweater, sweet perfume invaded his head, and then it was hard to know anything, let alone remember it.

"You're probably wondering why I came."

"I figured you'd tell me eventually."

She looked up at an angle and screwed her fingers together. "This is a little embarrassing. . . ." When she looked back at him, he smiled at her. "Well, you know I'm getting married in a week."

"Yes, you told me."

"Oh, I had this all planned, and now I'm chickening out. . . ." She bit her full lower lip, and Jason's heart went *clank!* and threw a rod. If a tuxedoed cartoon wolf had been present in the room, its eyeballs would have shot out of its head.

"Go ahead," he said.

"I should just come out with it."

"I would say so."

"Okay. Don't get mad at me." She took a big breath and let it out. "Here's the thing. Jack and I agreed that before we got married, we could each have one last fling, and I want you to be mine."

Pop!

His first reaction was to be flattered and to enjoy the fantasy of retaking her.

"I see," he said.

"I hope you're not mad. It was always so nice with us. I wanted that again before, well, you know, one last time."

His second reaction was starting to creep up, but he couldn't tell what it was yet.

"Well, it wasn't always so nice," he said. "That last year—"

"Yes, I know. But we've both grown since then." She leaned forward and took his hands in hers, her skin warm and dry, sliding over his. "Do you still find me attractive?"

The second reaction, once the nerve endings on the back of his hand had stopped shouting *hallelujah!*, seemed to be a sense of manipulation, but instead of displacing the sense of flattery, it just added itself to the mix, leaving him simultaneously eager and stubborn, hanging head-down in a waterslide, wanting to slide down, snagged on something.

"Anyone would. Find you attractive."

"I didn't ask about anyone. I asked about you."

The third reaction was a sense of cliché, but he decided to forgive this because she smelled good.

"I . . ."

She slipped closer. Where her fingers brushed his forearm, the hairs stood. She leaned in and kissed his jaw, near his ear. Nobody's face had been there in a long time. It was smooth and soft, pretty and feminine.

"Is Jack out having his fling tonight too?" he managed.

"I think so." She kissed his neck. Without thinking, he angled his head so she could continue, and his hand rose and stopped just short of caressing her hair.

The fourth reaction was the faint edge of a subtle sense of wrongness. The hand near her hair gestured *stop* vaguely, where she couldn't see it.

"He knows you're here?"

"He knows I'm somewhere. He doesn't know it's you."

She kissed his cheek and slid one hand behind his head to turn him toward her, and kissed his lips, her hand on his chest and sliding lightly down. In his imaginary hearing, water rushed and crashed, though the room was almost silent.

In the moment when he would have capsized in her kiss, he hesitated. She pulled away, looking at him.

"Don't you want me?"

The sense of cliché again.

"Like a . . ."

He couldn't think of like a what. He nodded.

Her brow furrowed attractively. "Then what?"

"I don't think this is going to work."

Cliché was contagious.

"Why not?"

He began to stand and decided sitting was better. "Because I'm . . ."

. . . I'm what? . . . not that kind of guy? . . . too conventional? . . . outmoded?

. . . your ex-husband?

Getting pissed off?

That was it. That last one. The fifth reaction.

"What?" she said, her eyes big and pretty, shaking her head slightly in confusion.

"I think that's all, for this." He shifted a little and stood, which was easier now.

"Why?"

"Just—I think that's all."

She stood. "I should have known."

The sixth reaction was an onset of boredom. "How about we don't need to get nasty with each other? I'm flattered. It just—"

"I should have known you wouldn't be man enough."

He opened the door. "That's true, I'm not. But there's a bar on Washington, near the beach walk. I understand that's where all the human vibrators hang out."

Her eyes and mouth set in lines that he remembered. She was going to knife him through the heart with whatever she said next.

"You're not half the man he is," she said. "Jack can fuck me like a real man."

Or maybe she was just going to say something stupid. Funny how the old things didn't hurt once you weren't the old person anymore.

"Probably not tonight," he reminded her.

She wheeled on his doorstep. She'd slapped him before, when they were married, but he'd never actually caught the wrist before. They stood facing one another, posed in the moonlight: angry, pretty hand frozen in his grip, dark eyes glittering. He considered laughing heartily like Clark Gable, but decided not to get frivolous.

"You'll always be a loser," she said. "Just look at this place."

"Marisa . . ." He released her hand. "What's the capital of North Dakota?"

"Bismarck," she said triumphantly.

"Go there," he said, and closed the door.

y the time morning dared interrupt him, he'd whipped his
irritation and insult into a full-blown raging snit. He calcu-
lated that over the course of the night, he had paced almost
four miles on the bedroom-to-bedroom circuit. Twenty-five feet
times two, once a minute, sixty minutes to the hour, six hours.

"Go bounding off after her *god*damn stick," he fumed in the
bathroom.

"*Half* the man," he shared with the stove.

"*Real* man," he muttered as he locked the front door.

He had a long, one-sided conversation with her in the pickup
on the way to Dwight's house. She occasionally interrupted him,
but mostly he cornered her viciously and she cried.

"Let's go," he said to Robert when Cora Smith let him in.

"You're in a good mood," Robert observed.

A little denim jumper over a yellow T-shirt blasted out the
open door at Mach 3 and jittered hyperactively by the pickup.

Jason looked back. "She's ready early."

"Remember, it's field trip day? I talked to Celia Weather last
night. We don't need to be there. The regular security guys will

hang around and the teachers have been alerted, but Lissa Court is on a photo shoot in New York."

"Good, fine, let's go."

Donna was happier than Al Sharpton in the Land of Microphones.

"Did you know Jupiter has a moon that's bigger than the whole Earth?" she asked. They turned out of the gate onto the hill road.

Jason muttered something. Robert said, "Did you know Jupiter has more than one moon, and people used to use them to tell where they were on the Earth?"

"Did you know that Saturn's rings are made of rocks and ice?"

"Yes I did," Robert said. "Did you know that when some stars burn out, they turn into black holes?"

Jason swerved around a bottled water delivery truck. Robert's hand lifted a little. "Uh . . ."

THEY DROPPED DONNA at school and watched her until Mrs. Kinsella waved at them.

"May I take a guess?" Robert ventured as they headed down the hill.

Jason gestured it's-a-free-country.

"Marisa?"

Jason angled his head slightly in anger and felt his jaw clench.

"I guess I guessed right," Robert said. "What did she do?"

Jason told him.

"Ouch." Robert watched Mulholland Drive go by. "Uh, where are we going?"

His answer came when they entered a wide, windowy Mexican restaurant in Los Feliz, nowhere near Dwight's house or

Donna's school, but very close, Robert pointed out after they were seated, to Griffith Park.

Jason glared at him. "Problem?"

Robert shook his head and tapped absently on the table, rattling the salsa bowl. He'd occasionally lock into the three-on-two pattern accidentally, but only for a bar or so, and then it would collapse. Jason's impatience increased with each fumble. Clearly, Robert was doing this to annoy him. He crunched an angry tortilla chip. His toes wanted to yell in his shoes.

Robert stopped tapping. "So how come this bothers you?"

"Because you're not isolating the patterns. The only way to—"

"No," Robert said. "The Marisa thing."

"Oh."

Robert waited while Jason overcame his annoyance with his own mistake.

"It bothers me because it bothers me, all right? I'm supposed to what, slobber on cue? The whole thing's just . . ." He tried to think of a nonjudgmental word.

"Just what?"

"I'm *thinking*."

Beyond my understanding. Without ethical basis. Contrary to the spirit of marriage.

He settled for: "Sick."

"To you."

Jason pointedly took a chip instead of the bait.

"So . . . did you?"

"Did I what?"

"Slobber on cue?"

Jason's thumbs conga-rolled the tabletop: rrrrrrrrrr-*bap!* "Are you really asking just to ask, or do you have some predetermined insight you're trying to shunt me toward?"

Their orders came. Jason spooned shredded beef, scrambled eggs, beans, and rice onto a hot flour tortilla, soaked it all in Tapatío pepper sauce, oversalted it, and folded it into a burrito.

Robert had the same thing, but he didn't make a burrito. "I have a predetermined insight that I'm trying to shunt you toward," he said. After forkfuls of hot machaca and sips of cold, sweet horchata, he said, "If you were doing anything you really wanted to do with your life, these little conflicts wouldn't eat you up so much."

"What are you talking about?"

"What do you do for a living?"

"I make music."

"Is that what you wanted?"

"Of course."

"So, you grew up thinking, One day I'll realize all my dreams by writing the music that goes under CD-ROM games. You thought, CD-ROM game music scores are the ultimate outlet for my artistic expression. I die a little, you thought, for CD-ROM games. CD-ROM games are my life, they are my breath and destiny."

Jason's vision was blurring. He gulped horchata, dousing the pepperfire in his mouth, but it flared again when the glass was empty. "I make a living at music. That's more than a lot of musicians can say."

"Are you happy with it?"

Of course, Jason thought. I'm pro. This is the goal.

"It's fine," he said. He drank half his ice water and wiped his eyes. His foot tapped four-on-the-floor with ghost eighths on the table leg, *buh*-puh *buh*-puh *buh*-puh *buh*-puh. "I don't understand your objection."

Robert looked at him judgmentally. "Yes you do," he said.

After breakfast flan—there was no such thing, but calling it that made it okay to eat dessert in the morning—they drove up a narrow, islanded boulevard that twisted at the top, and parked in a broad lot that overlooked the city. The observatory was white and copper-domed. Its big front lawn sprouted a hexagonal statue of six white stone scientists who all looked the same except that some had bushier eyebrows. Coin-operated telescopes dotted the brushy drop-off. There were no school buses there yet, only a few cars in the lot.

They leaned against the low wall between the lot and the drop-off, five yards from a soft drink vending machine. Jason bumped his knuckles rhythmically against a painted metal post that supported the shading latticework overhead.

Robert said, "What about the Marisa thing hurt you?"

"I'm not hurt, I'm fucking pissed off."

Robert looked at him patiently.

Jason said, "That she's able to do this to me, okay, you happy?"

"Why are we here?"

Jason stopped bumping his knuckles to aim a thumb at the lawn statue. "Ask Aristotle."

"No," Robert said patiently. "Why are *we*"— he pointed back and forth between himself and Jason—"*here*?" He pointed vigorously at the ground.

"Just doing our job." His heel thumped sixteenths on the concrete.

"Our boss told us we weren't needed here." Robert eyed him. "You always put your negative energy into something productive. Tell me if I'm wrong."

"You're wrong."

A little breeze came up and riffled the green treetops below. A bicyclist crested the entrance to the parking lot and coasted toward them, clanked the bicycle to the vending machine and secured it with a combination lock, and walked across the lawn in his helmet, into the observatory.

The tip of Jason's right forefinger rubbed against the pad of his thumb, cross rhythm with his heel: eighth triplets, accents on two and four. He noticed he was doing it only when he stopped to say, "I just don't understand."

"Different things work for different people."

Jason shook his head obstinately, but without conviction. Forefinger slid against thumb again, no particular rhythm.

Two yellow school buses pulled up off the twisting road onto the far side of the parking lot like lozenges coming off a conveyor belt. They parked near the statue. Teachers exited first and parsed the subsequent flow of kid-atoms into molecules that threatened to destabilize energetically and revert into individual little enthusiasm particles. Donna was the first kid off the second bus. She bore an important-looking clipboard and stood next to Mrs. Kinsella.

Robert said, "Here's a thought. Tell me what we're doing."

"We're watching Donna."

"Why do you think we need to, when the person in charge says we don't?"

Jason shrugged. A blue Oldsmobile pulled up the drive, leveled down onto the parking lot, and parked across the lot from them.

Robert said, "This is just you needing to get out of the house."

"You doing a thesis on me or what?"

"I was going to," Robert said, "but my advisors said it would be too unrealistic."

Jason glared at him. Robert maintained his amiable expression and was not engulfed by a fireball. It was irritating.

Looking at the lot, Jason said, "Have you seen any Bellweather people today?" His other forefinger rubbed his other thumb: unison part, irrational time signature.

"No. They stay back most of the time."

"Back where? We're on top of a hill."

Robert looked startled by the thought, and studied everything. He looked at his watch. "Hmm," he said.

"Yeah, hmm."

"There's only one entrance. Maybe they're down the drive."

The children were in rough double queues now, holding hands, roughhousing, complaining, and chattering. A *threet!* of Mrs. Kinsella's whistle commanded most of their attention; herded and worried by teachers and TAs, the queues caterpillared across the lot, over the curb, and onto the lawn. Donna walked beside Mrs. Kinsella, whose attention leaped from one transgression to another to another. Jason's fingers oscillated against his thumbs.

Robert said, "Donna's smart. I was teaching her about relativity—"

The door of the Olds opened, and Lissa Court got out and called, "Donna!"

Jason's fingers froze.

Donna turned and spotted her. She dropped the clipboard and shouted, "Mommy!"

Jason pushed away from the wall. Robert said, "Is . . ."

Jason took a few undirected steps, empty-handed, and then stopped and looked around, turned and quickstepped to the bicycle, and flicked the lever that secured the bicycle seat. The seat pulled out of the frame, attached to fifteen inches of metal seat post. He stepped onto the parking lot as Donna dropped the clipboard and started running across the lawn toward her mommy. Mrs. Kinsella didn't seem to notice.

Jason broke into a run, but Donna would reach the Oldsmobile before he did.

(Not going to happen.)

For a moment, he almost contained the thing. Then it cracked open like an ampule and rage erupted through his body. He surged toward the Olds to hurt Lissa Court.

She dropped to one knee and put her arms out. Donna raced into them, whump, and the arms went around her. Murderous grace gave Jason's legs speed. His lungs expanded, pulled in air for power.

(Not going to happen. Get the hell away from that child.)

"Donna!" Robert bellowed, vaguely behind Jason somewhere. Lissa Court's face came up out of the embrace and she saw Jason bearing down on her.

(Not going to happen. Get the hell away from my child.)

The bike seat spun against his palm: heft, bore, length, balance. He roared. The roar made perfect inchoate sense, went with the rhythm of the scene, tore his throat: Coming to get you. He held Lissa Court fixed in his sight, her eyes on him as she kissed Donna's forehead and disentangled herself. She backed away. Donna didn't understand why Mommy's hug had stopped. She tried to follow Mommy into the car. Two little hands, reaching.

The door closed as Jason got there. Donna whimpered "Mommy?" and knocked on the driver's window. The door locks clicked down as he reached for the passenger's door handle, and he came around the front of the car as the engine started, the bike seat twirling in rotations along its axis, alive in his hand, oily dirt coating his palm, arcing over his shoulder, a round attack, BANG on the windshield.

The impact left a mark on the glass, but the windshield didn't break. As the Olds backed away, Donna chased it, trying to clutch the fender and screaming until Robert got there and scooped her up. Jason stayed between Robert and the car and followed it.

(Not going to happen, god damn you.)

The car slowed in its retreat. Lissa Court was weeping. She looked at her daughter in Robert's arms. The bike seat twirled and spun in Jason's hand.

"Mommy, wait!" Donna screamed, her eyes and nose red and wet, her arms outstretched, the scream given convulsive vibrato by her sobs. Her mommy blew her a kiss and backed away without a glance at Jason, cut a turn, and disappeared down the drive. Donna sobbed and reached, six feet up in Robert's embrace. Jason stood holding his club, unused adrenaline gasping against the crash of his heartbeat, swallowing pain in his torn throat, watching the empty lot entrance, his vision blurred, shuddering, the muscles of his face pulled tight into an aching grimace, not enough air in the parking lot, his face hot and wet, *not going to happen*. The bike seat beat crazy time against the side of his knee. A white sedan with *Bellweather Security* in blue letters on the door came up the drive.

onna sobbed and hiccuped behind Jason, and he heard her
fists on Robert's shoulder. "It's all right," Robert's voice
soothed. "I know. It's okay." The Bellweather sedan pulled
around to where Jason and Robert were, and two men in blue
blazers, a redhead and a brunet carrying take-out coffee cups, got
out of the sedan and closed the doors.

Looking at Robert and Donna, the redhead said, "What's
going on?" He paused to sip his coffee.

Jason's legs carried him forward, and the bike seat flung off
to his left. The redhead's step faltered and he started to turn, but
Jason reached him and banged him against the chest, two-
handed. The man hit the car and his coffee splashed across his
front and spilled across the side of the car as Jason backpedaled
half a step in counteraction to the shove, settled into a wide
stance, and backarmed him violently across the jaw. The man
staggered sideways against the side of the car, and then someone
locked Jason from behind the upper arms and pulled him back,
off-balance.

"Ease it down, there, cowboy," the other man said behind

him. The redhead righted himself and glared at Jason. He brushed at his wet shirt and his right hand closed into a solid fist. He started to walk forward. Donna wailed.

"Don't, Kel," the voice behind Jason said. "We got children here." He shook Jason. "You shoulda thought of that too, asshole."

"Yuh—" Jason gasped. He looked back, as far as he could. Four classes of schoolkids were agog. Mrs. Kinsella's hand was to her mouth.

Robert's voice said, "It's okay, Donna," as she hiccuped. Loudly, he said, "If you had been here during the kidnap attempt, you might understand a little better what's going on. Would you mind letting Jason go?"

"What kidnap attempt," the man behind Jason said.

"Lissa Court was just here. Would you mind letting Jason go?"

"How long ago," the redhead said.

Robert said, "Two minutes."

"You going to cause trouble?" the man said, close to Jason's ear.

Out of breath and not about to cooperate, Jason nodded stubbornly.

"You know he's not going to cause any trouble," Robert said over Donna's weak crying. "He just saved Donna and he's upset. He's not somebody you don't know; you know exactly who he is, and she's getting away. Let him go, please. It's upsetting everybody."

The redhead said, "Let him go, Gerritt."

After a hesitation, the armlock disengaged. Jason carried himself the few unsteady steps to the sedan and leaned against its hood.

Gerritt said, "I think we need to be brought up to date. Kel?"

Kel nodded, pulled a cellular phone from his jacket, and dialed. Donna sobbed once, but she had exhausted herself. Her head sagged against Robert's.

Gerritt said, "What kind of car?"

"An expensive blue one, kind of sparkly," Robert said.

Jason said, "Ol—" Pain spiked his throat. He whispered, "Oldsmobile. New."

"License plate?"

Jason shook his head. Robert said, "No. Are you going to go after her?"

"No, the Five and the One-thirty-four are both right here. She hit a freeway entrance within thirty seconds of leaving the lot. She's gone."

FORTY-FIVE MINUTES LATER, Jason's control was sort of coming back. He sat on a stool and leaned against a display case of Laserium merchandise in the observatory mezzanine. Robert was a few feet across the floor, leaning against the outside of a walled pit in which a thin spike on the bottom of a massive Foucault pendulum repeatedly missed the first of a row of vertical wooden dowels by a hair's breadth. Other dowels were scattered in the pit, evidence of the passing of hours. The mad-scientist zap of a Tesla coil reverberated from an adjoining stone hallway, underscoring the echoing clamor of children on a field trip.

A straight-spined young LAPD officer who looked like a movie Marine had arrived. Donna was in the Bellweather sedan with Kel. She'd gone limply. Jason didn't know how she was.

Officer Chen said, "Why didn't you let the security company"—he checked his notebook—"Bellweather, why didn't you let them know you'd be here?"

Jason was giving his statement on paper because talking hurt. He wrote:

I didn't know we would be here.

"Why *were* you here?"

We're under contract with Bellweather to watch Donna, and we had nothing better to do today.

"You could've gone to a movie, hung out, right? Why watch Donna?"

I just answered that.

"Are you being uncooperative, sir?"

No.

Celia Weather clacked into the mezzanine, approached Jason, and said, "What did you do?"

Leaning against the wall of the dowel pit, Robert said, "He kept Donna from being kidnapped while Gerritt and Kel were off getting coffee when they should have been watching Donna. Please don't be rude to him."

"What time was this?"

Gerritt said, "Eleven o'clock."

Robert said, "Eleven-fifteen. Is Donna all right?"

Celia said, "She'll be fine. Kel's a family man. He'll take care of her."

Gerritt said, "It was eleven o'clock."

Robert said, "Eleven-fifteen."

"You calling me a liar, big guy?"

Jason nodded. Robert said, "Unequivocally." Gerritt took a half step forward, and Jason's hand went up and got the front of his shirt. Officer Chen stepped in and stopped everyone.

"Take your hand off his shirt, sir," he said. Jason released it. Gerritt smoothed the rumpled fabric.

Celia Weather said, "Was it eleven or eleven-fifteen?"

"Right around eleven," Gerritt said, ready to move on.

"Minute or two either direction." He squinted in the direction of the parking lot and pointed. "We came up the drive there—"

Robert talked over him. "It was not a minute or two, and it was not either direction; it was fifteen minutes in the late direction, and you were both carrying full to-go cups of coffee. Yours is probably gone, but Kel's should still be evident on his jacket and shirt, as well as on Jason's."

Jason looked down. Coffee-stained. Eighteen-dollar shirt.

She turned to Gerritt as he began to respond, and said, "We'll talk later."

Gerritt nodded as though he were in control of the situation.

Robert pointed outside. "We were over by that vending machine—"

Celia Weather said, "How do you know it was eleven-fifteen?"

"Well." Robert smiled. "Not only do I know it was eleven-fifteen because I looked at my watch when they arrived, but I know it was *not* eleven because I looked at my watch previously, when we were wondering earlier where the security people were, and it was eleven-oh-five then."

Gerritt said, "Your watch accurate?"

"We'll worry about that later," Celia said.

A clatter in the pendulum pit meant the noon dowel had succumbed. Robert looked at his watch. He displayed it. 12:00.

"Maybe the earth is fast today," Jason rasped. It hurt, but smart remarks were not without price.

Everyone looked at their watches. Officer Chen adjusted his.

Celia Weather said, "Officer, the custodial parent is Dwight Cooper."

"Dwight Cooper the rock star?"

"Yes. I am authorized to speak for him. He would prefer that as little uproar as possible —"

Jason put his head down on the display case and tuned out until a hand on his shoulder clicked him into focus. Celia Weather said, "Go home, get some rest, get cleaned up. Be at my office at two."

"NO GERRITT?" JASON asked softly as she gestured toward the chairs in her shiny office. He'd rested his voice and had a lot of hot tea and honey. As long as he kept it soft, he'd found, it didn't hurt to talk.

"Both Gerritt and Kelly have been released from my employ."

Jason paused in mid-sit, and then sat.

Robert said, "Do you mind if I ask why?"

"They left Donna unprotected for fifteen minutes in a high-risk public situation. Then they tried to cover the mistake. Either is grounds for termination."

Robert said, "Oh."

"As was attacking Kelly. Do you understand that?"

Robert said, "Yes."

Jason said, softly, "Then don't put me in that position again."

She pursed her lips. "I beg your pardon?"

Robert said, "I think what Jason is saying is that he would be happy to observe that guideline, and that his behavior sprang from his finding himself in a situation for which he was not prepared."

"I understand where his behavior sprang from, and I am not unsympathetic. I'm saying I don't want it to happen again."

Robert said, "I think that would be—"

Jason said, "Don't put me in that position again."

"I think what Jason is—" He subsided when Jason held up a hand.

"I asked before we took this job what would happen in the case of a kidnap attempt. You said it wouldn't happen. It did. You said you'd have security people there. You didn't. You said my role would be strictly deterrent. It wasn't. I'll use my best judgment and learn from my mistakes. I'll do what you require of me and I'll do what I say. What I won't do is feign apologetic beta male when you screw up."

Robert's gaze lingered on Jason and then switched to Celia Weather.

She rocked thoughtfully in her leather chair. "If we're going to butt heads every time you make a mistake, we ought to sever this relationship."

"If you're going to look for me to apologize every time you fail to properly manage things, plan on butting heads."

Robert looked at each of them intently. She rocked the chair forward. "I think it's becoming clear that this is not going to work out."

Jason nodded. "I agree. This is why I don't last at day jobs." He got up. "Thank you for the work."

"I'll forward your closing check."

Robert rose awkwardly and stood next to Jason, his fingertips staying on the chair back.

"Mr. Goldstein, do you plan to stay on?"

Robert looked at Jason and raised his eyebrows. Jason shook his head; no problem here.

"Yes."

"Fine. Take the rest of the day off. I'd like you back at the Cooper residence tomorrow."

"IF YOU'D MINDED, I wouldn't have stayed on," Robert said as they waited for the elevator.

"I know. It's okay. Thanks for trying to keep me out of trouble."

On the way down, Robert looked at him critically and said, "You don't mind butting heads, do you?"

"I mind it a lot, actually. Just not as much as I mind rolling over. Why, were you uncomfortable? How'd you feel?"

Robert chewed on that for the rest of the ride down.

"Like Jane Goodall," he concluded as the doors opened.

Fuckin' saved my little girl's life," the smoke-rough baritone said after Jason said hello. "You ever need a favor, ever, you just say it and it's yours." Twangs and electrical hums of people setting up a sound system came through the line.

"Thanks," Jason said, standing in his studio.

"Man . . . I can't tell you what you've done. You've saved my little girl's life. I won't forget that. Dwight Cooper pays his debts. You ever need anything, anything at all, you just tell me."

"That's, uh, thanks."

"I ain't bullshitting you. You think I am, but I'm not."

"I don't think you are."

"You don't, huh." Dwight laughed and coughed. "I'll talk to you later. Jason the hero. Fuckin' lifesaver."

"I didn't exactly—" Jason said, but the line was already dead.

WITH JASON OUT, Martin's schedule with Bellweather doubled. He asked Jason to look in on Leon in Long Beach.

It was evening when Leon let him in. Jason had called ahead.

Martin's mom hadn't been there, and she still wasn't. Jason asked where she was. Leon shrugged. How long had she been gone? A couple of days.

He called Martin at Dwight's house and told him.

"Put him on," Martin said.

Leon came out when Jason called him, took the phone, and uh-huhhed and I-dunnoed. Then he gave the phone back to Jason and went into his room.

Martin's voice said, "Got a small favor to ask."

"Sure, what."

"I told Leon to pack. Bring him up to L.A.?"

"Okay."

"I'd come down and get him, but I'm wrapped up here."

"Don't worry about it. I'm already here."

"Leave a note, okay? Just say I asked him to come visit, or something. I dunno. Just say something."

"Will do."

A pause. Then the ruffle of a sigh in the phone mouthpiece. "Man—"

"I know," Jason said. "I know. We'll pick you up when you're off at Dwight's."

"Yeah. Thanks, chief."

"No sweat. See you then."

They almost got out without a fuss.

Leon was waiting to get into the pickup and Jason was closing the camper shell. A dull green 1970s Camaro drove just past and its brake lights lit as it stopped in the street. The doors opened and Martin's mom and a big guy with a brown mustache and a beer gut got out. He looked like a construction foreman Jason had once worked for who cheated on his wife during work hours.

"Jason," Martin's mom said. "What are you doing here?"

"Martin thought you could use some company, Mrs. Altamirano."

"How sweet. Where are you two going?" A brittle smile.

Jason had never had much interest in lying, so he'd never practiced. "Well, we didn't know when you'd be back, so Martin invited Leon up to visit for a couple of days." He tilted his head toward the building. "We left you a note."

"I don't know...." She glanced at the construction foreman, activating him. He stepped around the Camaro.

Jason said, "We left you a note."

"I don't think Leon's going to be able to go. I'll have a talk with Martin." The voice seemed vague. The smile was still brittle. "You can go on home now." The foreman crossed his arms so the biceps bulged and watched Jason.

"Hello," Jason said to him.

"Hey."

When Martin's mom stepped forward, Jason realized she wasn't sober. He was slow that way; it always took him an extra few beats to figure it out. She said to Leon, "Go in the house."

Leon was standing next to the cab. "My stuff's already in the truck," he said to his mother.

"Got his stuff out," she snapped at Jason.

Jason sorted keys. "I'm sorry if—"

"That's enough out of you," she said. "I know what you're up to, and I do not appreciate your lurking around here."

"Mrs. Altamirano, I really didn't—"

The construction foreman said, "I think you better shut up, punk."

Jason eyed the guy and decided against. "How about I get his stuff," he said. He unlocked and raised the camper hatch.

The foreman walked closer and bellied up to Jason. "I told you to shut up, punk."

"Yeah, I heard you say that." A buzz had started, somewhere down around where he got mad. He pulled Robert's backpack toward him, unzipped it, and glanced in, as though that was what you did with backpacks. Just checking. The buzz got stronger and wasn't pleasant; he was misstepping. But he didn't know which thing was the misstep.

He held the backpack in his left hand while he reached into the bed and snagged Leon's bundle. "Leon, come get your stuff."

Leon came around and Jason handed the bundle to him without looking.

"You don't listen too good, punk," the boyfriend said. He cracked his knuckles. "I told you to shut up."

Jason arranged the opening of the backpack. The buzz got worse. In a normal voice, he said, "Le, get out of the way."

Leon backed away. "All the way away," Jason said. Leon backed farther. Holding Robert's backpack carefully, Jason turned to face the boyfriend, leaning slightly back because the guy was crowding him.

Martin's mom said disgustedly, "Oh, look at all the testosterone. What a couple of macho pigs."

The foreman said, "If you were looking for trouble, punk, you found it." He shoved Jason backward against the tailgate, banging his back into the protruding handle and making him half-sit against tailgate and bumper.

Jason pulled the pistol out of Robert's backpack and plugged it into the soft part of the boyfriend's underjaw.

The boyfriend froze.

Jason said, "This is called escalation, Moose." The buzz was in his arms and head. His stomach flopped like a tongue.

Martin's mom shrilled abstractly in the background. The boyfriend's arms went out slowly in pacification. Jason wanted to freeze everything, to not have taken the gun out. Schrödinger's Gun. Wrong universe.

"Hey, man, it's all good," the boyfriend said.

The buzz roared. His stomach sideslipped and rolled. "Don't placate me."

The eyes came up off the gun. Incomprehension and worry.

"Placate me," Jason repeated. "Don't."

Nothing.

"Appease."

Confusion.

"Mollify."

Nothing.

"Pacify. Never mind." His guts roiled. Oddly, his voice sounded normal. "Just put your hands down."

The boyfriend dropped the hands. As Jason registered the fact that the shrilling had gotten louder, Martin's mom appeared at his side and slapped his arm down, still screaming at him. The boyfriend came in for the gun, and Jason dropped it and shoved Martin's mom away from him. As she reeled, the buzz turned to rage that splashed like oranges against a wall. For a moment, he was able to keep it from penetrating. Then the boyfriend bent to get the gun, and that was what the rage needed. Jason shoved up onto the tailgate behind him and drove his knee into the boyfriend's face.

The man crumpled.

Martin's mom ceased squawking and looked at the boyfriend. The buzz was now a shudder that nearly buckled Jason's knees as he bent to pick up the gun.

"You stay away from me," Martin's mom said. Trembling as though hypothermic, Jason went to the open driver's door in a blur and placed the gun on the transmission hump. Behind him,

Martin's mom said, "You piece of shit." He got in the cab and looked through the passenger window. Leon was standing on the lawn, holding his bundle, looking at his mother. She said, "You want to be like that, Leon? You want to be a piece of shit too?" Leon looked at Jason.

Jason leaned over and unlocked the passenger door with wobbling fingers. Leon looked at his mom.

She said, "You know you're going to."

Leon looked at Jason again.

"Go on," Martin's mom said. "What are you waiting for? *Get in the fucking car, you little shit!*"

Leon opened the door and got in. Jason started the engine. In the rearview, Martin's mom was crouched over the boyfriend. Leon had his bundle tight against his chin. He was staring at the glove box. Jason forgot to disengage the parking brake at first. They left.

t the first pay phone, he gave Mrs. Altamirano's address to the emergency dispatcher while Leon waited in the pickup, and hung up when she asked his name. He and Leon didn't talk while they drove north. Leon looked out the window, tapping his fingers casually on his bag and bobbing his head a little as though listening to music.

A while later, around El Segundo, Jason got off the freeway, parked in the empty lot of a commercial printer, and walked deliberate circuits atop the white concrete wheelblocks that terminated the dark parking spaces until his shaking subsided. Jets from LAX rose overhead, carrying peanuts and in-flight magazines to faraway places where they would be happy.

There was a pay phone on the far corner near another unlighted commercial building. Cora Smith answered when he called to talk to Robert.

"Oh, they've left," she said. "Robert's not feeling very well."

He called the groovy beach pad.

"Jason! Mom's on the other line. What happened?"

"I don't know. Leon and I were getting into the truck and she and this guy pulled up—"

"Frank."

"I don't know his name."

"His name's Frank. You put him in the hospital, man, broke his nose or some shit. Mom's not being too clear. What the heck happened?"

"God, Martin, I wish I knew. He got in my face and I let it go, and then he kept it going and I just went at him. Maybe I made some mistakes. I did make some mistakes. I made some mistakes. I'm really, really sorry."

"Is Le okay?"

"He's quiet. She said some stuff to him. He's just sort of gone inside. He's sitting in the truck right now. Why did she do that?"

"I don't know, man. What about you? You sound shaky."

"I guess I am. I don't know how I am. I'm really sorry it went like that. Why did she do that?"

"I hear planes."

"I'm near El Segundo. I had to pull off the freeway and wig out for a few minutes. I called over at Dwight's a minute ago so Robert could be smart at me before I talked to you, but Cora told me he's not well."

"Yeah, he's upset because Donna hates him because he chased her mommy away. Also, we got canned. Listen, I don't want to keep Mom on hold. You're still coming here, right?"

"Yes."

"Okay, I'll see you when you get here."

"I'm sorry, Martin."

"We'll figure it out, chief."

· · ·

LOS ANGELES IS a city that never sleeps, but you have to like Grand Slam™ Breakfasts. Jason had been a high school junior when he'd first had the adult thrill of staying up all night at Denny's with people you weren't related to. Leon was twelve.

They were in a booth directly across from where Jason's pickup was parked under a street lamp. Musician's habit: Always eat where you can see your equipment. Robert was looking out the dark window at the headlights on Colorado Boulevard. Martin's arm was along the back of the booth around Leon, and Jason's elbows were on the table, his hands supporting a warm cup of coffee. The surface of the coffee didn't ripple anymore. He figured he must be feeling better.

Leon had been hyperactive from the moment they'd been seated, making loud nonsense talk and giggling. He calmed down a little when Martin finally put a hand on his neck and said, "Leon— chill," but his gaze still jumped around the place. He didn't want to talk about anything, and though he'd allowed a big hug from Martin in the Denny's entryway, he hadn't returned the embrace.

Martin said, "Dwight's coming home."

Jason sipped his coffee. "So they fired Bellweather?"

Martin nodded. "Daddy's home. No need for a security company."

"Was the tour canceled?"

"Yeah."

"Well," Jason said. "Let's sum up, shall we? We're all out of work, Martin's mom is furious with him—"

Martin shook his head. "Don't worry about that. She's mostly furious with you."

"Oh, good. Robert's distraught over Donna hating him—"

"I'm fine."

"— and I've attacked three people in two days."

Leon said softly, "Fick, fick, fick, fick."

Over Leon, Robert said, "Who's the third? I can think of Lissa and Frank."

"Kel."

Everyone nodded and drank their decaf. They'd forgotten Kel.

Leon was saying, "Futt, futt, futt, futt, futt."

"I'm not balanced," Jason said. "I had to pull off the freeway because I wasn't fit to drive. This is out of whack."

"I have a theory about you," Martin said. "Le—"

Leon stopped saying "futt" and fell silent.

Martin said, "I'm not mad at you, bro—I just can't think when you do that."

Leon bounced in his seat a little.

Jason gestured do-tell.

"Okay, check it out." Martin shifted in the booth a little, to face Jason better. "You've gotten really angry three times recently—"

"Two."

"Count with me. One: The kidnap attempt. You saw red, am I right?"

"Yes."

"Two: This thing tonight with Frank."

"Yes."

"Now you tell me what three was."

"I don't know."

"Robert told me you were really mad yesterday morning."

"Yeah, but that was about Marisa."

"Bingo." Martin leaned back.

"That's your theory? I attacked three people because I was mad at Marisa."

Robert said, "Not just mad at. Hurt by. Do you know what you were shouting at Lissa Court?"

"I wasn't shouting."

Leon picked up his spoon and started tapping his coffee mug with it.

"You said three things. The first, which you repeated, was 'Not going to happen.' "

"I don't—"

"Which, interestingly, seems also appropriate to your encounter with Marisa. The second was 'Get away from that child.' "

"I don't recall that one, either."

"The third was 'Get away from my child.' "

"I—"

That one felt weird.

"Le," Martin said, putting his hand gently on Leon's arm. "Please—" Leon dropped his spoon with a clatter. "Dig, about your thing with Marisa. One thing about Marisa, she always knew how to hurt you. Right?"

Robert raised his eyebrows and nodded as though that were an understatement.

Martin continued, "The best way to hurt people is to take a jab at their, I know this is stupid, inner child."

Jason looked at him patiently. Or not. "Inner child, uh huh."

Leon started again, very softly, "Fick, fick, fick . . ."

"I just told you it was stupid, Jase, okay fine, but check out the parallels: Marisa—a woman—tries to hurt the inner child you're supposed to protect. You tell her it's not going to happen and you—Le, come on, bro; if you want to say 'fuck,' just say it—where was I . . . uh . . . right, so you chase her off. Then Lissa Court—another woman—tries to kidnap a child you're supposed to protect. You tell her it's not going to happen and you chase her off."

"Outer child," Jason said seriously. "Yeah, don't give me the look; I'm listening. I can't take 'inner child' all that seriously, but I'm listening. Anyway, Frank's not a woman, and I attacked him. So it doesn't follow the supposed pattern."

Robert said, "Did Frank care whether Leon stayed or went?"

Jason looked at Leon. The kid had fallen silent. "No, he was the agent of Mrs. Altamirano."

"And Mrs. Altamirano is?"

"Okay. Female."

"Do you think it conceivable that your reaction wasn't entirely without relation to the pattern we've hypothesized?"

Martin leaned back and watched him. Leon stared at him. The kid looked very tired.

Jason drank some of his coffee. "Inner child," he said. "Bleah."

Finally, he nodded.

"Could be totally off-base," Martin acknowledged, his hands up. "Could be totally unrelated. I could be so full of shit, they could put a sign on me, says 'Andy Gump.' It's just a theory, is all. Just something to think about."

"I'll think about it." He considered Martin.

Martin said, "What."

"You said the other day that you feel like you're trying to catch up with me."

Martin shook his head. "Not about women. I love you like a brother, Jase, but about women, you are totally retarded."

Jason smiled. "Ah, but I'm rich. No, wait, I'm not. Enough about me. How're you doing with all this stuff tonight?"

Martin looked at Leon before he answered. Leon had closed his eyes. "Well, it's not news. Mom plays men, sometimes against each other. She's always done it, she's always gonna do it. You notice I didn't ask you what she said to Leon?"

Leon opened his pouchy eyes for a second, but then they closed. Martin put his arm around his little brother's shoulders. Leon tilted over and leaned against him.

Jason said, "I figured you already knew what she said."

"I already know. If you're worried about what I think about how you handled it, well, as much as I would have done it differently, my friend, I wasn't there. You were. I wouldn't have let it blow up that far, but I also probably wouldn't have left with Leon. You did what you thought was best." He extended a cocked hand. Jason grasped it. "We're cool," Martin said. They bumped fists.

Robert said, "It's good that Leon has people who care about him like this."

Jason said, "You're worried about Donna."

"Yes." Robert looked suddenly as though he were about to cry. "I tried to be honest with her, and to tell her what happened. I think you should always be honest with children."

They drank their decaf for a long while.

"Sorry it didn't work," Jason said. Robert nodded and wiped fingers under his eyes. Robert never hid his tears. Jason had seen him cry when they had come across a baby duck in the Venice canals, dead under the hinge of a wooden gate.

Jason said, "Have you been thinking about the kidnapping?"

Robert pursed his lips and redirected himself. "There are . . . things about it . . ." He looked sideways at Jason, his eyes still red, but his attention on the question.

"I know," Jason said. "Me too."

Martin said, "What, what things?"

Robert said, "Well, for instance. How would you kidnap a child on a field trip?"

"I dunno, I guess like she did. Get out of the car, call the kid, put the kid quickly into—" He stopped, then said with dawning interest, "Huh. Quickly into the car."

Jason said, "She didn't put the kid quickly into the car. She knelt and had a hug. That's lost time, during which she could have been caught or identified."

Martin said, "It could be a maternal impulse, say she just needed to hug her kid. Is that all you got?"

Robert said, "She yelled across the parking lot, too. Is that how you'd kidnap a child?"

"No, that would be stupid. But maybe she's stupid."

"Maybe so," Jason said. "But now, imagine that not only are you going to kidnap a child, but you're not you. You're an internationally recognizable supermodel, and the school has been alerted that you are a danger. Do you stand outside your expensive car, yell for the kid, and then hug her?"

Martin thought. Then he said, "Okay, you got a point."

Jason glanced at both of them and sipped his decaf. "How're your schedules?" he asked casually.

"My calendar is a vast, inkless tundra."

Martin put out a hand. "Whoah. Time out. Tell me what we're talking about here."

"I want to know Donna's going to be okay."

Leon stirred and subsided. Martin stayed frozen with his hand out, watching Jason. Jason knew that they were thinking the same things.

So was Robert: "Looking after Donna would be so utterly none of our business that to even consider considering it is to skip right past arrogance and hurl ourselves into a deep tub of hubris."

His hand still extended, Martin looked at Robert and then considered Jason a while longer. Then he sat back in the booth. "I got no argument," he said.

"Robert?"

Robert poured sugar in his decaf and clinked his spoon absently in it. He sighed. "This job was supposed to go on long enough to build up my savings. I care about Donna, but if I don't find work soon, I won't have enough money to live."

Martin looked at Leon. When he looked back at Jason, his expression was resigned. "I got my own to take care of," he said. "Sorry, chief."

Jason thought about his own money. When Celia Weather's final check and the Light Wizards' check came, he'd have enough to pay his back bills and six weeks of living expenses. He could gamble that money would come for the seventh week, but for that to work, the job would have to be starting around now. And there was no such job.

"I guess me too," he said.

They sat around the table, silent and irritable.

Martin said, "Well, this sucks," and they paid and went home.

Robert moved his blanket and pillow off his mattress and onto the living room couch, and Martin and Leon crashed in the bedroom with the banana clock and rain lamp.

The next morning, Jason made work calls. Light Wizards had nothing for him. Neither did two other game manufacturers he'd done minor things for before, nor three he looked up in the yellow pages and called cold. He gave up around noon and put together promotional packages for the three new contacts, and Robert took over the phone and called casting agencies. Martin took Leon and went to a movie.

In the afternoon, Jason and Robert walked to El Tarasco on Washington near the beach and had lunch. They took Ocean Front Walk for a while toward the Third Street Promenade and tried to have a conversation despite the assembly line of almost-naked girls on skates. They saw an action-adventure movie with a lot of explosions. It was very loud. When they came out of the theater and started walking home, it was evening.

MARTIN WAS SITTING on the step with a blank expression, smoking a cigarette. He didn't say anything as they approached.

"Hi, Martin," Robert said. Martin raised his eyebrows and continued to stare at the house across from them. It was only about six feet away, its three front steps and red, peeling door facing theirs over a short, oxidized chain-link fence.

"Uh, how you doing?" Jason asked.

"Oh, just fuckin' fine," Martin said. He took a drag. "Couldn't be better."

"What's happened?"

He shook his head.

Robert said, "What?" He sounded worried.

Martin glanced up at each of them.

Jason said, "Where's Leon?"

"In the house."

They waited. Robert put his hands in his pockets and looked worried. Jason leaned against the fence.

Martin stubbed out his cigarette. "Mom called."

"What did she say?"

Martin looked at him, took a pack from his shirt pocket, lit it with a lighter that was next to him on the steps, dragged on it, held it, breathed it out, and looked at Robert. Robert nodded, prompting.

Martin took the cigarette from between his lips and held it between two fingers. "She said if I want Leon that bad, I can have him."

"She didn't mean it," Robert said.

Martin raised the cigarette and took another pull, looked at the other house. "She meant it."

THE FRONT GATE squealed and banged, interrupting the silence. Marisa came around the front house.

"Hi," she said. She had her pulled hair back and she was

wearing a different outfit, this one gray and tailored to her figure, with a white blouse. "You all look terrible! Is everything okay?"

Robert said, "Hello, Marisa."

"Robert, I saw you on *Joanna*!"

"Hey, that's great."

Martin stood and brushed his seat.

"Hello, Martin. It's good to see you."

Martin said, " 'Scuse me," and went into the house.

Robert said, "I'm going to—" He pointed vaguely and went up the walk and around the front house. The gate clinked carefully.

Jason said. "I'm not up to this, Marisa."

"It'll only take a minute. I called yesterday, but you never picked up and I didn't want to leave a message. Can we go inside, please?"

He motioned her in reluctantly and followed her. They stood in the living room. Martin and Leon were in Robert's bedroom.

"You really look like something's wrong." Concern.

He nodded. Concern was, he realized, bait.

"Martin doesn't like me anymore," she said. More bait. No take. "I came by to say I was sorry. I had no right to talk to you that way. I just felt rejected. You understand."

He nodded.

"I hope we can still be friends. I really missed you. That's why I came last night."

"I'm flattered."

"I'd still like to—"

"Look, Marisa. It's just not going to—" Hearing himself, he stopped. Damn; Martin and Robert were right. "Not going to happen," he finished.

"But why not?"

"How tough do you want that answer?"

Her answer was a guess. "Probably . . . not very tough?"

"Then let's just leave it at 'It's not going to happen.' Go back to Jack, have your fling, have your wedding, and let's not do this again."

"Are you still mad because I slept with Paul?"

"No." He shook his head. "But it's one of the reasons I don't want you as a friend."

She didn't react as he expected. Her eyes dropped. "I can understand that." So. She thought it was wrong, too. It wasn't just him being parochial. "You've changed a lot."

He nodded.

"Well," she said. "Bye?"

The cue was to hug her. He just nodded. She turned awkwardly and left.

The gate banged. He sat down on the couch and picked up a magazine.

Martin came out of Robert's bedroom in jeans and no shirt and said, "Man, you're sure a lot nicer than I woulda been. I'da just throwed the bitch out on her dishonest, fucked-up, less morals than a fruit bat with a gambling debt, piss on your neck and tell you it's Chanel, manipulating, self-centered, tell-me-you-want-me, hello-sailor nasty ass."

He got a water glass from the cabinet, filled it from the tap, and leaned against the sink to drink it. Jason stared at him. A chuckle sneaked up from somewhere, and then he thought about it again and chuckled again. He sat there replaying it and chuckling each time. Martin sipped his water and watched, shaking his head in pity.

et up. Company's coming."

Jason didn't want to get up. "What company?"

"Just get up."

He heard Martin go into the living room and say the same thing to Robert. He sat up and pulled his jeans toward him from atop one of his synthesizers.

He was almost done shaving and Robert was still in the shower when Martin knocked on the half-open door and said, "Company's here."

Jason rinsed and toweled, put on his jeans and shirt, and went barefoot into the living room. Cora Smith was sitting with Martin on the couch. She had a glass of iced tea. A white box sat on the floor beside her.

"Hi, Cora," Jason said, surprised.

"Hello, Jason. I was just saying to Martin what a lovely area this is."

"We like it." He sat on a chair. "What brings you?"

"Well, Martin seems to think we can help each other out."

"Does he?" Jason looked at Martin. "How's that?"

Martin said, "Let's wait for Robert."

The shower was still running. Jason got up and went to the bathroom and knocked. "Robert!"

"Aaa?"

"Hurry it up!"

"Ah ohih aaa aa."

"He'll be out soon," Jason said, sitting again.

They chatted. Presently, the shower stopped with a clunk and soon Robert came out, the bottoms of his unfashionable khaki pants brushing the tops of his bare feet, a red long-sleeved shirt hanging untucked, and his hair clearly towel-dried with great vigor.

"I can't find my comb," he said.

Martin eyed Robert's hair. "You don't say."

Robert mussed his hair with his hands and stepped back to look through the bathroom doorway at the mirror, as though hairstyles were probabilistic and he might accidentally get one.

Jason said, "Come sit. We've just been making small talk until you got here."

Robert gave it another muss, squinted into the mirror, and joined them.

"It's nice to see you," he said to Cora.

"Hello, Robert. It's very nice to see you too."

"How's Donna?"

Martin said, "That's just what I want us to talk about. We got some, what, *compatible needs.*"

Jason said, "How so?" and looked at Cora holding her iced tea glass on her lap.

She said, "Martin tells me you have had some experience in looking into things and keeping quiet about them."

Jason looked at Martin. "Obviously not all that quiet," he said.

"Rag me later, chief, just listen."

Jason looked back at Cora. "You're worried about Donna."

"Yes, I am."

"We are too."

"Yes, I know."

Robert said, "Is she okay?"

"She's a very sad little girl right now."

Robert looked stricken.

Jason said, "So what is it that needs looking into?"

"That so-called 'kidnapping.'"

"Why 'so-called'?"

"I tell you, it just doesn't set well with me. I think there's something more to it, and I suspect—just a feeling, mind you—that Dwight and Johnny Ray may be involved."

"How?"

"I don't quite know. It's just a feeling." She shook her head and sighed. "He was doing so well."

"Doing well how?"

"He'd been off the drugs for nearly four years, since Donna was two. I thought he had made it, but then . . . I suppose it was the strain of this new tour. Dwight has never handled stress very well, even as a young man. He has always needed people taking care of him."

"Like you."

"I take care of one child, not two."

"Who takes care of Dwight?"

"Mostly Johnny Ray."

"Who takes care of Dwight when Johnny Ray's not around, like now?"

"He stays with other musicians. When he was on the drugs, he would often stay with his connections. Dwight's judgment has always been very poor. He trusts unscrupulous people with all manner of things." She shook her head.

"Who handles his money?"

"Johnny Ray."

"Wait, why does he stay with other musicians? Why doesn't he stay in his house when he's home?"

"His house? Oh, goodness, no. Lissa bought and paid for that house. Dwight will have enough income to live on for the rest of his life, but I do not believe he has saved any money."

It wasn't Dwight's house. No wonder it was so normal.

Jason extrapolated. "Who pays you?"

She looked pleased. "That's very good, Jason. You're helping my confidence. Lissa pays my salary."

"Why does Dwight have custody?"

She paused.

"It doesn't leave this room," Jason said. Robert and Martin nodded.

She looked at them and didn't answer at first. "It had better not," she said finally.

"It won't," Jason said.

"It won't," Martin assured her.

"Dwight has custody," she said, "because Lissa's a lesbian."

After a moment of silence, Jason said, "That's it?"

"That's enough, honey."

"Because the mother likes women, they give the child to *Dwight Cooper*? Oh, that makes a ton of sense. So, what was this Martin was saying about compatible needs?"

"He told me you're concerned about Donna, but you can't afford to spend the time. I don't have the time or energy, but I can afford to pay. I have a little put aside. I can't pay you as much as Celia did, but I will sweeten the deal"—she held up two fingers —"in two ways."

Jason was already sold. Robert and Martin probably were, too.

He smiled at her. She smiled back.

"What's the first way," he said.

"Martin is in need of child care. I will provide it for as long as you're doing this for me."

Robert said, "What's the other way?" but Jason already knew what was in the white box before she lifted the lid.

Looking in, Jason said, "I'm afraid we will require a two-pie deposit."

"It is the standard rate," Robert seconded regretfully.

"Three could be arranged," she said.

"Um," Jason said, "well, we do have to talk about—"

Martin said, "I told Mrs. Smith we'd be willing to do it if we could just survive during that time. Just cover our rent and stuff, nothing extra."

"Okay," Jason said, relieved. "That's all I need. Robert?"

"Yes!" Robert nodded enthusiastically. "That's good! That's fine!"

She smiled at him, and asked Jason, "Do we have a deal, then?"

"Are you sure you wouldn't want someone more professional?"

"I would not know who to trust. I do have one requirement."

"What's that?"

"Lissa must not know I hired you."

"Why not?"

"That poor girl always thinks she can handle everything herself. She would take it as a personal offense that I hired someone else to look after the safety of her only child."

"I see."

"There are some good reasons for her to feel that way, but"—she leaned forward slightly, so as not to be overheard—"she will overdo it. Do we have a deal?"

"Probably. Just two things first, to make it clear what you get when you get us."

"All right."

"First. I only have two speeds. On and off. If we start doing this, it clicks over to on. That means I won't take your money and do it halfway"—he remembered in time not to say "half-assed"—"but I also won't gear down even if you want me to. Is that acceptable to you?"

"You are a young man. I would expect nothing else."

"Second, if we come up against expenses, we'll call you. If you can't or won't pay them, we get stuck."

"I expect there to be expenses. Now, do we have a deal or not?"

"Yes."

They shook.

"That is fine," she said. "Will you start tomorrow?"

"We'll start now. How much do you tell Lissa Court? Do you report to her about Donna's health and grades and stuff?"

"Yes, I do."

"Did you tell her about the field trip?"

"No, I did not."

"Why not?"

"I might very well have, eventually, but it simply had not come up."

"Did you know she was in Los Angeles?"

"No. As far as I knew, she was out of the country."

"She lives in New York."

"Yes. That is where the fashion industry is."

"Tomorrow morning," Jason said, "we'll go talk to Mrs. Kinsella."

U p at seven the next morning, stagger around in search of clothes, and then Robert and Jason drove to Donna's school, parked across the street from the teachers' parking lot, and waited. There were no kids yet, and only two cars in the gray lot. A janitor and a wheeled barrel floated spectrally through the walkways.

"So," Robert said. "How are you feeling about Marisa?"

"Talked out."

"Oh. If we knew anything about sports, we could talk about that."

"How 'bout them . . . uh . . ."

"Right, them. I dunno."

They sat.

Jason said, "I still don't get addiction."

"Did you ever read 'The Wonky' by Cathy Bellamy?"

"No."

They sat.

Robert said, "On *Robbery/Homicide*, they always take coffee on stakeouts."

"Donna's really into science, isn't she?"

Robert gave him a sad look. "I was going to get her a microscope for her birthday."

"Were you really trying to teach her relativity?"

"Not just trying."

"You're not telling me she was getting it."

"Yes, she was. I mean," he amended, "it's not like she was grasping E equals m c squared, but we were getting into curved space and your basic time travel paradoxes and stuff like that."

"Huh."

"She's very smart and creative."

The lot was half filled and there were three kids on the playground when Mrs. Kinsella drove up and got out of a forest green Geo that looked like an athletic shoe with tires.

She turned when Jason called her name, and waited as they crossed the street. She was a large middle-aged woman in white Reeboks, and her whistle was around her neck on an orange ribbon. "Well, hello," she said. "I didn't expect to see you two."

"We didn't expect it either," Jason said, smiling. "We're no longer with Bellweather."

"Yes, I'd heard."

"Mrs. Kinsella, maybe you can help us. We're worried about Donna."

"Worried?"

Robert said, "Yes. I'm sure you know what her parents are like."

Her face hooded.

"Oh, we know," Robert assured her. "You don't have to say anything that would be a breach of confidence. But I think we understand each other, yes? Unofficially? I mean, for myself "— he leaned in slightly, conspiratorially—"I think Dwight's completely unfit."

She began to move away. "I'm sorry, but my attorney has advised me not to discuss this." She turned and walked briskly through the lot, toward the office.

"Mrs. Kinsella," Jason called. "How did Lissa Court know about the field trip?"

She quickened her pace.

"Attorney?" Jason said.

SITTING IN THE pickup truck, Jason said, "Why would she tell Lissa Court about the field trip, and why does she have an attorney?" They mulled. While they were mulling, the office door opened and a tall, fortyish woman in slacks and a flowered shirt came out, looked at the pickup, and walked toward it.

They got out and waited. She turned out of the driveway and went a few steps down the sidewalk, looked at the front of the pickup, and wrote on a piece of white paper. She capped the pen and walked back to the driveway. "I don't want to see you here bothering my people," she said. "If I see either of you again, I will call the police."

"Why?" Robert said, behind Jason.

"I'm the principal and I want you both out of here, now."

Jason said, "Why would Mrs. Kinsella tell Lissa Court about the field trip, and why does she have an attorney?"

"If you're not gone in one minute, I will call the police right now."

Jason said, "Mighty is your power over time itself."

She turned and began walking back through the lot.

"Effect before cause," Jason explained to Robert.

"Yes, I got it," Robert said. "We'd better go."

"Probably so." He stood and watched the principal go into the office. It had a window that faced the street.

"So let's go," Robert said. "I know you hate backing down, but . . ."

"Why would Mrs. Kinsella tell Lissa Court about the field trip, why does she have an attorney, and why does the principal want to run us off?"

They got back in and drove home.

Jason got Lissa Court's head shot out of the information packet Celia Weather had given him and called the agency number printed on it.

"Etta Earl."

"Hello, I'd like to get in touch with Lissa Court."

"Is this regarding a shoot?"

"No, it's personal."

"I'll be happy to take a message."

"I'd really rather talk to her directly. Is there a way for me to get in touch with her?"

"No, I'm sorry."

"No way at all."

"No. What was your name, sir?"

"Meriadoc Brandybuck."

"Mr. Brandybuck, do you have a message for her?"

"Yes. Please let her know that the One Ring has been found, but that it is in danger of falling into the hands of Bill Gates."

"Thank you, Mr. Brandybuck. I will let Ms. Court know you called. Please give my regards to Mr. Baggins."

He hung up. "Giving fake names is more fun when they don't know you're doing it," he said to Martin, who was leaning against the doorframe.

"Why'd you give her a fake name?"

"I suddenly realized that if I left a message that said, 'You don't know me, but this is about your daughter,' it might make her harder to track down, not easier."

"Oh."

"So I figured I'd just get weird and the receptionist would write me off as a crank call." He pondered. "How do you feel about New York in June?" he said.

"I like it. How about you?"

"I don't want to go alone, but we can't charge Cora for more than one person going. It would cost us some of our own money."

"Well, boss, for a change, we have some of our own money."

ora took Leon, and the flight took five and a half hours.
There was no immediate reason for all three of them to go,
but it seemed a good idea to go in force. And then, none of
them had ever been, and no one wanted to be working a dull day
job while his two friends jetted across the country on the trail of
a supermodel/kidnaptrix. Jason had asked Cora for airfare for one
person and the cost of as inexpensive a hotel room as he could
find. She'd agreed. The rest was out of pocket, split three ways.

The in-flight meal was gummy and the various food tempera-
tures were switched around randomly, but it was as good as what
they usually ate, so they ate it. The in-flight movie was the same one
they'd seen at the Promenade, so they didn't rent headphones.
Without sound, and with the helicopter crashes excised, it became
the story of a man squinting ruggedly and leaping over things.

"It's better than I remembered," Robert said.

Leon had been too cooperative about going with Cora.
Every so often, Martin would look at the credit-card-operated
phone mounted in the seat in front of them. None of them had
a credit card.

In Newark, they herded to the baggage carousel. Watching for their bags, Robert said, "I want an egg cream before we leave."

"An egg cream in New York is a bar mitzvah requirement, isn't it?"

"It depends. If you're Reform, you have an egg cream. If you're Orthodox, you learn Aramaic."

"What if you're Conservative?"

"You work on a kibbutz for a month and then become a civil rights attorney."

There was no baggage on the baggage carousel yet. Robert stooped so he could see a foot farther into the maw of the luggage disgorger.

Jason said, "I want to try the pizza while we're here."

"I think I could get custody," Martin said.

Robert and Jason looked at him. Robert shook his head as though clearing his ears of moths, did a take like a cartoon pig that's been hit on the head with an anvil, made a wobbly sound that went something like, "Oingyoingyoing," and said, "What?"

"You heard me."

Jason studied him. "You're serious."

"As a head transplant."

"Would she let you?"

"If the parent is willing, you go to the courthouse and you sign a paper. That's it."

"You think she'd really be willing?"

"I think she'd be more than willing."

Jason shook his head. "Why?"

Martin seemed to consider how to answer that. "Did you ever wonder why I spent so much time hiding out in high school?"

While Jason was trying to think about that, he flashed on a series of snapshots: Martin staying over at his house. Martin drawing on sketchpads in the park after school. Martin arriving at night games on foot.

"She didn't want you around," he said.

"Bingo presto, you get the Rice-A-Roni."

"You think she doesn't want him around, either."

"Have you seen her act like she wants him around?"

"No."

Martin nodded, mostly to himself. "I think I could get custody."

AT THE WINDOW of their room at the YMCA, looking down at a New York street, Robert said, "The traffic is yellow."

"Streets" ran east-west, and "avenues" ran north-south. Five people had told them that. Three of them had amended that it wasn't really north; it was "uptown," because Manhattan was tilted. One had added that the other cabbies couldn't drive. As far as Jason could tell, all these statements were true.

Robert said, "Do you think this is a bad neighborhood?"

Jason went to the dark window and looked out at the pedestrians and yellow cabs. Litter lined every crack and angle. "I don't know," he said finally. "My radar's calibrated for the West Coast. Trying to judge by the amount of graffiti and trash doesn't seem to work here."

"Maybe this is a good neighborhood."

"The mixture of commercial and residential is weird, too." Pink neon caught Jason's eye. "There's a donut shop."

"I'm starving," Martin said.

"Do you think it's safe?"

"I say we risk it."

As they crossed the sidewalk, a faint rumble rose underfoot and Jason looked around for a safe doorway and calibrated mentally; maybe a three-point-oh if they were near the epicenter. Maybe not even that big. The rumble subsided. None of the pedestrians seemed concerned.

"Oh," he said, realizing.

"I thought so too," Robert said.

"It must have been a subway."

"Oh, right," Martin said. "Duh."

"Or a subway train, or whatever they're called."

"I want to go on a subway," Robert said. "Are they as dangerous as people say, do you think?"

"I would know the answer to this how?"

They crossed and went into the donut shop. No one mugged them. The donuts were freshly made, and the neon sign Jason saw had been turned on to indicate the fresh batch. They looked hot and good, but they were tiny, and cost as much as the manhole-cover-sized apple fritters Jason used to get along his pipeline patrol route. He ordered a dozen and three cups of decaf and they went to a table.

"These are cute," Martin said, holding up a glazed between thumb and finger and examining it. It drooped a little. "Kinda squishy, though."

Robert took it from him and swallowed it. "They're good," he decided. He took another.

Jason took one. "It's almost impossible to screw up donuts. The worst that happens is you get deep-fried dough with sugar on it."

"So tomorrow, we begin our dastardly plan," Martin said, taking another donut. "Which would be what?"

"Two things. Find Lissa Court and ask her how she knew about the field trip, and contact Zeb Lindengreen. He's a string player I know on MUSE. He helped me with the fingerpicking parts for the Southern Gothic Mansion segment of *Ghost House*

II. We have dinner once a year at trade shows. Right before we left, I suddenly realized he was probably playing around Dallas about the same time Dwight was, so I e-mailed him. We left before I got a response, so I need to call him."

He and Martin each took another donut. Then the donuts were gone, so they threw the box away. They sat a while until the donut people began to put the chairs up on the tables and sweep the floor.

"They're closing." Robert interrupted his imprecise two-handed tapping on the tabletop to puzzle about this. Jason looked at Martin's watch. Martin turned it to let him see. Midnight.

Outside, they waited for a woman in a white Dart to make a ten-point U-turn and then go the wrong way on the one-way street. The flow of pedestrians had thinned.

"I thought the foot traffic was supposed to be just as heavy at night here," Jason said. " 'City that never sleeps,' and all that."

Robert shrugged. "Maybe this is the wrong part of Manhattan."

"The map says the whole thing's only twenty-something square miles. How big's the actual non-sleeping part, a block?"

"It's kind of like Hollywood," Martin said, looking around. "Only not as weird. Sort of."

"Nobody can drive, and the donut shops close," Jason said as they crossed the street. "Guess we're not in L.A. anymore."

The conventional belief in Los Angeles, propagated by visiting New Yorkers who also liked to mention how phony everyone was but themselves, was that Manhattan traffic noise would keep out-of-towners awake until they became "real New Yorkers," which transformation was apparently attended by brass bands of cherubim who turned cartwheels and said things like "So how you like bein' a Yankee fan?" But the lack of police helicopters was such a lovely change that Jason, Martin, and Robert slept beautifully. They woke at noon, still on L.A. time.

The door security woman at the Y pointed them toward a diner that had hatstands between the booths, cigarette smoke in the air, and an efficient waiter named Lenny who said "youse" and wasn't kidding.

They sat at the window and tried to ignore the smoke. The radio was set to an oldies station, and the Beatles sang "Mean Mr. Mustard" in low-fi.

"I think those are Irish cops," Jason said. He was looking back into the diner at four out-of-shape men in ill-fitting uniforms.

Martin looked at them. "They look like water and power guys."

Past the front window, two Middle Eastern men got into an argument on the sidewalk next to an incense stand manned by a dreadlocked black man in a ragamuffin hat. An Orthodox Jew in fedora and overcoat stepped around them and continued on his way.

"It's like central casting," Robert said.

"I know it," Martin said. "I'm looking for someone to yell 'Cut!'"

Jason watched with them. "I guess now we know where all the clichés come from."

"Have you ever heard of 'egg on a roll'?" Robert asked, looking at his menu. Stevie Wonder started "I Wish." Jason sang along under his breath, skipping the part about being a little nappy-headed boy, because he hadn't been.

They ordered. Lenny looked at them funny when, after being asked what kind of toast he wanted, Jason said sourdough.

"White, wheat, rye."

"Oh. Uh, white."

"No sourdough," Robert said when Lenny left. "Weird."

"I don't know how," Jason said, "but we need to get to where we can talk to Lissa Court. I thought of pretending we're the publishers of a new fashion magazine and we want her for the cover."

"Maybe that could work," Robert said.

"But then I thought if we did that, we probably wouldn't get to see her until the shoot. I even had names for us. Robert and I were going to be Lewis and Miles Archer. That was the only thing I really liked about it, though, and the names won't work because the receptionist is apparently literate."

"Not to mention that we don't know anything about fashion."

Jason and Martin both looked at Robert silently. He was

wearing dark green corduroys and a wrinkled orange button-down shirt that wasn't buttoned down, and under the table were Velcro-fastened blue shoes, sockless.

"Yes," Jason said. "Well, there's that, too."

Martin said, "So what do we do?"

"I don't know, exactly. We just need to talk to her . . ."

"What if we really hired her for a shoot?"

"With what? She must get tens or hundreds of thousands for a magazine cover."

They brooded.

"Hey," Martin said. "Could we get me hired at her agency as a temp?"

Breakfast was much less expensive than they were used to. When they left, Lenny told them to have a nice day. He said "youse" again. As unlikely as it seemed, at least one person apparently really talked like that.

"THIS IS GOOD," Jason said at the copy place, looking at it.

"Not only is Martin the only one of us Lissa Court hasn't seen before, but after the free week is up, we can actually start charging them."

"This could take a while," Martin said. "What if they don't take us up on it soon? I gotta get back to Leon."

"Then we think of something else. But I hope they do. We can't just hang here for weeks on end, spending Cora's money."

"Or ours."

"That too."

They rented voice mail at the copy place, added the phone number to the flyer, copied a few onto pink paper, and mailed one to the Etta Earl Agency with a cover letter from Robert Goldstein, executive account manager. It was Friday. On Monday, Mr. Goldstein would make a follow-up call.

hen they got back around five o'clock, the desk clerk gave them a message from Zeb Lindengreen. Jason called him.

"I e-mailed you, but you probably left L.A. before you got it," Zeb's rough smoker's voice said on the phone. "I wanted to invite you and your friends to a pickin' party tonight, around eight until whenever."

"Sounds good to me. Hold on a sec." As though it weren't a stupid question, he said to Robert and Martin, "You guys free tonight?"

Martin said, "Sure." Robert looked at him as though it were a stupid question.

Jason said, "We'd love to." He grabbed a notepad off the side table. "How do we get there?"

Zeb's directions included such arcane instructions as "Cross the platform" and "Walk toward the rear of the train." Jason figured they would become clear later, so he just wrote everything down.

The desk clerk told them how to get to a subway station a block away. At the specified corner, two green globes on posts demarked a rectangular hole where concrete steps descended.

"Properly warned, ye be," Jason said. It was what an animatronic talking skull in a tricorner Jolly Roger hat said to you in the Pirates of the Caribbean ride at Disneyland before your boat-on-a-track took its first plunge.

There was a booth with a guy in it down there, under the sidewalk.

Jason wondered, "How do we pay?"

They stood and watched as people came down the steps, slid yellow cards through turnstile-mounted card readers, and entered.

"It's those yellow cards, Spock," Jason murmured. "We must get some of those yellow cards."

Robert cocked an eyebrow. "Captain, logic dictates that the source of the cards should be close at hand."

Martin said, "Yeah, like in this booth here."

Jason felt too stupid to ask the guy in the booth to repeat what he'd just said about discounts and extra-ride incentives, so he slid ten dollars into the tray, nodded at whatever the guy said, and the guy slid out a card and a dollar. Martin and Robert did the same, and they went through the turnstiles.

There were train rails down there, under the sidewalk, where trains did not belong.

Sweating people stood very close to the edge of what had to be the "platform," which was no more than the part of the floor nearest the four-foot-deep trench that contained the tracks. To the far left and right, the tracks entered tunnels. A hanging sign at the platform's edge said F DOWNTOWN BROOKLYN.

Wind blew.

Robert looked confused. "Why would there—"

The wind picked up and the flat, silver front of a train appeared in the left-hand tunnel like the plunger of a syringe, pushing air. Jason reconsulted his written directions. "I think this is our train."

"We're going to downtown Brooklyn?"

The train whizzed rumbling by and its brakes screeched. No one stepped back from the edge of the platform, so Jason didn't either. There had to be twenty cars; subway trains were apparently actual trains. The doors slid open, releasing a few people and some cold air. They stepped in. Center-facing plastic seats, and metal poles for gripping. The floor was slightly sticky, and backlighted advertisements for podiatrists and jeans ran the length of the car. It was like a bus, only it was a train.

Martin said, "I think we're going downtown *to* Brooklyn, not to downtown Brooklyn. Downtown is a direction here."

An overhead loudspeaker clunked and a male voice said, "Nazza fodeezee, peeza keeza kozodos." Clunk.

The poles were there for a reason, Jason figured, so he grasped one. An electronic chime sounded, bing-bong, and the doors closed. The train jerked forward and a tall actor who hadn't yet puzzled through the metal pole issue did so now.

The windows went dark as the car crawled into the dirty tunnel, a themeless kiddy ride at Kafka Land.

Each time the windows lightened and the train stopped, Jason looked for the station name, checked the wall-mounted subway map, and counted the remaining stops. In twenty minutes, they exited and stood on a platform under tiles that spelled *Bergen.* The chime reverberated underground, and then the train closed its doors and its motors turned, their rising whine bouncing against the tiles as it accelerated away.

" 'Walk toward the rear of the train,' " Jason read. "So that's what that means." They walked back in the direction from which the train had come, and found a set of turnstiles and an exit there, and another booth with a guy in it, and concrete steps, which they went up.

They came out of the sidewalk and looked at Brooklyn at night.

"Looks like Manhattan," Martin said. "Only shorter."

Robert was looking across the street. "Is that a bodega?"

"That looks like a liquor store. Isn't a bodega like a warehouse?"

"No, it's like an endangered whale."

Martin and Jason looked at each other, trying to get it.

"Beluga," they explained to each other simultaneously. Martin rolled his eyes.

Robert said, "That's what old-fashioned trucks driven by dolphins would sound like."

Jason looked at Martin. Martin said, "Beluga, a-ooga."

Jason nodded and consulted his directions. "Walk north to Atlantic."

They all looked around.

Martin said, "Is there some way we're supposed to know which way is north?"

Jason looked at the directions. "Yes. If we don't get to Atlantic, we went the wrong way."

As it turned out, their first guess was good, and they continued to a treed street of three- and four-story brick buildings. They all had front steps, some with people sitting. A few had planter boxes within the gates. Only one had live bluegrass streaming from its open windows.

They went up the steps and into a dark little wooden foyer with an up staircase to the right and an open single door to the left. Through the door, half a dozen men made a circle, picking and bowing.

Turned three-quarters away from the door was Zebedee

Lindengreen, with shiny wire spectacles on his face and green sandals on his feet. Either his clothes had too often been laundered as one big load or he'd found a clothing store that sold listless gray, to match his hair. Jason knew some of his history. He'd been a first-call studio banjo player in the early 1980s, but in a year he burned out playing the *same* damn *thing*, *day* after *day* and they *don't* want *any*thing *new*, and chucked it. There was a story about the chucking, too, something about fingerpicking Penderecki on a Teddy Handrell track. Jason couldn't remember all the details.

Zeb had bounced around since then, playing occasional gigs, teaching, and writing articles for left-wing magazines. Jason had met him first as a disembodied personality on the MUSE message boards, and then corporeally at a music trade show.

And before all that, there was something about Dallas in the 1960s.

The pickin' party was Jason's first, but it was familiar. Gatherings of musicians and spouses tended to pattern themselves after the archetypal ur-jam, same as it ever was, back to the beginning of time. If there had been a jam session during the first 1^{-43} second of the Big Bang, the wives would have been curled up in one of those other six dimensions, trying to have a conversation.

Wives, not spouses. Sexist as that was, it was usually true.

"What song is this?" Robert said, raising his voice.

"I don't know," Jason shouted back. "To me, an evening of bluegrass is one long twang with brief intermissions."

Martin was concentrating, one forefinger chasing something familiar in the beat. "I know this," he said. "I know I know this. From when I was a kid." They watched him subvocalize lyrics no one was singing. At the chorus, the forefinger froze. "I got it." His lips formed the words of the chorus almost silently, *ain't got*

time to kiss you now, my mule has— He stopped. "It's 'Ho, Mule.'"
Gloom flickered. "Mom taught me."

Jason gave him a regretful look, and Robert nodded in sympathy. Martin shook the mood off, or appeared to. A tall, neat man with a slight hunch in his long neck and shoulders had risen from the spouse conversations and was approaching them. "It's Jason, right?" he said. "I'm Gary. And these are your friends?"

"Martin. Robert. Hal," Jason said. "Hal and I met at the NAMM show one year when Zeb was working the AxCess Pitch Tracker booth. I haven't seen you since then, though."

"One NAMM was enough. I think he only brought me to show me how much I'd hate it, so he could leave me home the next time. Come on in. There's beer and soft drinks in the kitchen."

The kitchen was past a circle of women sitting on chairs, leaned in toward each other to talk. Drinks were in coolers on the floor. Robert dug through melting ice and came up with a glass bottle with a soaked yellow paper label.

"Manhattan Special," he read. "Espresso coffee soda." He shrugged, twisted the cap, and glugged. Jason squatted to examine the cooler, and Robert tapped his back. Jason looked up.

Pointing at his drink, his eyes aglow, Robert promised, "You want one of these."

THEY CARRIED THE second round of Manhattan Specials into the living room, where an Asian man was sitting on the couch with the head of a Chinese bowed instrument tucked into the hollow where leg met trunk. The instrument had a neck as long as that of a guitar, but skinny as a dowel, with only two strings running down it, the fibers of the bow captive between them.

Jason stopped walking and felt his eyebrows go up. "That's an erhu."

Zeb asked the man something; the man nodded uncertainly. Zeb smiled.

" 'Old Joe Clark,' " Zeb called. "One, two—"

Bluegrass band and erhu launched into something loud and strange.

"He can't play the dominant," Zeb shouted after a repeating clash. "Make it major."

It got stranger.

Chinese bluegrass. Jason looked at everyone. Robert's expression was joyful. Martin's was *what the* . . . Zeb's sweating face was smug. The spouses were on their feet, happily surprised. The band's eyes were on the erhuist, whose brow wrinkled as he concentrated fiercely on following altered chords, chords that would have sounded plain old wrong if the band hadn't been tight and accurate playing them, and if the plaintive scrape of the erhu had woven less confidently through their transitions rather than doing the traditional little turns and ornaments that made it seem right.

Jason leaned toward Martin and pointed at the instrument. "The sound box is covered in snakeskin. That's what gives it that tonal color."

"Uh hah," Martin said.

The erhuist didn't know the song, so he missed the cue for the ending and it fell apart. Applause splashed up around the room. The band grinned. The erhuist declined invitations to continue and waved demurely at the applause.

"Jason!" Zeb cried. He unstrapped his banjo, climbed around things, and embraced Jason.

"Zeb," Jason said. "These are my friends Robert—"

"That was great!"

"Why, thank you, Robert!"

Robert elbowed Jason. "Now that's what music is all about, wouldn't you say, Jase? That that's what music is all about?"

Jason ignored him and said, "—and this is Martin."

"Martin seems a little less sure it was great."

"Lemme put it this way: I'm still not even used to rap. You gotta give me a little time for stuff to sink in."

"It's true," Jason said. "When I play my Sugar Hill Gang records, he yells at me to turn them down."

"I'd tell you to do more than that with them," Zeb said.

AS IN THE mythic ur-jam in the time before time, the music went on until early, and as some people started kissing cheeks goodbye, others who worked second-shift jobs showed up. Midnight, the music changed to low and sweet and conversations got pleasant.

Usually at that point, you either sat on lawn chairs in the back yard around the barbecue and had a breeze and the quiet music, or you sat at the kitchen table and ate leftovers. But Jason had never sat on a stoop. He hadn't, in truth, been sure what one was. Martin and Robert were inside.

Zeb's sandals smacked the stone as he came out into the illuminated dark.

"Are these brownstones?" Jason asked.

Zeb sat. He was drinking beer. He tilted the bottle to point with it. "No, these are all brick."

"Oh." Apparently, brownstone was the building material.

"There's some beautiful architecture around here. You should try to see some while you're here. Speaking of which, what *does* bring you here? You said in your e-mail you wanted to pick my brain?"

"Yeah. You were playing around Dallas in the sixties, right?"

"That I was."

"Dwight Cooper was playing then, too."

"I sat in with him on a few tunes and vice versa."

"I was just wondering if you could tell me anything about him."

"Not a lot. Good singer. Miserable human being. That's what I think, anyway."

"Miserable how?"

"In its truest sense. Unhappy."

"Any idea why?"

"I know he came from a hard background. His mom was a prostitute and his dad was a drunk. Mom ran off when he was little. I'm no psychologist, but that couldn't've helped. How is it you're interested?"

He told Zeb in broad strokes. "So we've been hired to just sort of poke around and make sure the little girl's okay."

Zeb let the story sink in a little before answering. "Well, at least it's a good cause."

"Yeah. I don't know what else I want to know, though. Brothers, sisters?"

"Not that I know of. Well, unless you count . . . what was his name . . ."

"Who?"

"The guitarist. He was sort of like a brother. He played with Dwight for a good while and then did some solo albums when the band broke up. It was one of those guitarist names. . . ."

Jason waited so he wouldn't influence the process. Zeb gave up.

"John Ray Hoffer?"

Zeb pointed his bottle. "That's it. How do their mommas know to name them like that? Dwight gave him a nickname, too . . . Tornado. Something like that. You know, 'cause the boy could blow. No, it was Hurricane—Hurricane Hoffer, that's it. You know what, I probably still have his solo records."

"I didn't know he did any."

"Oh yeah. I was reviewing for *String Picks* around that time. That was what, ten years back. Man." Zeb paused and shook his head at the ten years. Laughter bubbled in the apartment.

"How were they?"

"They were good." It was both an acknowledgment of their value and an implication that they were not great. "Sort of Eric Johnson meets . . . I dunno . . . Dickie Betts."

"How'd they sell?"

"You ever hear of them?"

"No."

Zeb shrugged. There's your answer. "I'll look tomorrow and give you a call if they turn up."

"I'd appreciate that." More laughter came from inside. "What was it like playing in Dallas in the sixties?"

"Well, if you were a liberal Brooklyn fag named Zebedee," Zeb said, "it was awfully interesting."

They slept in on Saturday. Lenny remembered their orders from the day before and said, "The usual?" when they came in. They hadn't known they had usuals, but it was too much a black-and-white movie moment to turn down.

Donovan sang that they called him Mellow Yellow.

Jason called Cora Smith from the pay phone outside the diner and brought her up to date. Martin came out and spent ten minutes talking to Leon, asking a lot of brotherly questions and apparently getting very little in the way of response. Then, since they had a weekend to kill before they could get back onto tracking down Lissa Court, they walked around and went to the top of the Empire State Building. There was more smog visible from there than Jason had seen since he was a kid, when there was still such thing as a third-degree smog alert in Los Angeles.

"Man," Martin said. "This place is *tiny*!"

Jason said, "They sure built it up, though. Every block is like downtown. I wonder why they expanded up instead of over."

"To stay on the island," Robert said.

"Island," Martin snorted. "Fiji is an island. Manhattan is a little piece of mainland cut off by a river."

"The Indians thought it was an island."

"Yeah, the Indians didn't have aerial photography."

Back on the sidewalk, Jason said, "How was Leon when you talked to him?"

Martin shook his head. "That expression you used the day you got him . . . 'gone inside.'"

"He still is?"

"Yup."

"Not much you can do from here."

"Nope."

That was depressing, so Robert waited a suitable time before saying, "I want to find a deli and have an egg cream."

"There's a deli on the ground floor here."

"Not a deli we're already at. One we find."

They walked. There were a lot of people walking. After an hour or so, they hadn't found a deli. They asked a gnome lurking in a newsstand where they could find one. He gave them exact directions which they followed exactly and which put them onto a corner with no deli, where they asked a friendly countergirl the same question. She considered it seriously and gave them precise directions which they followed precisely, and which put them onto a block with several department stores and no deli. They asked a goateed passerby with tattoos. He told them two blocks that way and turn left. They did. Office buildings. No deli.

There was a bookstore, however.

JASON WAS LOOKING at music magazines when Robert appeared beside him with an oversized paperback. Martin was off somewhere in the art section.

"I found it," he said, showing Jason the cover: *The Naked Eye and Other Stories* by Cathy Bellamy.

"Found what?"

"The short story I asked you if you'd read." He opened the book to where his thumb had been keeping it. "Listen."

THE WONKY

TED BOUGHT THE wonky on the gray market, in the back of
a shop, making the deal over the technician's workbench. He
stood looking indisceringly at the old vise and the clipped
solder ends while the proprietor went to get it from somewhere, not the storeroom.

He hurried to his car and unboxed it, spilling cardboard
shipping ears and plasticine-wrapped warranty cards on the
floorboard, prying the styrene carton-stabilizers from it, fin-
gernailing the tape off the inner plasticwrap.

He pulled it free and beheld it.

He pulled the string and held his breath.

"Take me to Morocco," it said.

The Moroccan sand was bright and costly. Ted sat on a chaise
near a pool with Byzantine mosaic tilework, the carrying case
next to him, chained to his wrist.

Tunisia was the same.

. . .

The purchase of the forty-foot motor home took some fina-
gling and a bribe to the loan officer. While the officer left to
have the paperwork rubberstamped, Ted opened the case and
pulled the string.

When the loan officer came back, Ted shot him.

Then he pulled the string.

. . .

They were on a flight to Ontario that evening. The carrying case had a hidden compartment inside and its shell was an unremarkable gray that baffled X-rays. Ted took it into the bathroom. When he came out, he shot a hole in the bulkhead. Everyone who didn't pass out screamed and beat their knees in fright. The equalization of pressure sucked air from the cabin.

Armed and unmolested by the crew, Ted opened the case and pulled the string. The sound of a little thunderclap was lost in the panic of the despairing plane as the wonky vanished.

. . .

A scented blue slip of paper appeared in mid-thunderclap and fluttered in the bouncing air. I can't say whether Ted saw it. It was not discovered by the investigating divers.

You should assume it was the explanation.

. . .

"I'M SUPPOSED TO get what from this?" Jason asked when Robert had looked expectant for a few moments. "That short stories don't need endings anymore?"

Robert closed the book meaningfully and went back to where he'd gotten it.

BY THE TIME they carried their bookstore bags through the lobby, they'd seen some extra parts of Manhattan they hadn't intended to see, and their MetroCards were exhausted. There was a message from Zeb with the check-in counterman: Found the CDs. Come get them if you want them.

unday morning, he took the subway back to Brooklyn. Zeb gave him the CDs and loaned him a portable CD player, assuring him it would be safe to use on the subway. Probably. Jason waited until he got back to the YMCA. Robert and Martin weren't there. He looked out the window vaguely and listened.

Neither *Mother's Fresh-Picked* nor *Hurricane Warning* seemed to contain anything of significance, either as clues or as music. They were, as Zeb said, good, and Eric-Johnson-meets-Dickie-Betts seemed not inaccurate.

Since all the music was instrumental, the CD booklets contained no lyrics, just lists of credits and the names of instruments Hoffer must have been endorsing then.

Jason didn't recognize any names in the credits, but he'd never paid attention to rock music, since every song seemed to be a reworking of every other song. He'd once said this to Robert, whose response had been shock and a vague opinion that "alternative rock" was essentially new.

No, Jason had said, the production's different, the composition's same old.

Okay, Robert had said, play me something different, then.

Jason had played him Thomas Dolby, *Budapest by Blimp*; Steve Reich, *Different Trains*; and Frank Martin, *Petite Symphonie Concertante*.

Those are cool too, Robert had said, and appropriated them. He was still playing Hootie sometimes, but Jason had hope.

He wondered what that short story had been about, and why Robert wouldn't just tell him the moral instead of making him guess.

WHEN HE FOUND them at the donut shop, Robert was leaning forward on the small table to peer at the vertical pages of a large hardcover book that Martin had propped up for viewing. Martin was on the other side, his fingers wrapped around to cover, Jason assumed, the caption. The newly purchased paperback of conversational Hebrew at Robert's elbow was already severely creased and dented. He'd never figured out how Robert did that.

The painting displayed in the open pages of Martin's book was blue, with controlled horizontal arcs and slashes.

Robert looked up at Jason. "What do you think this painting is of?"

Martin said, "No fair getting help. What do *you* think it is?"

Jason sat and put his own book on the table. "I'd be cheating anyway if I said. I saw it at LACMA a couple years ago."

Robert leaned in close and peered intently for about ten seconds. Then he said, "I give up."

Martin shook his head. "If you don't at least take one guess, I'm not telling you what it's called."

"I could just go back to the bookstore and look it up," Robert said. "It's not as though this is the only place the information exists."

"This was the last copy and you know you're too lazy."

Jason said, "What a fortunate moment for my entrance. Martin, what's it worth to you not to tell him at all? He still owes me an explanation."

Robert said, "Now, that's not fair."

Martin considered it. "We could deal. Buy me lunch."

"Just tell me what the painting's called."

Jason said, "What was the point of reading me that story?"

Robert looked reluctant. "It would really be much better if you interpreted it yourself."

Martin leaned forward over the top of the book. "Whaddaya know, that's just what *I'm* tellin' *you.*"

Robert narrowed his eyes and looked at each of them.

"I think I'll wait," he said.

Martin closed the book. "Y'all do whatever you like," he said, "but, uh, this here book don't leave my side, you understand."

"That's fine," Robert said casually. He picked up his paperback.

They read. They went and ate dinner. They went back to their room and fell asleep.

TEN A.M. MONDAY.

They had their usuals. Robert hunched over a spiral notebook at their table and wrote a script for the phone call to the Etta Earl Agency. Martin studied the paintings in his book, too absorbed to converse.

"Okay," Robert said finally. "What do you think?" He handed the notebook over.

Jason took it and read it twice. The second reading was to buy time before answering.

"It's good," he said. "Mind if I . . . suggest a little?"

"Sure."

" 'Fantabulistic orbit into the exciting inner stratum of the mind of a brilliant designer . . .' " He nodded. "It's . . ."

"Too much?"

"Not for some things, but I think a little for this." He gestured politely for the pen and Robert handed it over. He studied the page for a moment so Robert would think he was considering it seriously, and then drew a line through it.

" 'Our spines are prehensile.' " He looked up. "I don't get it."

"Yeah, maybe that wasn't clear. . . . It means, like, bending over backwards. I should have used 'flexible' instead."

"Ah." Jason nodded. "Gotcha." He studied it without really studying it. "I don't think it works. You mind?"

Robert gestured go-ahead. Jason hesitated, as though he was making sure that striking it wasn't a mistake, and then drew a line through it.

His eyes fell on "take you to unparalleled heights of artistic genius."

He nodded silently, eyes straight on the paper.

Robert said, "What are you thinking?"

"Well," he said. "I like this. But I think maybe we're . . . taking the wrong, uh, approach for . . . the, ah, target audience."

"I was keeping in mind what you said about the receptionist being literate."

"I see." After reading it through again, he held the notebook up. "This is good? You know? But I'm starting to think simple. I think simple might be the way to go."

"Like what?"

"Like . . . Something like . . . 'Hello, this is Robert Goldstein from Graphics Pros, following up on my letter to you. May I send over a graphic designer for your one-week free trial period?' "

Robert nodded slowly. "I think I see where you're going."

Jason could see him trying to comprehend it. "I guess I can see that." He thought longer. "But—"

Martin, still studying his book, cut him off pointedly with a little "uhp!" sound.

"I don't know. It seems—"

"Uhp!"

"—a little—"

"Uhp!"

Robert peered at Martin in annoyance. Martin, either engrossed or ignoring him, turned a page and looked at the next painting.

"Or," Robert said, "we could use Jason's."

"There you go."

JASON CALLED FROM their room. The Etta Earl Agency wanted to know whether they had anyone who could do a CD-ROM with pictures of all their models on it.

Certainly. He'll be there this afternoon to introduce himself. Is this the right address?

When Jason hung up, Martin said, "Um, I can do thin-line/thick-line, light and shadow, warm-color/cool-color, or I can do lay-it-out-nice-and-straight. I ain't never birthed no CD-ROMs."

"I have," Jason said. "Or at least I've been around them enough to get by. We'll have a coaching session."

Robert said, "I could've made that phone call."

HALF AN HOUR later, Martin stood by the door and presented himself in slacks, jacket, and tie.

"You sure that's not too formal?" Jason asked.

"No, it's good," Robert said after a moment of serious consideration. "You're thinking West Coast. They dress like that out here."

"Even for something like this?"

"Yeah, it's okay, trust me."

"All right, if you say so. Martin, you feel confident?"

"Seventy-two DPI, RGB JPEGs, no bigger than six-forty by four-eighty, rasterize all fonts, and look serious when I lie through my teeth."

"Go get 'em."

Robert said, "Martin, you can leave that. I'm not going to look at it."

Martin flourished the art book. "Right. Buhwhat am I, buhstupid? See y'all around seven if I buhdon't buhget confuhbused on da buhsubway."

When the door had closed behind Martin, Robert said, "Our little boy is growing up."

"And turning into Old Weird Harold."

"What's the painting?"

"What's the point of the story?"

They looked at each other.

Jason said, "Well. What do you want to do the rest of the day? Where do you want to go that you've always heard of?"

Robert considered.

Jason said, "The Statue of Liberty? The Met? A police precinct?"

Robert thought. After a while, it was clear that neither of them cared.

Jason went to the window. The pink neon sign was on. "Fresh batch," he said.

Robert picked up his book. "Let's go."

• • •

"FIGURED I'D FIND you here," Martin said, standing by the table. His tie was loosened and his jacket was over his shoulder.

Jason said, "Who is this accountant, and what can he possibly want with us?"

Martin rubbed the side of his nose with his middle finger.

Robert said, "How'd it go?"

"I'll tell you on the way to the shoot."

"What shoot."

"I'll tell you on the way."

Standing, Jason said, "Don't tell me we got lucky the first day."

"I been around models all day," Martin said. "Don't say 'get lucky.' "

enny's was a dark, scuffed bar someplace or other in Manhattan that took two trains to get to. A dark-haired woman in her thirties bent behind a tripod, taking pictures of Lissa Court, who sat at the bar in flared blue jeans and a chainmail shirt made of small gold links. The skin of her breasts, arms, and stomach shone pale through the links. A darkly handsome low-fat wedge in a gray blazer stood with his back to the camera, as though approaching her. Exotic music played on a boom box: an excellent field recording of pygmy women chanting and rhythmically splashing river water. Jason had it at home. Two baggy-pantsed young men quietly lagged quarters on the carpet out of camera range, and a dark-haired, fortyish woman was sitting at one of the tables with a worn tackle box, watching. Lights, goboes, and reflective materials were clamped to a flock of tall stands and turned toward Lissa.

Without looking away from her camera, the photographer said, "Is one of you Martin?"

Martin said, "I am."

"Have a seat."

Lissa and the low-fat wedge looked toward Martin's voice, but the lights kept them from seeing anything.

The wedge said doubtfully, "Sarah? How's the hair? Is the hair good?"

The photographer was busy adjusting her camera. "Sean, if the hair were any better, it would be God's hair and you would be bald."

Sean was stopped. "So it's good, right?"

"It's beyond good, darling. I wish you could see it."

"Me too, if it's that good!" Sean grinned at Lissa Court, sharing his sly joke. She smiled beautifully at him until he looked in the photographer's direction. "If it's that good, I want to see it too, Sarah."

"Well, you can't, sweetie," the photographer said. "You can't be here and there at the same time. It's one of those laws of thermodynamics you really can't break."

"Laws of thermodynamics?" Sean thought he was on a roll. "I think you're making that up." He winked in the general direction of the two assistants.

The photographer said, "You're right, Sean. It's not a physical impossibility; I'm just a big meanie."

"Yeah." Sean seized the opportunity for a pout. "That's what you are. You're just a big meanie."

"Christ," Martin whispered to Jason.

The photographer said, "Okay, beautiful, stop pouting and let's get back to work."

"You too, Lissa," Sean joked. Lissa beamed the revolving smile at him again, a lighthouse for male vanity.

"Oh, Sarah," Sean said, looking back at her, his eyebrows emoting gratitude, "you're so good to me."

"I know, Sean. Now turn that luscious, masculine bod around and give me some o' that hunky shoulder of yours. Lissa, what you were doing was great. Let's start there again, only this time . . ."

"The photographer's good," Jason whispered to Martin as the shoot got back underway.

Martin said, "Yeah."

"Really nice voice, too," Jason said. In a moment, Robert turned to look at him.

WHEN THE PHOTOGRAPHER had taken a series of shots of Lissa Court being approached by Sean, she said, "Okay, guys, set up the next one. Frannie, makeup?"

The dark-haired woman was already up from the table and crossing the floor with her tackle box.

Sean said, "Sarah . . ."

The photographer said, "Yes, Sean . . ."

"That suit . . ."

"The suit looks wonderful on you, Sean. Trust me."

"Okay . . ."

Sean went through a door to the side of the bar as Frannie started working on Lissa. The photographer removed her camera from the tripod, detached and stowed its lens, took another lens from a case, and walked over to meet them. She wore a loose brown blouse over black leggings, and silver earrings. It all looked expensive.

"Which one's Martin?" she asked.

Martin said, "I am. Nice to meet you."

She gestured apologetically with the camera and lens instead of offering her hand. "Sarah Fletcher."

"This is Robert and Jason."

"Etta was talking about a CD-ROM, but I was too busy to pay attention."

"Right. She wants to do a CD-ROM portfolio of all the models. We're thinking of including a day-on-the-set section, like a magazine article. Robert does narration, and Jason's a composer. We just wanted to sort of soak it up and see what we can maybe do with it."

"Okay," she said, beginning to screw the lens into the camera body and turn away. "Well, do whatever you want as long as you stay out of the way."

Jason said, "Do you know who in your family made arrows?"

She stopped and looked at him. "Somebody male," she said. "And you know what a fletcher is."

"I'm showing off. I thought it would be bad form to ask you out without impressing you first."

He wasn't looking at Martin and Robert, but he felt the jaws drop.

"Oh, a little chest-pounding," she said. "I like a man with one foot in the jungle."

"What a shame. How serious are you with this one-footed jungle man?"

She looked off-balance for a moment. Then she returned to attaching the lens. "You're fast."

"I had coffee before we came."

"Always do that. It works for you."

"Do you drink coffee?"

"Is water wet?"

"Well, no, actually."

She looked at him.

"Things water touches are wet," he explained.

She looked at him some more.

"I could impress you some more with my erudition," Jason said, "but I only know four more things, and then I'd be left with just my personality."

"I'm done here around ten."

"I know where to get coffee and tiny little donuts."

"Oh, don't tell me that. Now you only have three things left."

After half a moment, he said, "You're fast too."

"And I haven't had any coffee."

"This is you without coffee?"

She smiled. "Yup."

"Oh." He paused. "Maybe I'm in trouble."

Her smile broadened. "Yup."

"Shall we when you're done here?"

"Yup."

His own smile was too wide. He could feel it stretching his lower face, but he couldn't make it smaller. "Good," he said.

"Sarah . . ."

She crossed her eyes briefly and then turned around. "Yes, Sean?"

The wedge was standing in a green suit, thick arms spread helplessly, chiseled eyebrows tragic. "I look like AstroTurf Man." He leaned slightly away from the assistants, as though that would help them get by with the light stand they were moving.

"Oh, Sean, you look beautiful. You definitely do not look like AstroTurf Man. Lissa, tell Sean how gorgeous he looks."

Lissa Court stood. Now that the lights had moved, the room was visible to her, and she was staring at Jason and Robert. Frannie the makeup woman stood next to her, looking where Lissa was looking, a rouge brush still poised.

"What do you want?" Lissa said.

Sarah turned to see who she was talking to. The assistants stopped moving lights and looked too.

Sean said, "*Sarah*, I have a *prob*lem here."

Jason said to Lissa, "It can wait until you're done."

She stared at him. The makeup woman's rouge brush still

hovered where Lissa's face had been. Sean clued in that something was going on and looked where everyone else was looking, his arms still spread.

Sarah said, "You're disrupting my shoot?"

"Yes," Jason said. "I'm sorry."

"I'm sorry, Sarah," Lissa said. "Let's just keep going. If they want to talk to me, they can wait until we're done. Outside."

"That's where we'll be."

As he passed her, Sarah said softly, now looking through her viewfinder, "Does this mean coffee is off?"

"Maybe late. Not off."

She looked at him and smiled. Solar flares erupted past the orbit of Mercury and ignited the wings of slower-moving angels.

As they left, Sean said behind them, "If Lissa can have a personal drama, I think I should at least get a different suit."

THE BAR WAS on a corner. Robert was at the front door and Jason and Martin were at the side, watching a gray metal door behind a black iron security door. Robert popped his head around from the front of the building every so often just to maintain contact, and then popped back out of sight. It was cold. There was little traffic because the side street dead-ended.

"You surprise me, chief."

"Think how I feel."

"Leave it to you to go to a fashion shoot and fall for the photographer. I didn't even notice her. I was too busy trying to be too cool to look at Lissa Court's nipples."

"Lissa's not my type."

"I wouldn't've thought Sarah was, either."

"Why's that?"

"Well she ain't exactly skinny little Marisa."

"So my type moves around. Isn't she cool?"

"She's smart, you can tell that."

"I used to think Marisa was smart."

"Why?"

"I don't know. I guess because the alternative was that she was dumb, which wasn't an attractive thought."

"Especially since it would make you a guy who goes out with dumb women."

"Marries dumb women. Even worse."

"Why did you marry her?"

Long pause.

"Sorry, what?"

"Never mind."

A LITTLE LATER, IT was five after six by Martin's watch, which made it five after nine in New York.

"What are you going to do if you two really hit it off?"

"What do you mean?"

"She's in New York. You're in L.A."

"First I'll worry about coffee tonight. Then I'll worry about cross-country relationships."

"Okay, good deal."

"Did you hear that voice?"

"Uh, yeah, uh, good voice."

Nine-fifteen.

"I noticed you don't talk much about your mom and Leon."

"You noticed that, huh?"

"Yeah."

"Well, it's like, what am I gonna say? Hey, c'mere, look at my messed-up family? Hey, take the Altamirano family tour: On your left is Dad. Dad took off when I was two and I haven't seen him since. He gave me my last name and—hold on—here it is—this lovely Chevrolet key ring! —Oh . . . look at that . . . Well, it used to say Chevrolet. Please keep your hands inside the tram, there, young lady. Thank you. Next, on your right, you'll see Mom. Mom drinks too much and goes through way too many boyfriends. What is it she's doing there—? Why, it looks as if she's getting ready to go out. This mating practice is a common behavior for this particular female. If we're lucky, we might get a glimpse of one of her young. *Let's* see . . . hmm . . . No, maybe not tonight. The offspring must be with another female so this one can go party. No flash pictures, please, ma'am—it startles them.

"That's all you're missing when I don't talk about it."

Nine-thirty.

"What are you going to do for work if you get custody of Leon?"

"I dunno. But I'm thinking I could pull it off. I spend way too much money now, so if I cut back, I could probably make it. What worries me is housing."

"So stay in Venice with us."

Nine-forty.

"Should I go back to Etta Earl tomorrow?"

"Good question. Let's see how this goes."

The gray door opened in and the iron security door swung out and Lissa Court shot straight at Jason. Her nails came up and raked his forearms as he raised them to protect his face.

"You *fuck*!" she screamed. "You goddamn *fuck*!"

He didn't have a reaction ready, so he just kept his arms up and blocked her reasonably well. Frannie the makeup lady, standing in the doorway, dropped her tackle box and hurried after Lissa.

Lissa's hands slapped at his head, hitting his forearms and

elbows. "You go to hell. I have *nothing* to say to you!"

Frannie's soothing pulled her back a half-step. "You go to hell," Lissa said.

The snap of Jason's defensive reaction was over and he was feeling mean.

"You—" he started, and stopped when anger banged up through him. Not blowing up would be a good goal.

"Don't you say a word to me, you fuck," Lissa said. Frannie cooed softly at her and pulled lightly on her arm. "You're no better than a kidnapper, keeping a little child from her mother. How much is he paying you?"

Bang went the anger. "Look," he said. "We—"

"You have nothing to say to me! How much is he paying you?"

Bang. "I think—"

She stepped closer and shouted, "Not a thing!" Her eyes were wide and her lips trembled.

Frannie touched her shoulder. Lissa whirled upon her. "God*damn* it, Frannie, stop *pulling* my goddamn *arm.*"

Robert came around the corner from the front. Lissa saw him and launched herself toward him. Frannie ran after her. Robert looked surprised, but drew into an easy stance and pivoted aside so she passed him. He shot Jason and Martin a helpless what-should-I-do? look as she caught herself. Frannie reached her before she could recover and fly at him again. She put her hands on Lissa's shoulders and spoke to her very softly.

Jason said, "We're at the Y in Chelsea under the name Keltner. Come talk to us or not."

"*Fuck! You!*" Lissa yelled past Frannie.

"Fine," he said. He was shaking. He turned to walk away, and saw Sarah Fletcher in the gray open doorway, behind the iron rods of the security door.

They looked at each other, fifteen feet apart.

A rip of disappointment started in Jason's stomach and tore slowly upward.

"Maybe . . . not tonight?" he said.

"Maybe not ever." She turned and went back into the bar. In his mixed-up, adrenaline-spiked haze, the loss was misery.

Jason finally spoke in their dark room.

"I just don't get any of this."

Robert snored.

Martin's bedclothes rustled. "It's family, chief. Family's always a big mess."

Jason didn't answer.

Martin said, "What exactly don't you get?"

"You want a list?"

"Don't be coy, you know I do."

"Okay." Jason ordered his thoughts. "I don't get Lissa showing up at the field trip. I don't get her paying for the house and for Cora. I don't get Dwight leaving Donna in the car while he shoots up, not to mention the basic cliché of just being a burned-out rock star. I don't get the court giving Dwight custody because Lissa's a lesbian. I don't get Mrs. Kinsella being in contact with Lissa. I don't get Ed. I don't get Frank. I don't get why banks charge you twenty bucks for a bounced check, I don't get super-models, I don't get serialism, I don't get new age music, I don't get why a nineteenth-century orchestra is still standard, I don't get deism, I don't get atheism, I don't get politics, I don't get how a microphone can possibly cost four thousand dollars, I don't get why I'm wasting my time on CD-ROM game sound-tracks instead of real music and don't have a romantic relationship."

"You left out my mom."

"I was trying not to be impolite. I don't get her, either."

Robert znorfed and tossed. The pay phone rang briefly out in the hallway before a woman picked it up and spoke in a low voice. The door stopped her consonants, but her vowels came through as an inarticulate burble.

Jason said, "There was a message from Light Wizards on my machine when I checked it earlier. They have another CD-ROM music job for me. I need to let them know tomorrow."

"You gonna take it?"

"I just don't know."

The phone handset was replaced on its switchhook energetically. The woman stood outside their door in the hallway, talking loudly with another woman about a man who'd punched someone in the mouth.

"What I don't get," Martin said, "is why you didn't go back in there and talk to Sarah."

Jason remained silent.

"What is it," Martin said, "like a pride thing or something?"

"She said no."

"You still like her?"

After some time, there was a little rustle that was Martin shrugging, and he said, "Your life, Tarzan."

"Yeah."

The two women in the hall left. Silence pressed in. Jason slipped into a Technicolor adventure in which he and Danny Kaye had to protect the people of Ottowa, California, from someone called The Shoe.

"I," Robert's voice proclaimed regally, startling Jason awake, "am King of the Clodhoppers!"

Martin about killed himself snickering.

Jason's dream lingered, and he associated clodhoppers tantalizingly with The Shoe until he awoke completely and realized they weren't related.

"YOU KNOW WHAT else I'm wondering?" Jason said later, still awake.

Martin was asleep.

Jason said, more softly, "I'm wondering how Hoffer knew Dwight was at Ed's."

I suggest an alteration of our usual tactics," Robert said at the counter over their usuals.

"How so, Your Majesty?"

Robert cocked his head at Martin. "Why do you keep calling me that?"

Martin smiled puckishly and drank his orange juice. The Who were singing on the oldies station that they hoped they died before they got old. They hadn't managed it, but the royalties were probably a consolation.

Jason said, "What kind of alteration of our tactics?"

"I suggest we do not just walk up to Hoffer and say, 'How did you know Dwight was at Ed's?' I predict that that would just make him defensive."

Jason thought about it, poking his eggs into a tessellation of triangles. "Yeah, that's about what I'd be likely to do," he admitted. "What do you think would be better?"

"I'm not sure about that. Maybe make friends with him?"

Jason subdivided the triangles.

Martin said, "He did say he owed us one."

Jason nodded absently, darkening alternate triangles with black pepper. "Yeah," he said. Then his hand froze. He looked at the pay phone outside the front window.

"Uh oh," Martin said. "He's got an idea."

Robert said, "Do you? What is it?"

Jason dangled the pepper shaker from its cap and twiddled it as he thought. The idea was still good. He stood up and went out to the pay phone. Robert and Martin watched him through the window.

The Strawberry Alarm Clock were singing about incense and peppermints when he came back a few minutes later.

"Oh well," he said, sitting. "I was calling Hoffer to ask him to play guitar on *Ghost House IV*."

"Oh, good idea," Robert said.

"That's what I thought, kill two birds with one gig; do the job and get close to Hoffer at the same time, but he wasn't there. I left a message."

"What do you want to do now?" Martin said.

"I dunno. They have pie here."

"Good plan."

They ate pie and listened to Aretha sing "Respect." Then the Tokens sang "The Lion Sleeps Tonight."

Martin shook his head. "The mighty jungle."

Jason said, "I'll play you the Manu Dibango/Ladysmith Black Mambazo version when we get home."

The DJ came on and back-announced the songs in a silky voice, very close to the microphone to give himself lots of extra bass. Then he said, "Just a moment," and there was dead air.

He came back on and said, "We're interrupting the music for a moment here to bring you an unconfirmed report. John Ray "Hurricane" Hoffer, longtime guitarist for the Dwight Cooper Band, is reportedly in critical condition from a gunshot wound at County/USC Hospital in Los Angeles. John was one of the founding members of the band, and was recently on tour with them. Are we . . . yes, we're looking into it, and we'll let you know what we find out. While we try to confirm that story, here's an old one from Uncle Trouble and the gang. This is 'Give Me a Sign,' going out to Johnny Ray and his family from all your friends here at New York's finest oldies."

wight answered when Jason called Cora.

"Yeah," He sounded bad and panicky.

"This is Jason Keltner. We—"

"Jason the hero. You gotta get off the line, man."

"We just heard on the radio that—"

"Get off the line. Listen, you come here."

"I'm in—"

"You come here, man. Get here quick."

"Could I—"

The line clicked and went dead.

Jason hung up and looked at the pay phone. A whitish square of adhesive adorned the handset where a sticker had been, minus little divots where thumbnails had busied themselves. He wondered what the sticker had said, to compel people to try to peel it off. Maybe it had advertised the adhesive.

He went back in and sat at the counter. "I got Dwight. He said he had to clear the line and that we should go there, and then he hung up. He didn't sound good."

Martin said, "What about Hoffer?"

"He didn't say."

"Did you talk to Cora?"

"He hung up before I could ask. I didn't call back because he said to keep the line clear."

Robert said, "Why would he want us there?"

"No clue."

"Are we going back?"

Jason stared at the counter before answering. "It's got to be what, eight hundred dollars apiece for a same-day flight? We can't take on that kind of expense without Cora's approval."

"Right . . . and we can't get Cora's approval without tying up the line."

Martin said, "Doesn't he have call waiting?"

"You'd think." Jason put his head back and looked at the slow whirl of the black ceiling fan as he tried to think of options. He didn't think of many. "Okay," he said. "Unless we find an amazing fare in the next few minutes, I'll fly back today and you guys follow as soon as it's reasonable. If that turns out to be the wrong decision and Cora doesn't approve, I'll eat the expense."

"If that happens, I'll split it with you," Martin said.

"Yeah," Robert agreed, standing up. "I'll call for the fares."

THREE A.M. ON the coast was foggy and familiar. Jason took a taxi from LAX to where his pickup was parked in Venice, and drove to the Hollywood Hills with his wipers on intermittent. Martin and Robert had standby tickets the next day. If Cora disapproved, they'd be out more than five hundred dollars each.

He'd been out of contact with news for over six hours. He tuned the dashboard radio to KFWB. It had been a rock and roll AM station in the 1950s. Now it was all meaningless newsbites, all the time. The same professional voices Jason had heard since he was a kid said nothing about John Hoffer. Reception came and went in soft bursts when he got into the dark hills. In the twentieth century, the staticky bursts might be music if you listened to them that way. Jason wondered what might be music in the twenty-first.

The gate opened when he buzzed down. The hollow that contained the house was like a giant bowl of dark, damp air. As he drove down, Jason felt as though he were sinking in it.

HE PARKED NEXT to the only vehicle down there, a big black motorcycle with water beaded on it. The front door was cracked. He knocked. The light inside was dim.

He stood on the step in the eucalyptus-scented mist and wondered whether to enter. Unseen crickets sang in ensemble behind him.

"Come in," Dwight's voice said, near the door. The voice was wrong, scary-wrong, cranked up and overtightened down. There had been no footsteps.

"Dwight, it's Jason."

There was no answer.

"You told me to—"

The door jerked open and Dwight crouched in the entryway, thrusting a double-barreled shotgun up at Jason's face. Warm air flowed out and was buffeted by the fog. The eyes that looked up through streaks of disheveled blonde hair were feral. Jason couldn't see their pupils, but they would be dilated. He froze.

"The fuck you want with Uncle Trouble," Dwight growled.

Putting his hands up might seem threatening. Jason spread his fingers and moved his hands slightly away from his hips to show harmlessness.

Dwight wobbled the shotgun. "What the fuck you want!"

"You told me to come."

Dwight studied him suspiciously. "Stay where you are," he said.

Jason stayed where he was.

Dwight's eyelids drooped unevenly and closed.

He jerked awake immediately. "The fuckin' hero," he said, jabbing the shotgun toward Jason.

"Uh . . ."

"The fuckin' hero!"

"If you say so."

Dwight laughed. "If I fuckin' say so. If I fuckin' say so."

He lowered the shotgun.

"If I say so?"

"I—"

"UNCLE FUCKIN' SAY SO!" Dwight roared.

The crickets shut off.

Dwight's eyelids drooped again. There was a moment when Jason might have taken the gun from him, but it passed as he tried to visualize the space Dwight's index finger was in and whether it would push or pull on the triggers, depending on how the gun was handled.

The eyelids opened and the shotgun bobbed back into aim. "You the fuckin' *hero*?"

"Okay," Jason said. "If that's what you want, okay."

Dwight studied him again. Jason tried to feel helpful so Dwight would see whatever he was looking for.

"Yeah," Dwight said, looking closely for Jason's response.

"Okay," Jason said.

"Okay."

Dwight was still studying him, but the charge went out of the air.

A cricket started up.

"Okay," Dwight said.

Jason said, "Can I have the gun?"

"Yeah, okay." Dwight handed it over and swiveled on his heels, a move too graceful for the awkwardness of his standing and moving into the house. The crickets came back in hesitant chorus. Jason hadn't intended to ask for the shotgun.

The gun was heavy. Jason didn't know how to unload it—or how to tell whether it was really loaded—so he carried it cross-body, its barrel in the crook of his left elbow, like carrying a cat. Port arms, he remembered from somewhere, but he wasn't sure he had it right. He stepped out of the cool fog and into the still, warm house.

At the step down to the living room, Dwight spun on the hardwood to face him. "You gonna help, man."

"Help with what?"

"You gonna fuckin' help."

"Help with what?"

Dwight probed behind himself with one semi-responsible foot and then misjudged the carpeted step down into the record-lined living room anyway. He fell loosely backward and did a jelly-limbed little sideways run across the carpet, chasing his center of gravity. He caught it for one swaying moment. Then he tried to take a step and his feet hooked together and he fell. Minus the horror, it would have been Buster Keatonish. He drew himself sloppily up until he was sitting, loosely cross-legged. Jason stood above the living room in the entryway with the shotgun at port arms or whatever, his stomach getting queasy.

"Where's Hoffer," he said.

Dwight's face crumpled. "Johnny Ray . . . ," he moaned.

"Is he at County/USC?"

"Oh, Johnny Ray," Dwight said. His eyes were wet.

"What happened?"

Dwight was shaking his shaggy head. A tear streaked down his cheekbone into his short beard. "Shoulda gone." His forehead wrinkled. "Shoulda gone." After a second, Dwight was crying. "Poor Johnny Ray," he said. "Poor Johnny Ray."

Jason said, "Where did he go?"

Dwight sat on the living room floor and cried.

"Dwight," Jason said sharply. "Where did Johnny Ray go?"

Dwight sobbed. His eyelids drooped closed.

"*Dwight!*" Jason yelled.

Dwight's eyes came half-open.

"*Where did—*"

He stopped, loosened his clenched grip on the shotgun, and put it less aggressively. "Where did he go?"

The gaze that met Jason's bespoke heart-stopping torment. Jason's breath caught.

"Went to get her." Dwight mumbled. Each soft word held a human body of pain.

Dwight's eyelids closed and his body sagged.

"Get whom," Jason said softly.

"Oh no," Dwight murmured sadly. He was out before his back hit the carpet.

Jason stood with the shotgun. "Whom" hung falsely in the room.

A shudder rattled him.

THE KITCHEN HAD a three-gallon aluminum stockpot, into which he put all the ice from the freezer. He filled it the rest of the way with water, lugged it sloshing out to the living room, and dumped it on Dwight's face. The ice cubes bounced like little rocks. Dwight came up drenched and choking righteously.

"Hey, man," he whined.

"Hey, man," Jason said. "Where's Donna?"

Dwight looked at him for a moment and then slumped toward the puddled carpet. His eyes began to close.

Jason clonked him on the side of the head with the empty stockpot. The eyes opened and one forearm went up feebly to fend off the blow. "Hey, man," Dwight complained.

"Where's Donna?"

"To get her," Dwight said, fading out again.

Jason clonked him again. Dwight, awake again and nearly riled, said, "The fuck, man."

"You close your eyes, I bonk you with a pot. That's your world until you tell me where Donna is."

"Fuckin' hero," Dwight said, "gonna help," and he slipped into half-sleep again.

Jason's anger built. He put the pot on the floor and looked at his hands from two miles away.

"Okay," he said softly, turning his anger cold. He'd left the shotgun in the kitchen. On purpose.

He nodded slowly. Rage was still hidden behind the cold, and if he wasn't careful, it would be destructive. No more uncontrolled fury. Make a plan, do the plan.

"Okay," he answered himself.

Make Dwight tell.

Good plan.

He'd once been in an anechoic chamber that a psychoacoustic researcher on MUSE had allowed a few people to visit. There was no such thing as silence in all the world. In an anechoic chamber, not only did you not hear things, but you didn't sense the walls, floor, and ceiling the way you sense them in a normal space. The chamber was utterly absorptive and utterly weird. If you stood still and tried to listen, it raised the hair on your neck.

Then you noticed a high whine.

The human nervous system is electrical. It operates at a frequency within the human audio range. If you switch off the audible external world, you start hearing your nerves.

In the soundless vacuum of Dwight Cooper's living room, Jason picked Dwight up gently and noiselessly by the front of his leather jacket and placed him quietly against the wall.

"Where is Donna?" he asked politely. The room seemed to absorb his voice.

"Took her," Dwight said. "Johnny Ray went."

"Who took her?" Jason said.

"Don't call the cops, man, can't call the cops."

"Who took her?"

"No cops."

"Dwight—"

"No cops, no fuckin' cops."

"Who took Donna?"

"I dunno, man, I dunno, there's a note."

"May I see the note?"

"In the kitchen. No cops, man."

"Thank you."

Jason released him, and Dwight swayed and dropped onto the carpet. Where his back had been, the plaster was cracked.

Jason's footsteps seemed loud and reverberant as he walked through the kitchen. The note was by the phone, where he could have seen it if he'd looked while he was filling the stockpot. It was laser-printed in a generic font on white paper that had been crumpled and dirtied. He began to reach for it, but stopped and read it with his hands behind his back.

If you contact the police or FBI, we will kill your daughter. Keep your telephone line clear and wait for instructions.

He looked at the phone. Was it tapped? That might be how they'd know if Dwight called the police or FBI.

He went back to the living room. Dwight was out.

"Dwight," he said. "We have to call the police."

He got close to Dwight's ear and bellowed, "Dwight!"

Dwight was out.

He had to call the police.

Her father said not to. The note said not to or she'd be hurt.

He stood looking at the note. Doing nothing wasn't acceptable either.

He knew some people who weren't cops.

If he left the house, no one would answer the phone if the kidnappers called. But he shouldn't call out on the house phone because the kidnappers might have it tapped.

He left Dwight unconscious on the floor and sped his pickup down the dark, twisting roads. It was a good little truck, but it was squirrely even on dry curves, and twice he almost ran it off the oily, dew-slick road and down the unseen slope.

There was a new ache in his biceps and forearms. He noticed it when he steered. As though he'd been doing heavy lifting.

That thing about making a plan and doing it really worked. He'd have to remember that.

FROM THE PAY phone at the deli where he'd eaten with Robert, he got Norton Platt's answering machine.

"This is Jason," he said. "I need to talk to you as soon as possible. I'm at Solley's Deli in Van Nuys. This pay phone won't take incoming calls. It's a twenty-four-hour restaurant. I'll be a customer here until someone contacts me."

He took a booth and ordered a cup of coffee. Platt had to have some way of getting his messages quickly.

The full cup of coffee was still very warm when his waitress came to his booth and said, "Is your name E. T. Mensah?"

Jason said it was.

"We don't usually do this," she said as he started to slide out of the booth, "but you have an urgent phone call."

"ASK ME ABOUT Mom's colectomy," Platt's voice said.

Jason was standing at the register. The phone cord ran back behind the counter. The cashier was somewhere else, but two waitresses were right there. He said, "How'd Mom's colectomy go?"

The waitresses moved away a little to give him more privacy.

"I'm booked right now," Platt's voice said. "What do you need?"

"A parcel that wasn't diverted previously has been diverted."

There was a long pause.

"Sorry," Platt said. "Too cryptic."

"Um . . ." Jason tried not to look around furtively. "List your major crimes."

"Okay, murder."

"No."

"Rape."

"No."

"Unauthorized franking."

"No."

"Uh, kidnapping."

"Yes."

"Ransom note?"

"Yes."

"Adult victim?"

"No."

"Is law enforcement involved?"

"No."

"Threat of retribution if they are."

"Yes."

Platt sighed. "I'm booked. My first suggestion is call the police. If that's not an option, my second suggestion is hire Carl."

"How do I find him?"

"What time is it . . . He may have just left. I'll track him down. You should get a cell phone. Where's the rendezvous?"

"Uh . . . in the Hollywood Hills." He gave Platt the house address. "How much does he cost?" The cashier came back and looked annoyed. Jason put up a forefinger to indicate one minute, and tried to look apologetic.

"Free initial consultation. You work the rest out between you. I'll find him—you head out there."

"I should be there within fifteen minutes."

"With luck, so should he."

"Thanks."

"Good luck."

A silver Cadillac idled fluidly in the entry driveup. Water droplets hung vibrating on the tailpipe in the gray light before gaining enough mass to blow off, and dew clung in a semicircle to the rear window, striped from the defogger wires. Jason stopped his pickup behind it. The dome light in the Caddy came on. The driver was wearing a fishing hat and a red windbreaker. A gloved right hand waved, and the dome light turned off.

Walking past the Caddy to the security keypad, he looked at Swofford and pointed down the drive. Swofford nodded.

Where the big black motorcycle had stood in front of the house, there was only a small dry patch of driveway.

"Thanks for coming," Jason said as Swofford got out of the Cadillac.

Swofford scratched his head, moving the fishing hat around on his skull. "Who's been kidnapped?"

"Donna Cooper, the little girl who lives here. Her father is Dwight Cooper, the rock star."

"Never heard of him."

The front door was still open. The stockpot was still there on its side on the mushy, wet carpet, but Dwight wasn't. They stood in the entryway.

"Where's her family?"

"Her mother lives in New York. She's Lissa Court, the model."

"Never heard of her."

"Dwight was passed out on the floor here an hour ago. The motorcycle that was here then is gone. I don't know where the woman is who takes care of Donna, Cora Smith, but she was also taking care of my friend Martin's little brother, Leon."

Swofford nodded.

Jason said, "I heard on the radio in New York that a close friend of Dwight's, a member of his band, is in the hospital with a gunshot wound."

"What's that person's name?"

"John Ray Hoffer. They also call him Hurricane."

"Never heard of him. Norton said there's a note."

"It was in the kitchen." He led Swofford there.

Swofford unfolded bifocals from a case in his shirt pocket and read the note with his head tilted back, not touching it. He put the glasses away. "Did you touch it when you read it?"

"No."

Swofford looked at the shotgun on the counter. "Is that Mr. Cooper's?"

"Yes."

"You touch it?"

"Yes."

"Has anyone called the police?"

"I haven't."

"Why not?"

"The note says not to and her custodial parent insisted they not be called. I called Platt instead."

Swofford grunted.

Jason said, "Dwight has custody, but Lissa seems more responsible, and we can possibly reach her."

Swofford took a small pad of paper and a pen from his windbreaker and picked up the phone.

"Before you do that—" Jason said.

Swofford paused.

Jason said, "If there's a phone number currently stored in redial, you'll flush it if you dial star-six-nine."

"I don't have a way of getting the redial number, and it would waste too much time to go back and get the right equipment."

"I can get it."

"Without ringing the phone on the other end?"

"Yes."

Swofford handed him the phone. "Be quick."

Jason put it to his ear and pressed the redial button.

Dit-dah-dah-dee dit-dee-dah dit-dah-dah-dee.

He depressed the switchhook before the call went through and gestured for Swofford's pad and pen.

Dit-dah-dah-dee. It wasn't the little Bachlike figure of 1-213, the Los Angeles area code. He pressed the touch-tone buttons, finding the digits by ear the way he found any remembered piece on a keyboard. It was tricky; each of the touch tones contained two pitches.

Not that tricky, though, if you had an ear. And a history of wasting time writing music for telephone keypads. He gave Swofford the pad and pen back with the number written on it. The area code was 805. Valencia/Newhall.

Swofford dialed star-69, scowled, didn't write anything down, and hung up.

" 'Cannot be dialed?' " Jason said.

Swofford nodded. "It usually doesn't work."

"I want to hire you," Jason said, "but I don't know if I can afford you."

"How much can you afford?"

"I can't do a day rate because it's too uncertain how many days. I can only hire you for a flat fee. I have two thousand dollars. It's possible that I can come up with more in time, but right now that's all I can commit to."

"Do we have any help?"

"Robert and Martin, when they get in from New York sometime later today."

"All right," Swofford said. "You give me the two grand and I'll try to find her. I'll take expenses out of my fee. If the parents decide to call the cops, we say 'okay' right away and back off."

"Fine. I'll pay you as soon as we can get to the bank. What's first?"

"I can start trying to track the kidnappers or I can look for the caretaker and your friend's brother. I can't do both."

"It's my call?"

"You're the one signing the checks."

"I'll look for Cora and Leon, you look for Donna. Does that make sense to you?"

Swofford shrugged. "Everything makes less sense than calling the cops. This in particular . . . it splits our focus."

"How bad is that?"

"Until we have leads to act on, it's probably reasonable."

"All right, then that's the plan for now."

"Before anything, first thing I need from you is a written account of everything. That means everything. Once you leave, I need an hourly check-in, every hour on the half-hour." Swofford withdrew a business card from his windbreaker and gave it to Jason. "This phone number."

"Something else you should know," Jason said. "The mother may have made a kidnap threat previously."

"I'll keep that in mind. The cops should be called, and they should be called soon."

"I know," Jason said helplessly, "but it's not my decision."

FROM BEING HIRED by Celia Weather to watch Donna, to quitting, to being hired by Cora, to meeting Lissa Court, to his encounter with Dwight, Jason spent half an hour writing down everything he could remember. While he did, Swofford had brief conversations with phone company people and also confirmed that John Hoffer was at County/USC Medical Center. He'd been shot in the abdomen. He'd also been shot in both hands. He remained in critical condition, unconscious, and was not expected to survive.

"Hands," Jason said.

Swofford said, "You say he's a guitarist."

"Yes."

"Whoever shot him knew that."

"That doesn't narrow it down. A lot of people know he's a guitarist."

Swofford handed over his cell phone. "Call the mother."

Jason looked at the oven clock. A little after 6 A.M. Nine o'clock in New York.

"Etta Earl."

"Hello, this is a friend of Lissa Court's. She has a family emergency. How can I get in touch with her?"

"Mr. Baggins, have you found the One Ring yet? Ms. Court has been very concerned."

Jason blinked.

"I have a phonographic memory," the receptionist said.

"Voices are like photographs to me. I'd suggest you don't call again, because I will have the call traced."

"No, it really is—"

She hung up.

Swofford said, "I'll call in a few minutes."

Jason nodded and called the groovy beach pad. There was no answer, but holding the phone, he suddenly had an intuition so strong it was almost déjà vu. He could almost feel Cora and Leon sitting in there, looking at the ringing phone by the couch.

He stood in the silent living room of the groovy beach pad
with the front door open. So much for preternatural instinct.
Cora and Leon weren't there.

He found the phone and checked his voice mail, still standing. His first message was from Martin, his voice half-buried in
airport clamor, saying that the radio had confirmed John Hoffer's
hospitalization. "See you, bud. We should be flying out soon."

The second through sixth were hang-ups.

Someone knocked on the open door behind him, and Jason
jumped. He hung up and turned to see a brown-haired man in
olive Dockers and a pale yellow golf shirt leaning in from the
step.

"You don't answer your phone?" the man asked in a voice
that was supposed to sound casual. He was tall, corporate-
handsome and Nautilus-fit.

Jason put the phone on the couch. The guy wasn't setting
off any of his alarms. "Uh, can I help you?" Then he aimed a
thumb at the phone. "Were those hang-ups you?"

The man took the step through the door.

"I'm Jack West," he said.

"Imelda Marcos."

"Jack West," Jack West repeated, as though Jason just needed a little prod and then he'd get it.

"Hi. Flannery O'Connor. What do you want?"

"Jack West?" The man shook his head slightly, spreading his hands in a don't-you-know-the-name.

Jason put his up in a you-stumped-me. "Okay, Jack West. You're Jack West. If you don't have a Jack West complete sentence for me, I'll have to Jack West ask you to leave."

"Keep away from my fiancée."

Jason felt his eyebrows go up. "That's your complete sentence?"

"You're Jason Keltner, right?"

"Right . . ."

A no-nonsense Jack West pointed. "I don't want you near her."

Jason squinted. The guy didn't look any clearer blurry. "Did you really come all the way from New York to tell me that?"

A nonplussed Jack West frowned. "What do you mean?"

Jason frowned too. "Did you not come here from New York?"

A tentative Jack West shook his head slowly. "I don't know what you're talking about."

"Okay. Let's back up here." Jason pointed. "You're Jack West. We've established that. And your fiancée is?"

"Your ex-wife," Jack West said. "*Ex-*," he re-emphasized, "wife."

"Oh! Now I get it. I thought—" Jason raised an apologetic hand. "Never mind. I have no interest in Marisa."

Jack West had in his possession sworn testimony to the contrary. He shook his head regretfully.

"Jack West, I really don't have time to do 'Oh yeah?' 'Yeah.' 'Oh yeah?' with you, so here's a synopsis: Marisa came here twice, both times uninvited. The first time, she said that you and she were both having little 'flings' before you got married."

"That's—"

"When I said I didn't have time, Jack West, I wasn't kidding. I was flattered she wanted a 'fling' with me, but I threw her out. The second time—"

"The—"

"—she came to tell me how much I'd changed and tried to make nice and get a hug. I threw her out."

"Why should I—"

"I don't care why you should, and I don't have time."

"I don't like—"

"*I don't have time*," Jason said sharply.

Jack West stepped closer, claiming another few feet of Jason's living room. "Look—"

"You look," Jason snapped, and stopped. A snap wasn't the right tactic for efficient riddance of Jack Wests. He softened it and put up an open hand. "Look, believe it or not, I am not a problem for you. I do not want Marisa. I have not touched Marisa. I would prefer that Marisa find a comfortable hammock in Switzerland and stay there until the universe implodes. You're here to have a man-to-man and have it all out, but there's nothing to have out. That's going to have to be enough for you."

"You just stay away from her."

"Jack West," Jason said solemnly, "if Marisa comes around here yet again, I will throw Marisa out. Yet again."

Jack West was still not happy, and he didn't like that Jason was still casting Marisa in a guileful light, but he was a reasonable man who liked being seen as a reasonable man.

And he knew Marisa.

"All right," he said slowly.

Jason said, "I'm sorry to push this, and I can see that you're frustrated, but I'm really in a hurry."

With an effort, Jack West clicked his comportment a notch further into evolved reasonability. "And you're not coming around." He nodded, contingent upon Jason's confirmation.

"I'm not coming around," Jason confirmed.

"All right."

"Okay."

A masculine Jack West offered his hand.

Jason thought it was tacky, but he shook. Agreement reached on Marisa Accords. In political move, Keltner cedes rights to unwanted territories.

Jack West nodded, his treaty ratified. He disengaged and turned to the door.

"I'm sorry," Jason said.

Jack West waved behind himself without looking. Poor man. He had Marisa and he was Jack West.

The gate banged. Robert would be proud. Jason had gotten rid of Jack West without being a guy about it. Maybe if Sarah had seen how well he'd—

He called Swofford to check in.

"Your buddy Dwight wiped out on his bike," Swofford said. "Stoned to the gills. He's on life support."

J ason said, "Is anything not going to hell?"

"He wrapped it around a tree halfway down to Hollywood. You saw how slick those twisty roads were this morning. First decent moisture in a long time, floated up all the oil and gunk. Not that he needed any help losing control; he had more chemicals in his blood than blood. Shattered left arm, leg, hip, ribs, head trauma, everything . . . internal organs . . . he's busted up good. The bike's a paperweight. A guy walking his dog called it in on his cell phone." Swofford paused. "If Cooper was on his way to a meeting with the kidnapper, he missed it."

"What happens . . . if he missed the meeting?"

"The responding officer said he had fifty-some bucks on him, so it wasn't a ransom meeting he was going to. He might have been on his way to acquire instructions. If so, they'll call here again and see where the hell he is. They'll be mad."

"Mad enough to hurt Donna?"

A pause. Swofford cleared his throat.

Something vibrated through Jason, from the center out, in waves. It seemed to dissolve his muscles.

Swofford said, "We can't know."

Jason tried to breathe.

"Steady," Swofford said. "Keep it steady or you lose your effectiveness."

"Yeah. Okay. Okay. So. Did you reach Lissa?"

"No. That receptionist has caller ID. She knew I was calling from the same number as you. I don't know if I convinced her to pass the message on. She said she would, but she might be lying."

"Damn."

"I don't know whether I want to kill her or offer her a job."

"What will you say to the kidnappers when they call?"

"I'll say Dwight was in a motorcycle accident and ask what they want."

"Hm."

"You got a better idea, I'm dying to hear it."

Jason tried to think. He couldn't. "No. What was Dwight on?"

"Far as I can tell, a better question is what wasn't he on?"

"Any word on Hoffer?"

"No. What's the status on the search for the caretaker and the little brother?"

"I just got here a few minutes ago—I've barely started."

"Start."

" 'Bye."

Start where?

HE TURNED ON Robert's rain lamp so there'd be some sound in the house, got a notepad from his studio, sat on the living room couch, and leafed to a blank page. Across the top, he wrote *Ways to look for Cora and Leon*. He drew a fat black dot on the first empty line to indicate that he was about to write the first of several effective strategies. He was still looking at the black dot and the empty line when they came to the front door.

I didn't want to go out" Cora said, seating herself stiffly on the couch. Leon went straight into the kitchen when Jason said hi. Jason heard him open the refrigerator. "But there was no food in your house and we hadn't eaten since yesterday."

"You were here about an hour ago."

"Yes."

"Are you okay?"

She was rubbing her hands together, softly. "Yes."

Leon closed the refrigerator.

"Can you tell me what happened?"

"We were getting out of the car after picking Donna up from school."

"You, Donna, and Leon."

"Yes. Leon goes with me to pick her up. We had all just gotten out of the car when two men stepped up. They were dressed in black, wearing ski masks. One of them grabbed me from behind and put a gun to the back of my head while the other grabbed Donna. They were wearing gloves. The man who was holding Donna got into the front with her. She was struggling.

The other made me get behind the wheel. He got in the back and made me drive out the gate. When we got to the road, he told me that if I called the police, they would kill Donna. He told Leon he'd better keep quiet, and poked him in the chest. He said they would be in touch and told me to get out. I wanted to do something, but the man holding Donna kicked me away, and the man behind me got out and opened my door. He pulled me out. He threw me down the drive." Her hands slid against each other softly. "They drove away."

"Nothing's broken?"

"No. I'll be fine."

Her hands, he saw now as she gently rubbed them, were scraped and scabbed. Her elbows would be, too, but her sleeves covered them.

Robert had aloe vera gel in the bathroom above the sink for when he got sunburned. Jason went and brought it out.

"Thank you." She unscrewed the wide plastic cap and dipped into the transparent green gel. Scent seeped into the still air. Perfume didn't make sense in a first aid product. Maybe it was natural. She smoothed the gel over her hands.

"When I got up, Leon was standing there, and they were gone in the car with Donna. There was a paper dropped on the driveway. It said that if we called the police, they would hurt Donna." She shook her head. "Perhaps I should have called them anyway."

"What did you do?"

"I tried to call Lissa, but could not reach her. She is in Palermo, Italy, and she was not in her hotel room."

"We haven't been able to reach her either."

"Who is 'we'?"

"I called a man named Swofford who's not police, but... well, he's professional. But he's freelance, not cops. I trust him. He's very good."

"Do you think he might find her?"

He didn't know what to do with the question until he realized that she was asking for reassurance, not information. He nodded, hoping his confused hesitation had looked like thought. "It's likely. When did this happen?"

"Yesterday at about three o'clock."

"And you've not called the police."

"No, I have not, and I am not sure that was right." Her forehead furrowed. "They said they would harm her. . . ."

"Did you recognize either man?"

"No."

"You're holding up better than I would."

"I've been through a lot more than you have."

"I have two pieces of bad news." He took a breath. "John Hoffer has been shot, and Dwight crashed his motorcycle this morning. They're both in the hospital, in very bad shape."

She looked down and tsked once. "Oh," she murmured. Her face didn't change, and she didn't cry, but Jason had a sense of deep sadness. She shook her head. "That is very bad."

He called Swofford.

"I hope you've got something," Swofford said, " 'cause I got shit."

"Cora and Leon are here."

"Introduce me and put her on."

Cora said hello and listened, then said, "Yes, we're both all right," and began to recount the kidnapping. Jason noticed extra silence in the kitchenette. He got up and heard Leon move away, and the creak of a cabinet. When he looked in, Leon was peering at a shelf of resealed dry goods left from when Robert had decided to learn to bake bread. His back was to Jason. Three surfing weasels were silk-screened onto the back of his T-shirt.

"How you doing, Le?"

Leon shrugged, looking into the cabinet. "Okay."

"Can you add anything to what Cora told me?"

"Nope."

"Did you recognize either of the men?"

No response.

"It must have been bad, being ambushed and seeing Donna kidnapped and Cora hurt."

Leon shrugged.

"I'm sorry you had to see it."

Nothing.

"Well, I know this sounds lame, but if you want to talk . . ."

Jason waited. As he decided to give up on the conversation, Leon said, "Will they hurt her?"

"I hope not."

Leon stared at the bags of flour and meal.

"Where'd you go out to eat?"

"Some place." Leon shrugged. "I dunno. By some boats. Why aren't you trying to help her?"

"I am trying to help her."

"Yeah, right." Leon wiggled the cabinet door and stared in.

"I should buy food more often. We don't really have anything here, as you can see."

Leon stopped wiggling the door.

When Jason was sullen, Robert or Martin would bring it to his attention and leave him alone, and he'd eventually make an attempt to get over it. Maybe that was better than what he was doing with Leon.

And then, Leon's most vivid experience of him was the ugliness with Frank. The realization made his lips tighten. No surprise that the kid didn't want to talk to him.

"All right," he said. "Well, I won't bug you anymore. If you think of anything nobody's mentioned about the kidnapping, maybe you could say something."

"You pull guns on people."

Cora called, "Jason?"

Jason stood looking at Leon.

"Jason?" Cora called again.

"Yes," he said. "I did."

Leon looked at him.

"Jason, Mr. Swofford wants you."

"I'm sorry." Jason pointed toward the living room. "I have to . . ."

Leon turned back toward the cabinet. Jason went into the living room and took the phone from Cora.

"Yes," he said.

"Call waiting beeped. We have contact."

"What did they sound like?"

"A computer speech program. No background noises; they probably jacked the computer directly into the phone. I didn't need to tell them why I answered the phone instead of Dwight."

"How much?"

"One million."

"Delivered how?"

"To be arranged. They'll call the day after tomorrow at noon with the details."

"How do we get Donna back?"

"We get that info when they call."

"Do we know she's okay?"

"No."

"Have you reached Lissa?"

"No, but Cora's information will help. I have people I can call in Italy as soon as we're done talking. They'll track her down in Palermo."

Jason felt resolve tighten down around his fear. All of this had already felt real, but now it was real and current. The kidnappers were in direct contact and making demands. Behind them somewhere was Donna.

He said, "If we don't find Lissa in one hour, I call the police. I'm through waiting. That's it."

"Ten-four. Think she's got the mil?"

"I have no idea. We're coming in. See you in thirty minutes."

Jason hung up as Cora stood and went into the kitchen. He leaned into Robert's bedroom and looked at the banana clock. Eleven-forty-five. Donna's mother didn't know she had until a quarter to one before Jason acted in her place.

wofford's cell phone rang with ten minutes to spare. He told Lissa who he was, said, "Yes, she's here," and gave the phone to Cora. Leon was watching TV in the record room.

"Yes, baby," Cora said. "It's true. Yes." She listened for a few moments. "Yes. I understand. I will. Yes, he is. All right, just a moment."

She held the phone out toward Jason. He breathed in deeply, held it, and then let it out and took the phone.

"Yes."

"If I find out you had anything to do with my baby being taken, I'll have you killed."

"I didn't."

"You are not to call the police. We will pay the ransom. I do not want some *Cops* reject trying to be a hero and getting Donna hurt. We will pay the ransom and get her back safely. Do you understand?"

"I understand, but it might be wiser—"

"We don't have time for this. You are not her mother. I am, and I will handle this. You are not to call the police. I will be on the next flight out. Do not do anything until I get there."

"Understood."

"You think I'm coldhearted."

"No opinion. Do you have a million dollars?"

"That is none of your business. I will handle it. Is there anything else?"

Jason said to Swofford and Cora, "Anything else?" Both shook their heads.

"Nothing else," he said to Lissa.

She hung up.

"I hate this," Jason said. Swofford took his cell phone back and turned it off.

Cora said, "She doesn't want the police called."

"Does she have the million?" Swofford asked.

"She said she would once she called her insurance company."

"Then we'll have the police involved whether she wants them or not," Swofford said. "No insurance company is going to hand over a million and say, Okay, don't call the cops."

"Best to call them now?"

"Yes. But it will antagonize the mother further."

Jason put his hand out for the cell phone. "I'll call. She can't be less enamored of me than she already is. I'd rather keep her wrath focused on just me. That way, she still might be willing to take suggestions from you."

Cora said, "If the insurance company will be calling the police anyway, maybe it's best if you both stay on her good side."

As Swofford weighed that, the cell phone rang. He went to the kitchen table as he thumbed the phone and answered. "Yes." He uncapped his pen, flipped a notebook page, and wrote. "Thanks." He hung up, capped the pen. "That last-called number you got off the kitchen phone belongs to Kevin Washburn,

Newhall, California." He stood and took his red windbreaker off the back of the chair. "Heard of him?"

Jason and Cora shook their heads.

"Going or staying?" Swofford asked him.

"Staying."

"You should go," Cora said. "I'd feel better if you went with him. Leon and I will stay here and wait for Lissa."

"What if the kidnappers call?"

Swofford's windbreaker was on. He got his fishing hat off the table. "They're not due to call. If they do, I can take the call on my cellular. Norton has it all rigged." The hat was on his head and his keys were in his hand. "Going?"

Cora nodded at Jason. "We'll be fine. Go."

"All right." Without thinking about it, he surprised himself by kissing her on the cheek. She gave him a solemn pat on the arm and he followed Swofford out the door and into the quiet silver Cadillac.

"Thomas Guide in the glovebox," Swofford said.

LOS ANGELES HAS no center, which means it also has no outlying parts. Everything is scattered everywhere, and a lot of it looks like suburbs. It's not. That's the city. Although its entertainment business is clustered, its art, music, business, industry, crime, wealth, poverty, and leisure are spread in lumpily Gaussian distribution over five hundred square miles.

So a gargantuan, columned brick mansion on a huge dirt lot between two cookie-cutter tracts out in Newhall wasn't weird.

Well, yes it was.

"That," Jason said, "is the most ridiculous house I've ever seen. And I live in Venice. How much you think that mutant cost?"

They were in the Cadillac, idling on the unpaved dirt street in front of the lot.

Swofford appraised the house. "Figure around five fifty, out here. In Cooper's neighborhood, eight-five, easy, maybe a mil."

The landscaping wasn't done yet, but the earth had been graded and string was staked and flagged where things would go. The lot sloped up behind the house. A little yellow Bobcat earth mover perched near the top of the incline with its blade frozen aloft, and a chain-link fence ran the perimeter, its gate coupled with a heavy chain, padlocked.

Something small and white popped up and back down near ground level, almost behind the house. A duck, Jason realized when it happened again. In, he saw, a tiny rectangular lake. Dwarfed by the rising square walls of the tracts on either side, the lake looked like the permanent rivulet at the bottom of a large, poorly draining bathtub.

A dark green Ford Expedition gleamed dustily on the dry, graded dirt where the circular driveway would go.

"Gate's locked," Swofford said. "Can't walk up and knock on the door."

"Do we not say hello to Mr. Washburn after all?"

Swofford scratched his head through his fishing hat and pursed his lips. "Let's just sit here for a while and see if he cares."

"I keep having the feeling I've heard his name before."

"Keep thinking about it."

Swofford turned the radio on and got static; they were too far from home to pick up the preset station. Scanning through the AM frequencies found them a restaurant review. They listened to it. It had crab cakes in it. Jason liked crab cakes. He got hungry.

"Ever been to New Orleans?" Swofford asked him.

"Nope."

"The Royal Café, in the French Quarter. Outstanding crab cakes. You can sit out on the balcony and eat crab cakes, listen to the street music, and watch the girls."

"The complete cultural experience."

Swofford glanced at him.

Jason said, "Strangely, I wasn't kidding."

Swofford snorted and turned back to watch the house. The restaurant guy was speaking in enthusiastic detail about ladyfingers and thin custard. He went on about it. Swofford's stomach growled. He turned the radio off.

Two small oblong bars were set into Jason's door, in a backward L. He experimented with the lower oblong. A motor purred under his seat and he sank half an inch. Amused, he touched the upright. His seatback tilted.

Swofford was looking at him.

Jason said, "Nice seat." During the drive there, he'd been too busy navigating to pay attention to the car interior. Now he looked at it.

"We're facing northeast," he said, looking at the green *NE* in the rearview mirror. "And I see the outside temperature is seventy-one degrees." He turned and studied the nice day through his window, then peered again at the rearview's LCD display. "Does it say whether it's raining?"

"For a guy who wants to be a wiseguy, you're not very snappy."

"I'm not trying to be snappy; I'm just self-entertaining. Hey, look—the interior temperature is sixty-eight degrees."

"That's the target temperature for the AC."

"Target temperature. And I thought I was moving up when I ditched the Plymouth for a car with power windows."

"You finally junked that thing?"

"Stored it."

Swofford's grin started. "You stored it? Didn't that cost more than the car's worth?"

"I have plans for it."

"Oh, really. Like what."

"At first I was thinking I have enough broke artist friends that it would come in handy, but now I think I'm going to give it to Leon. He'll be driving in four years. He and Martin could fix it up together. It's easy to work on. No electronics, no fuel injection, lots of room under the hood. It doesn't run great, but it runs. I already replaced the most damaged body pieces from junk. It's paid for. I figure a mid-sixties sedan might be pretty cool for a kid graduating from high school in two thousand five."

"You got it on blocks and the whole thing?"

"Up on blocks, rags in the tailpipe and carburetor, removed the battery, all that. You a car guy?"

"I used to race formula cars, but I decided to keep my money for retirement instead. Now I just do regular oil changes on this thing. And traffic school."

"You get a lot of tickets?"

"I teach."

Jason looked at him, not sure. "No kidding."

"I was on my way to a class this morning when Norton called."

"An ex-spook who teaches traffic school. How'd that come about?"

Swofford turned the radio back on and settled in his seat, watching the ridiculous mansion.

"Ever seen people drive in New York?" Jason said.

"They're worse in Boston."

A van with "Benjy's Aquariums" on the side rolled up to the gate and honked. One side of the mansion's double door opened and a tall, goateed bald man in black lightweight workout clothes came out. He walked down the graded driveway and opened the gate, and the van drove up to the little lake. A man and a woman got out and started unloading green frondy things and plastic bags of koi and putting them in and around the water.

The goateed bald man looked at the Cadillac and went back in.

"We staying or leaving," Jason asked.

In a minute, the bald man came out again with a friend in a blue Gold's Gym sweatshirt and crossed the lot. The friend had a bushy black mustache.

Swofford said, "Try to follow my lead. If it comes down to it, you take the little one." He got out. Jason opened his door and went around.

They stood on the dirt on the driver's side. Neither of the approaching men was the little one. One of them was the big, tall one, and so was the other one.

"Something we can do for you?" the goateed man asked. His workout clothes were made out of synthetic material that looked like it used to be a parachute. His head was shaven. A thin silver chain flowed over his collarbones where the black workout top gapped. There were hard muscles there, and no hair.

"We were just looking at the house," Swofford said. "How much did that thing cost?"

"You'll have to move on."

"Public road." Swofford smiled.

The man shook his head.

His scruffy friend with the mustache said, "Why don't you two get in your nice car and get out of here."

"Not a very friendly tone."

"I ain't very friendly, Gramps."

"I'm sure you have other fine qualities."

"Other fine qualities." He elbowed the bald man. "Hear that, other fine qualities."

"Mimicry, for example," Jason said.

"And who the fuck are you?"

"Marley," Jason said. "Banana Marley."

Mustache laughed incredulously. "The fuck kind of a name is Banana?"

Jason frowned. "'Marley' is the part people usually make fun of."

Goatee said, "Leave the guy's name alone. You gentlemen just get back in your car and drive out."

Swofford said, "We'd like to speak to Mr. Washburn."

"Mr. *Wash*burn," Mustache exclaimed. "You want to speak to Mr. *Wash*burn. So you wasn't just sittin' here looking at the house."

"We was doin' that," Jason said, "while we was decidin' whether to approach Mr. Washburn."

Goatee said, "What do you want to talk to Mr. Washburn about?"

"Money," Swofford and Jason said at the same time.

Goatee pondered.

"Whaddaya think," Mustache said.

"You two stay here," Goatee decided. "Mikey, you stay with 'em, make sure they don't leave."

Mikey said, "You got it, Beauregard," and assumed a vigilant aura.

Goatee turned and walked off toward the gate and house. A six-inch rat-tail braid dangled at the base of his skull.

"His name's really Beauregard?" Jason asked.

"Yeah, *Banana*."

Swofford and Jason said nothing. Beauregard was halfway up the graded dirt.

"Nice house," Swofford said.

"It oughta be, enough suckers like you coming along."

Swofford nodded. Beauregard went into the house.

Mikey ran an admiring finger along the edge of the Cadillac's hood line. "You guys must be in *deep* kim-chee, you still got this nice car."

"What makes you say that?" Swofford said tersely, staring ahead.

Mikey waxed pedantic. "You see, guys in your average kim-chee, they got nothing, on account of they liquidate their assets to keep from getting their assets liquidated, you catch my drift. But guys in *really* deep kim-chee, they still got all their nice shit." He leaned in toward Swofford. " 'Cause liquidating it ain't enough to bail their sorry ass out."

"How interesting," Jason said admiringly.

Mikey shrugged. "You're in the business long enough, you learn stuff."

Beauregard came out of the house, across the dirt, through the gate, and across the road. He looked annoyed.

"What's your name?" he asked Swofford.

"Thurlow."

Beauregard went back across the road, through the gate, up the dirt, and into the house.

Jason said, "How do you like working for Mr. Washburn?"

"It's all right. The bennies are good."

Jason was trying to remember what drug that was when Mikey added, "Not everybody offers dental, you know?"

Beauregard stomped out of the house. They watched him approach.

"You got ID, Mr. Thurlow?" he demanded tightly. His face was pink.

Swofford withdrew a brown wallet from his windbreaker and gave Beauregard a driver's license.

"I need yours, too."

"Sorry, I didn't bring any."

Beauregard took Swofford's driver's license up to the house.

"Ol' Beauregard gets a reamin'!" Mikey crowed when the door had closed.

In a minute, the door opened again, and they were waved in.

KEVIN WASHBURN LIVED in a house where everything was new. The walls were bare and blank. Some of the carpet had never been walked on. The microwave had not yet held food. A glossy computer hutch contained a new computer, and a huge-screen TV and Dolby Surround system sat unassembled along the wall, their cables bundled. Washburn seated them on virgin couch.

"Nobody called to say you were coming," he said in a soft voice. He was a tall, slender, young-looking man in his forties with a thin beard, protruding ears, and a neck that angled forward off his torso. He sat with his long forearms on his knees, hands clasped, and examined his visitors. His shirt was pink and long-sleeved.

"We hadn't yet decided whether to bother you," Swofford said.

"Time is fleeting. Where did you get my address?"

"A mutual friend whose name I don't wish to divulge right now."

Washburn sat up and spread his hands. His cuffs pulled back a little, revealing an expensive-looking gold watch on a thick, brown band. "Business is based on mutual trust, Mr. Thurlow."

"I thought business was based on mutual need."

Washburn's eyes twinkled. "So it is. What is it you think I need?"

"Money."

"It's a gas. And what is it you think you need?"

"Money."

"And how do you propose to fulfill both our needs?"

"I was told you were a guy to make high-risk, high-interest loans. I want some money."

"What kind of money?"

"One million."

Washburn's eyes twinkled some more. "One million?" he asked in his soft voice. "Are we brothers? Do I suffer your wounds? Are we Ching and Ing?" He turned to Jason. "What do you say?"

"Chang and Eng," Jason said.

Washburn stared at him. "You have no manners." He turned back to Swofford. "Who gave you my name?"

Swofford shook his head. "I gave my word."

"Words are just dust," Washburn said. He rose. "Dust in the wind. Gentlemen."

Beauregard and Mikey took their cue to step forward as escorts. Swofford and Jason rose.

"It's been a pleasure," Washburn said.

"Only for a moment," Jason said. "And the moment's gone."

THE FRONT WHEELS scutted the dirt and pulled them back onto the road.

Swofford said, "So Cooper's last call was to a high-dollar loan shark. You get anything else out of that?"

"Yeah. He's been listening to Dwight songs. *Words are just dust* is from 'Flat Busted Heart.' *Are we brothers, do I suffer your wounds* is from 'Southbound Freight.' So is the Chang and Eng reference, and Dwight drawls it so it sounds like Ching and Ing. Annoys me every time I hear it on the radio."

"Washburn's screwing with us."

"I don't think so. *Time is fleeting* is from Rocky Horror, and *Dust in the Wind* is Kansas. There was another one . . . oh yeah; *Money, it's a gas* is Pink Floyd. I think he's one of those guys who thinks seventies songs are deep, so they just show up in his speech. If he'd been screwing with us, they would have all been Dwight songs."

Swofford grunted.

"Don't feel bad," Jason said. "If we're ever on the trail of a bad guy who speaks in Lawrence Welk lyrics, your insights will be extremely valuable."

Swofford's mouth twitched minutely, but he didn't laugh. "You figure out where you heard his name before?"

"No, and I wasn't sure anyway."

Around Woodland Hills, Swofford said, "What the hell is Banana Marley?"

Jason winced. "It came out before I could censor it. The refrain to 'Buffalo Soldier' by Bob Marley and the Wailers is the same as the Banana Splits theme."

A while later, Swofford said, "Your brain is connected wrong."

"You think mine's messed up," Jason said, "talk with Robert sometime."

issa Court let herself in at almost midnight, looking wide
awake and exhausted. She dropped a duffel bag in her entryway and looked into her living room, where Leon was
watching TV. Then she looked at the three people in her kitchen.
Swofford stood, reminding Jason to do the same.

"I'm Carl Swofford, ma'am," he said. "You already know
Jason."

"I do not want the police involved in this," Lissa said, stalking
through the short hall into the kitchen. "I will handle it. If they
want money, we will give it to them. The only thing that matters
is getting . . ." She broke off. Her anger almost went away. But
it came back. "The only thing that matters is getting Donna
back."

"Ma'am," Swofford said, "calling the police is the only sen-
sible move."

"If what they want is money, then we'll give them the
money."

"Well, ma'am—"

"*No!*" Lissa shouted. "*No! I will handle this!*"

The kitchen was silent. There were no street noises, no kids shouting. The house was set too far down, and the streets weren't the kind that kids could play on. Branches rattled in a puff of wind. A walnut dropped onto concrete nearby.

Lissa stood frozen in the kitchen door. Cora stood and walked to her, then touched her cheek briefly. Jason saw Lissa notice the scabs and scrapes, saw her tears begin to well as she gently took Cora's wrist in both hands.

"Don't think," she said to Swofford, "that because I'm a woman and I'm crying, I can't handle my own affairs."

"I don't, ma'am. I have no reason to think you're not a capable woman."

"That's right." She dried her eyes furiously on the back of her hand. Cora touched her cheek again, softly, and moved away a little.

"That doesn't mean you're capable of handling a kidnap situation."

She stiffened.

"I don't mean to offend," he said. "But unless you've had training I don't know about, handling kidnappers is not your area of expertise."

She looked as though she wanted to tell him off, but he was making too much sense.

"I will not call the police," she said finally. "This is a big enough problem without involving a bunch of testosterone-headed, swaggering men with guns in it. And before you tell me they're not like that, save your breath. I've had plenty of experience with cops, and so has Donna."

"I was going to tell you that there are some like that, but that most aren't, and the one I'd call isn't."

"Whose decision is it?"

There was a long moment of silence.

"All things being weighed, ma'am," Swofford said finally, "it's yours."

"All things being weighed?"

"Right. If it were a question of Donna's immediate safety, there'd be no question. We'd call the cops. If not you, then me, right now. But the two problems with paying the ransom instead of calling the police are one: the kidnappers will not be apprehended, and two: they're free to make a second attempt after the hostage is returned. The risk to Donna's *immediate* safety, however, is about the same."

"I don't care how you rationalize it," Lissa said. "I just don't want them involved."

She waited for an answer.

"Unless the situation changes," Swofford said, "I will—with great hesitation—respect that."

"What about you?"

Jason said, slowly, "I haven't decided."

"You'd better decide. Which side are you on?"

"I know which side I'm on. What I'm trying to decide is whose you're on."

"So speaks the man who attacked me for visiting my own daughter."

"I misjudged."

"Misjudged . . . Try thinking with the big head sometime."

"So speaks a woman who decides she's more capable than the police."

Bitterness pulled the corners of her mouth down. "Are you going to call them or not? That's all I care about from you."

"The custodial parent says no," Jason said, sort of to Swofford, but really trying to talk it through. "The non-custodial parent says no. The kidnappers threaten harm if the police are called. The danger to her is about the same, either way?"

"The immediate danger is," Swofford said. "The danger after her recovery is greater."

"What's it going to be?" Lissa said.

"You're wrong," Jason said. "I'm sorry. You're just wrong. They should be called right now."

Nobody prompted him. They just waited.

"Why'd Mrs. Kinsella tell you about the field trip?"

"She can't visit her son either." She shook herself. "What difference does that make?"

He couldn't tell what was right. "I won't call right now," he said. "But if that changes, I won't even notify you. I'll just call them."

"That's not good enough."

"Too bad."

"I am her mother!"

"That's why you get even this much from me."

"You and I," Lissa said, "will have an accounting when this is over."

"You got that right."

SWOFFORD STAYED AT the house. Jason took Leon back to Venice. The kidnappers were due to call at noon the day after next.

The ransom would be paid. Donna would be returned. There would be no trouble.

J ason's sleep was disturbed by nightmares that whisked through him and awakened him, then stood at the boundaries of memory and exhaustion and mocked him. It was the same nightmare every time, he sensed, even though it seemed like different dreams. The night stretched interminably. He succeeded in partially relaxing his neck and shoulders by concentrating on very tiny portions of their musculature and making them loosen. With each nightmare, they knotted again.

At four-thirty in the morning, he gave up on sleeping and put clothes on. He turned the kitchenette light on and looked into the gloom of Robert's room. Leon was splayed on the mattress in a tangle of bedclothes. It looked uncomfortable. As he moved back into the living room, he heard rustling. He looked in again. Leon was looking at him.

"Can't sleep?" Jason asked.

Leon shrugged.

Jason didn't know what to do for a twelve-year-old who couldn't sleep the night before a ransom payment.

"Want to go for a walk?" he asked.

Leon shrugged.

"Put your clothes on," Jason said. "I'll show you the canals."

CLOUDED MOONLIGHT RIPPLED on the surface. The narrow sidewalks were half-overgrown from both sides, from the small banks that sloped down to the water and from the untended yards that faced it. Their footfalls scuffed the concrete walks and thumped gently over the wooden footbridges, absorbed by the thick air. Ducks slept along the banks. A few drifted and paddled. The ocean boomed softly half a mile away.

"That's my favorite window in the canals," Jason said quietly as they passed the parabolic wooden arch. After a moment, Leon glanced back at it, trudging in his jeans and hooded sweatshirt.

They came out on Washington, near The Cow's End, where the inlet flowed under Washington, perpendicular to it.

Jason put a hand on Leon's shoulder to halt him.

"What," Leon said. Jason pointed. Perched on one of the valved pipes that overhung the inlet was a white bird the size of an egret, its beak tucked under its wing.

They looked at the bird, then walked the two lighted blocks on Washington to the beach. Misty haloes surrounded the street-lamps and obscured the end of the fishing pier. Jason walked toward it. Leon followed.

The pier was much longer than it looked, even in clear weather, and wider.

Two old men were fishing over the edge, two-thirds of the way out.

"Morning," Jason said.

"*Buenos dias.*"

Leon mumbled something.

At the end, Jason leaned on crossed arms against the side.

Leon stood with his hands in his sweatshirt pockets. He said, "What kind of bird was that?"

"In the canals? I don't know."

They leaned on the armrail at the end, watched and listened, and then walked back. One of the old men was cleaning a small fish.

"Hey, look," Jason said as they left the pier and walked up the cold sand. He turned, pointing back at the breaking waves. Very faint electricity had glowed briefly inside a big one as it crashed, so dim as to be uncertain. The old men were two dots along the pier edge.

"Did you see it?"

"See what."

"The glow. Did you see it?"

"No."

"Keep looking."

They stopped walking and faced the ocean. There was a string of smaller waves. Leon got a set look. "I think you're shittin' me."

A big breaker was gathering.

"Keep watching."

It rolled and arched. Dim green flickered within the dark foam as it broke against the flat sand.

"Whoah!"

"I haven't heard of a red tide right now." Jason turned and started walking. Leon followed him, looking back. "But maybe it just happens sometimes."

"What's that," Leon said when they were back on the beach walk.

"What, a red tide? When you get that glow, that's what it's called. It's bioluminescent plankton. Little single-celled sea organisms that glow. I've seen it brighter than this."

"Like animals?"

"Sort of."

They walked north in the dark on Ocean Front Walk, past two-story residences on their right. A strip of grass lined the walk on their left. Past it was the bike path and a dark gray swing set silhouetted against the dark gray beach. The sound of the breakers bounced against the building fronts.

"Why's it called red tide if it's green?"

"Beats me. You want to see my other favorite window?"

"I guess."

The building was two stories, with a modernist waterfall, a five-foot-high rectangular speckled stone the breadth of the building's front, over which flowed a nearly invisible eighth-inch sheen of water. Above that was a massive rectangular window with a red frame, facing the ocean.

"It swivels at the middle," Jason said. He pointed. "See the hinge? The entire thing rotates open until the glass is suspended horizontally by the center pins." He simulated with his hand. "It's like the entire wall opens up so the sea breeze can flow through the house."

"Cool."

Dawn was still to come, but it was lighter.

"Let's stop by the house, get some money, and go get coffee or something before we head back to Donna's house."

Leon shrugged. "Okay." Mist clung to his eyelashes in beadlets.

Halfway back on Venice Boulevard, he asked, "Do we have to go there?"

"Yes, we do."

"Why can't I stay here?"

"Because it would be irresponsible of me to leave you by yourself."

"I get left by myself all the time."

"I know, but you're in a different city now."

Jason hoped Leon wouldn't challenge that, because it didn't mean anything.

Leon didn't. "Do you think she's okay?"

He sounded very worried. "Yes," Jason said. "I think so."

"Do you think they'll hurt her?"

"I don't see any reason they would. Do you?"

"Sometimes people hurt people, even when you don't see why."

"That's true."

IT WAS LIGHT when they got back to the groovy beach pad at six-thirty. Robert was paying a cab driver when they turned onto Ocean from Venice Boulevard.

"Welcome back," Jason said when they were closer.

Robert looked exhausted. "Thanks," he said. The cab drove away.

"Where's Martin?"

"I don't know. We got separated in Saint Louis. I don't know if you got the message, but Hoffer is definitely in the hospital."

"You're way behind. I'll tell you about it on the way out."

"Out?" Robert said dully. "I can't do any 'out.' I haven't slept since before you last saw me."

Leon said, "I wouldn't be by myself, if he's staying too."

"Want to stay here with Leon?"

"Sure." Robert nodded blearily at Leon. "We can find some things to do a little later."

"I'll bring you up to date first, and then I'll take off."

. . .

"WOW," ROBERT SAID when he'd finished.

"Platt sent someone over to assist Swofford while I was taking Leon home and getting some rest. I'm not due to relieve him yet, but I want to get back."

It was six-thirty.

RUSH HOUR TRAFFIC hadn't hardened yet, so he got to Lissa Court's house a little after seven.

Norton Platt's familiar primered Suburban was next to Swofford's Cadillac. He parked alongside.

He met Paul Reno coming out of the house.

They looked at each other a long moment.

"Jason," Paul said. He had keys in his hand.

"Paul."

The look went on.

Jason said, "So, you . . ." and made an empty gesture.

"I'm fine."

"That's good."

"I need to get going."

"All right, well . . ."

He found nothing to say.

Paul unlocked the primered door and got in. Before he closed the door, he said, "What did you do with the money?"

"We split it three ways. I finished my music setup, Robert finally got his head shots done and started up his acting classes again, and Martin got a car and spent the rest on his family."

Paul just looked at him.

Jason said, "I'm getting music jobs, and Robert's had some acting roles. That wouldn't have happened otherwise."

"Great." Paul closed the door and started the engine. He backed the Suburban out, and Jason watched it climb the ascending drive. The engine was pinging a little. Unburnt exhaust darkened the eucalyptus scent.

He went in.

"Platt sent you Paul Reno?" he asked Swofford, who was at the kitchen island with his cell phone and notes.

"That's right."

"Well . . . how'd he do?"

"He showed up when he was supposed to."

"I guess that's good."

"You're early."

"I was up." Jason leaned in the kitchen doorway. "Where's Lissa?"

"In her bedroom, on the phone. She's finalizing the money."

"And Cora?"

"In her room. Supposedly resting. Probably praying. Have a seat. Read a book. There's nothing else to do right now. Norton sent along some crossword puzzles"—he picked up a blue booklet and tossed it back onto the island—"but they stink."

Jason pushed from the doorframe and walked across. He picked up the booklet.

Swofford said, "I checked on the guitarist. They don't expect him to last the day."

Jason sat on one of the tall chairs around the island and flipped open the booklet. " 'Tom Cruise or Alpha Centauri,' " he read. "Four letters." He looked up at Swofford. "I see what you mean. Why do you teach traffic school?"

"It's a long story."

" 'Four letters,' " Jason read. " 'O Christmas blank, O Christmas blank.' "

He didn't think Swofford would respond.

THUGS

I was sitting in the Crazy Horse, a famous strip joint in Paris. I was an American drug buyer. I was there with a man named Pierre Cardin. I was not really an American drug buyer, but he was not really named Pierre Cardin.

We were drinking imported whiskey because it was expensive. He had a supply of heroin, and he had been told I had a demand. I had stopped taking a paycheck from Uncle Sam only a month before, and now I had been hired for this job. Now I was in Paris.

He told me about his supply. He gave me a sample, which I would take away with me and test. I was the buyer, so I paid for the whiskey. We watched the girls and drank the whiskey.

I NEED TO back up.

St. Paul. Two degrees out.

I was indoors, in a coffeeshop on the other side of the bridge to the civic center. I was still on Uncle Sam's payroll. A guy named Hubie was meeting me to talk about testifying about some murders.

Hubie's supposed to be there at noon. He gets there at almost one. I'm sitting there with a plate of runny eggs for an hour, thinking of the places I'd rather be than a coffeeshop in St. Paul in two degrees above zero, getting secondhand smoke in my eyes and lungs and taking tiny sips of bad coffee for an hour. It's been a few years now, and I'm thinking, What am I doing this for? Is this what I joined up for?

Hubie shows up. He's huge, six-seven, three-fifty. Very ugly. Buzz cut and goatee. He's in this huge orange hooded ski jacket that makes him look like an orange dirigible, with the hood pulled and tied so just the middle of his face is in a little open circle in the middle. Ugly little blue eyes. He comes over to the booth and slides in. There's not enough room, but he wedges himself in there.

"What you got for me," he says. He turns his torso toward me when he says it, as much as he can the way he's stuffed into the booth. He's still in the jacket, with the hood on, so he can't just turn his head.

So I say, What do *you* have for *me*? He says he wants fifty thousand to even say hello. I say no. He says okay, I'll walk. I say don't let the door hit you. He orders pancakes and says we can talk while he eats. He's cocky. Like he's got leverage. He unties the hood. He's got those little foam headphones on under the hood. One of those idiots who's always got the headphones on, it's part of his dossier.

He talks with pancakes and bacon in his mouth. He says he wants this, he wants that. He says maybe he wants relocation.

I tell him relocation is only for guys with serious information.

He says, serious information, he's got so much serious information, he could put away half the state of Minnesota.

I act doubtful, sure you could. He gets offended: If I say it's serious, it's serious.

I don't know, I say. Give me an example.

So he puts himself at the discussion that preceded the murder of a local politician.

We already know that, I say, although we didn't.

Bullshit you know that, he says. How's this: He names a federal agent who turned up dead in the river two years previously. I know you don't know shit about that. I'll give you the trigger man, the driver, and the guy who called the hit. It's not just my word, he says. I got proof.

Okay, let's see the proof.

He wants guarantees.

I won't make any until I see the proof.

He says, okay, let's say it lets you put away the guys that killed that agent.

I tell him maybe we can do something, but no promises.

He kind of tips himself over so he can get into the pocket of his ski jacket and he wrestles out a cassette and hands it to me. He says it's just a few tastes of what he's got, and I can take it away and listen to it before I give him an answer.

I take it and leave. He's still back there, wedged in by the edge of the table.

The tape's pure gold, if it's real. Conversations about hits, conversations about all kinds of criminal activity. But it's a lot of bits taken from other tapes. We need the originals.

I meet Hubie again and make the deal. He'll hand over the originals, we'll get him set up in a nice ranch house in Arizona. I ask him how he got the tapes. He pulls back his hood and says, "These ain't headphones." All that time, nobody noticed that they weren't plugged into the headphone jack, they were plugged into the microphone jack.

We make it all nice and official. He hands over almost a hundred cassettes.

Hubie's all over these recordings. Hubie driving, Hubie taking orders, Hubie farting, Hubie eating.

Hubie participating in a rape.

Hubie participating in the murder of a local politician.

Hubie participating in the murder of a federal agent.

The tapes are gold. I'm getting kudos for turning them up. I'm sick to my stomach. I'm setting this waste of life up in a nice ranch house in Arizona.

Before that, I was already on my way to burning out, but I didn't know it yet. Maybe you never know it, it just all seems normal, only normal gets worse and worse.

It was like somebody turned my head a few degrees and I suddenly saw it all from a different angle. Who was I really helping? That's why I joined up—to make a difference. Save some lives. Make the world safer. I cried all the way home. If I really wanted to make the world safer, I'd have shot him through the head.

THAT WAS A few months earlier.

MY FRIEND PIERRE Cardin had a taste for the Crazy Horse's whiskey, I think more than he had for the girls.

His heroin tested all right. I made him an offer. We bartered and he named a price. I accepted. We agreed to meet the next day on the Cour de Commerce St. André, at the iron tripod that they used to use to mount horses. I would buy his heroin there.

I was there. He wasn't. I sat and waited and looked at the remains of the medieval city wall. You could still see a section of tower above one of the shops, and part of an old well. Pierre never came. I never found him again, at the Crazy Horse or anywhere else.

There was another reason for testing his heroin. It was to see whether it was part of a shipment stolen from a man we couldn't find. We would hear he was in Dakar, and then he would not be there. Paris, London, New York. One of our agents infiltrated his organization, but we had lost contact. The heroin tested positive as part of that shipment, so Pierre was a link to the man we couldn't find.

The agent was shot the night the shipment was stolen. He was found with eight other dead people in an apartment in Montparnasse.

Someone on our team told Pierre not to meet me. Nothing else makes sense. Someone came forward with information, which Pierre paid for. Maybe it was the same person who sold out our dead agent.

No lives saved. No difference made. Pierre finds another buyer, or gets killed himself. The world is no safer.

If we had got him, so what? There is always another one. Nothing stops it. The world doesn't get any safer.

Intrigue makes no difference. Exotic locations just give spies and wartime journalists head rushes, and good stories that get them laid.

Mostly, it's bullshit.

A t eight-thirty, the gate bell chimed. Lissa Court came downstairs.

"They're expected," she said, and buzzed the gate open.

Jason and Swofford watched through the front window. A nice Grand Marquis came down the drive and parked, followed by a white van. A woman in her forties, in a tan jacket and skirt, got out of the Grand Marquis, carrying a briefcase. No one got out of the van.

Lissa opened the door as the woman clicked up the front steps.

"Hello, Lissa," the woman said sweetly. She kissed the air by Lissa's cheek. "I know you said you're in a hurry, so why don't we sit down, and you can just sign the papers and I'll be out of your way."

They went into the kitchen. Swofford cleared his notebook and cell phone off the island, and the woman unsnapped the briefcase there and opened it. She looked at Swofford and Jason and hesitated.

Lissa said, "Some privacy, please."

They went out into the front room and looked out the window at the cars and the white van. Lissa closed the slatted French doors to the kitchen.

"Here," they could hear the woman saying, interspersed with rustlings of paper. "Here . . . and here . . ."

The doors opened, and the woman came out. She went onto the front porch and waved. Both van doors opened and two men in blue uniforms got out. One was carrying a brown leather satchel. The other was carrying a rifle, and looked all around the area as they walked past the other cars and up the steps into the house.

The satchel was given to the woman, who lugged it into the kitchen.

Swofford nodded at the men. They nodded back. Jason was tempted to nod, but felt unqualified.

The woman came out of the kitchen again, with her briefcase, and thanked the men, and they all left. The Grand Marquis and the van went up the drive and out the gate.

Jason went into the kitchen. Lissa Court was sitting at the island with the leather satchel open. She was looking into it.

Swofford came in behind him. "How much?"

"Eight hundred thousand dollars," she said very softly, still looking at it. "The insurance company won't pay unless the police are involved," she said. "It's their policy."

"Is eight hundred thousand all you have?"

"The rest is upstairs."

"How much of a loss did you take on the house?"

She was still staring in the direction of the bag. "I was going to live here with Donna someday."

Swofford took one of the seats around the island. "In four hours," he said, "it will be too late to call the police. I will respect whatever you decide. But please—let's call them."

She looked at him for a long time. Her eyes were rimmed and tired. The electric motor of the old-fashioned oven clock hummed.

"No," she said. She closed the satchel and buckled it, slid off the seat, and carried it out of the kitchen.

In the entryway past the kitchen door, she put it down and turned.

"I'm going to make the right choice for Donna this time," she said. "Not the right choice for me."

She hefted the satchel again and took it upstairs. Swofford looked at the surface of the island. His mouth curved unhappily.

Jason said, "Is there any use for me here, or am I just in the way?"

"There's no use for you right now. I'll tell you if you get in the way."

THE CALL CAME at noon.

Lissa answered it. Swofford picked up the kitchen extension. Jason listened ear-to-ear.

A halting computer voice said:

If you do not follow directions, the child will die.

Lissa Court's voice on the other extension said, "Who are you?"

In the Ralphs market parking lot at Ventura Boulevard and Woodman is an unlocked black Bronco without license plates. Open the back put the money in and close the back. Return to your home, you will be contacted.

Lissa's voice said, "I—"

The child is hidden in a very unsafe place. If we are delayed, the child will die.

The line disconnected.

· · ·

VENTURA BOULEVARD IS the closest thing to a Main Street that the San Fernando Valley has. It runs along the base of the hills for miles, mostly stores and restaurants in one- and two-story buildings.

The Ralphs lot was full and busy. A mid-eighties black Bronco with no plates was parked in the lot, facing east, against the side of the supermarket near its truck docks, next to an old Falcon. They stopped behind it in the Cadillac. Lissa got out and went to the trunk while Swofford popped the lid from inside. The Caddy jiggled when she hauled out the satchel. She put it on the ground behind the Bronco, opened the back of the Bronco, and wrestled the satchel in behind its rear seats. She closed the back. She didn't look around the lot. She got back in the Cadillac.

Jason touched her shoulder from the back seat. She didn't snarl at him. He took his hand away before she could.

THEY WERE BACK at the house at twelve-thirty. There was no message.

The phone rang at one o'clock.

You can find the child where you left the money.

The line clicked and went dead.

"DONNA," LISSA SAID as they opened the back of the Bronco.

It was empty. The carpeted surface behind its back seats was open to the ground, hanging down in two hinged panels. The drive train and undercarriage had been cut away to accommodate a straight drop to the ground. Swofford looked underneath and straightened.

"Radio trigger," he said. "Drive up behind, trigger the panels, scoop up the satchel, drive away. Their vehicle could block the view so the man getting out wouldn't be seen."

Lissa was folding the seats forward, looking under them. "Donna!"

Swofford got on his back under the Bronco.

"No other panels, and the engine's in the engine compartment," he said when he slid out. He stood and brushed himself off. "She's not in this vehicle."

"DONNA!" Lissa shrieked into the parking lot. "DONNA!" A few people looked on their way across the lot. Most didn't. "Where are you, baby! Oh, god, where—"

Jason started, and held up a hand for quiet.

"Oh my god," Lissa wailed.

"Listen," Jason said, his hand still up.

"Baby, where—"

"Listen!"

They all froze and listened. Traffic went by on Woodman and Ventura. Engines, radios, brakes. A Corvette with a custom stick shifted gears as it passed. A boy in a Ralphs shirt banged a shopping cart into a line of them and trotted across the lot to grab another.

Swofford said, "I don't hear anything."

"Call her again," Jason said.

"Donna!"

"I heard it," Swofford said, turning around, trying to get a bead on it.

"What did you hear?" Lissa said. "What did you hear? Did you hear her?"

Jason said, "Once more."

"Okay," Lissa breathed once and seemed to calm herself. "DONNA!"

Thump.

Low frequencies aren't directional. Where the hell was it? Jason turned slowly and concentrated, not seeing. Years of headphone practice.

"Again, please."

"DONNA!"

Thump.

He turned tentatively toward the old Falcon and cocked his head. Lissa and Swofford were facing the other way.

Thump.

That was a lock.

"There," Jason said.

Thump. The Falcon wobbled.

"The trunk."

Lissa bent over it, her hands splayed on it. "Donna, baby, it's Mommy—"

Thump.

"Did you feel it?" Lissa cried. "I hear you, sweetheart, Mommy's here. . . ."

Swofford had the Cadillac trunk open and a crowbar out. He wedged the straight end under the Falcon's trunk lid and twisted. The metal bent, but there was no leverage. The thumping grew frantic, and then stopped.

"Sweetie, it's okay, Mommy's here. . . ."

Swofford reversed the crowbar, got the curved end hooked into the bent metal, and wrenched. The edge of the trunk lid came up. He repositioned it and wrenched again, and the trunk bent up a little.

Lissa fell to her knees on the pavement and spoke into the

small opening. "I love you, Donna. It's okay, baby. It's okay, everything's okay."

The latch was still holding. Swofford went to work on the other side of the trunk until the trunk lid was bent into a V, the latch still holding in the middle. The thumping was now constant. He got the curved end in just under the point of the V and shoved it down. The latch pinged and the trunk popped open.

Donna was duct-taped. It was all the way around her head, strapping her mouth. It tied her wrists, knees, and ankles. Her eyes were dazed, her face wet. Dirt from the trunk stuck to it. Lissa reached in and lifted her out.

Just clear of the trunk, Lissa stopped, still half-bent. A thick red multifilament cord tethered Donna's abdomen into the trunk. Jason and Swofford leaned in. The cord was tightly knotted to the lower latch.

"Get—" Swofford said, but Jason had seen the bolt cutters when Swofford got the crowbar, and he was already heading for the Caddy's trunk.

Lissa angled Donna up so Jason could get the blunt jaws at the cord. He cut it.

"Into the Caddy," Swofford said. Lissa carried her to the Cadillac and got in with her. Swofford threw the bolt cutters and the crowbar back into his trunk, and brought out a folding knife. He knelt by the open front passenger's door and slit the duct tape, and Donna's limbs fell loosely from each other. Her arms went up sloppily and she clung to Lissa. He carefully chose a spot behind her ear and gently sliced the tape that strapped her head. It loosened around the back of her hair, but still adhered to her mouth.

He shook his head. "I don't want to hurt her, taking the tape off."

"It's okay," Lissa whispered to Donna, holding her tightly and rocking her. "It's okay." Tears wet her face and Donna's. Donna's fingers went shakily to the tape over her mouth and pried weakly.

"Let's get going," Swofford said. "Before someone asks what we're doing here."

Jason got in the back. Lissa worked gently at the corners of the tape. Swofford closed Lissa's door before getting in and driving out of the parking lot.

J ason drove home alone.

He stopped at his bank and withdrew two thousand forty dollars. It was dusk when he came out. Streaks of pale gold this early, it would be a good sunset.

It had deepened to dark yellows when he got home. There was a note taped to the bathroom mirror in Robert's writing: *Sunset*. It was written in thick black marker on a Denny's placemat that advertised key lime pie. Robert never wrote notes on note paper.

He called Swofford and left him a message: Got your pay, want an update, dinner's on me if we keep it cheap and local. Swofford called back a few minutes later and said Italian. Jason gave him directions and left Martin a note. Then he walked through the sparkling canals toward Robert's sunset-watching place on the beach.

The cheaply painted buildingfronts that faced the ocean were lustrous in the honeyed light. Robert was a silhouette on a silhouetted swing set against the glittering wavelets, halfway down the colored sand.

Jason slogged across the sand and took the swing next to Robert's. They didn't speak.

The ocean blazed amber. Shadows of seagulls crossed it and flicked over the sand and the luminous buildingfronts. Jason had always heard about the green flash that happened when the last bit of sun disappeared, but he'd never seen it, and didn't this time.

Afterward, he sat with Robert in the cool gray.

Robert pointed vaguely northwest over the sea. "The land bridge the native Americans crossed from Asia was that way."

"Native Americans?"

"Well, native Asians. Their children would have been native Americans."

"Oh." Jason looked that way. "Are you taking continental drift into account?"

"You really take the romance out of inaccuracy."

"Sorry."

Robert was silent for a while. Then he seemed to force himself to turn toward Jason. "I don't mean to pry it out of you since you're obviously upset, and I came here so you'd have someplace to come meet me and not talk, but . . . how did it go?"

Jason shook his head and didn't speak.

"Does that mean bad? Or does it mean you don't know?"

"She's back with her mother."

Robert let out a long breath. "That's good. How is she?"

"I don't know. I'll tell you all about it, but give me a little time."

"Okay."

"Where's Leon?"

"Martin got home while you were gone. They went to counseling."

"Didi?"

"Yeah. I gave him her number and she had a cancellation this afternoon, so they went right out."

A few clouds were still edged orange. Jason watched families pack their cars in the parking lot on the other side of the pier. "A cancellation, huh?"

"Yeah. I think my unresolved issues can wait a week."

"I may want that number."

"Three ten—"

"I don't need it right now."

"Oh. Right."

"I'm meeting Swofford at Alejo's at seven to pay him and find out how Donna is. I left Martin a note. Want to walk over?"

"Sure." Robert got up and shivered, and dusted his pants.

It was a fifteen-minute walk. Alejo's was in a corner mall with a Fatburger and a 7-Eleven. It was the size of a donut shop, with fluorescent lights and reverberant surfaces. Loud and small, good and inexpensive.

It was packed. Martin and Leon were against the back wall, sitting behind two small tables that had been moved together. They were the last two against the right wall. Robert and Jason worked their way past the line of people waiting for tables and dodged a couple of fast-moving waiters. Robert pardoned himself as he displaced a pair of women in their fifties at the next table in order to slide in next to Leon.

"Hey," he said to Leon. He took a hunk of bread from the basket on the table and dipped it in a bowl of olive oil and crushed garlic.

Leon followed suit. "Hey."

Jason turned one of the rear-facing chairs so its back was against the right wall and sat sort of sideways, half-facing the women at the next table.

"You expecting a saber-tooth tiger attack?" Martin asked him.

"Jase sit wrong way," Jason said. "Cave not safe."

"How is she?"

Jason didn't want to talk about Donna, but he tried to shake off his aversion. "I don't know. Back with her mom. There were no marks on her. She seemed to have been drugged."

Leon said, "She was drugged?"

Jason looked at him. Leon looked from Jason to Martin. Oil dripped down his hunk of bread, onto his wrist.

Martin said, "I guess he's been part of all this too, so go ahead and talk."

"She was hidden in the trunk of a car. They drugged her so she wouldn't wake up in there."

Leon said, "What kind of drugs did they use?"

"I don't know," Jason said. "The doctor wasn't there yet when I left."

Martin said, "I'm surprised you didn't stick around."

Jason shrugged a little without looking at him. "My presence distressed her."

After a bit, Martin shook his head. "Sorry, chief. Hey, Le, you're dripping."

Robert said, "At least she's safe now."

"Safe," Jason said. "Safe. She's not safe. They can come back and do it again anytime they want. They got a million dollars. Why not make it two? She's not safe. That's not safe. She's not safe."

Leon, wiping his arm with his napkin, looked around the table at each of them before saying, "I don't get it."

Martin said, "Well, sport, it's like this. Because Lissa just paid the kidnappers off instead of calling the police, they're still out there. So they could come back and kidnap Donna again if they thought they could get some more money out of it."

"But they got a million dollars!"

"That's Lissa's reasoning, too," Jason said. "But I don't think it works that way. People are greedy. If something works once, they want to do it again."

"So you think they'll come back?"

His voice was alarmed.

"Probably not," Jason said. "But they could."

"Would they hurt her?"

"I don't know. She didn't seem physically hurt when I was with her, but as I said, the doctor wasn't there yet."

"And she's still not safe," Robert said.

"What would it take to make her safe?" Martin said.

"Nothing. Catch the kidnappers."

"Could that be done?"

"They're gone with the cash. It wasn't marked in any way. I don't see how we could find them. And Lissa still won't go to the police."

"Could Swofford do it?"

"I don't know."

"What does he think of everything?"

"I think he thinks she made the wrong decision, selling her house and paying the ransom without calling the police, but she's the parent and it was hers to make."

"So that's it? She just stays unsafe forever?"

"I don't know."

Silence hovered over the table.

"So," Robert said. "How'd you like Didi?"

"Well," Martin said, "we didn't talk about much. The first session, they just get your history and stuff. I thought it went okay."

"What did you think, Leon?"

"I think it's BS."

"You know," Robert said, "sometimes even stuff that's BS can help you."

"Maybe I don't want to be helped. Maybe I just want to be left alone."

"I wish I could give you that, bro," Martin said. "If you can think of a way I can leave you alone and still make sure you get all fed and clothed and educated, hey, I'm all ears."

Leon said, "Well, I just think it's BS," softly.

Jason said to him, "Maybe you ought to give it a little more time."

"Yeah, right."

Swofford squeezed back through the tables and bodies with a bottle in a paper bag. He put the bag on the table and turned the seat next to Jason so it faced sideways a little before sitting.

"Cave extra safe now," Robert said.

"How is she?" Jason asked.

"The doctor said there's no apparent physical abuse. She doesn't seem to have been molested. She was drugged, and she seems to have been out since she was first taken. She has no memory between the kidnapping and her being found."

"I guess that's good," Robert said.

"Good for her," Jason said. "Bad for finding the kidnappers."

Swofford said, "Six-year-olds don't give great information anyway."

Leon said, "Are they going to kidnap her again?"

Swofford thought before answering. "Maybe I should tell you no," he said. "But you're old enough I won't BS you. The truth is, I don't know."

Leon nodded slightly. "Okay," he murmured. He blinked a few times.

"Dinner time," Swofford said, opening his menu. "Hunger just makes bad conversations worse."

They ordered.

While they waited, Robert said to Leon, "So, you think counseling is BS."

Leon shrugged.

"Do you really?" Swofford asked.

Leon shrugged again. "I guess."

"I was thinking of going myself. But you don't think I should?"

Leon shrugged.

"Look," Swofford said. "Is it your honest opinion that it's a waste of time, or isn't it?"

Leon seemed to actually think briefly before saying, "I don't know."

"Do you think maybe it would be good for some people, even if it's not good for you?"

Leon considered. "Yeah, maybe."

"All right," Swofford said. "Thanks."

The waiter brought wine glasses. Swofford pulled the bottle out of the bag and poured. He paused at Leon's glass. Leon looked at Martin.

Martin seemed to be struggling.

"I don't know," he said finally. "I don't want to set a precedent, but he is almost thirteen. . . ."

"I've drunk beer," Leon insisted.

"Like that helps."

Jason remembered Leon's Bud Man T-shirt.

It was Robert who cut the tension. "If you give him just a taste, I'll show you the Jewish blessing over the wine."

Martin looked mostly relieved. "Okay, just a taste."

Swofford poured. Leon was intent on his glass.

Robert whispered, "Don't sip until after I say it." Leon nodded.

Robert waited until everything was settled. Then he looked thoughtful, hesitated, and recited:

"Yesimcha Elohim ke-Sarah Rivkah Rachel ve-Leah. Yevarechecha Adonai veyishmerecha. Ya'er Adonai panav elecha vichuneka. Yisa Adonai panav elecha veyasem lecha shalom." He nodded once.

Jason said, "Do we say 'amen'?"

"Oh yeah. Amen."

They all sipped. Jason could never tell good wine from bad wine, so it tasted the same as usual. Leon made a face but very quickly hid it and put his glass down.

"Now," Swofford told Leon, "don't drive for at least an hour."

Their food came. They ate. On their way out, Swofford stuck his head over the counter and thanked the chef.

"THANKS," JASON SAID as he handed the envelope over. They were sitting in Swofford's car on Venice Boulevard, around the corner from Alejo's, at a meter.

Swofford opened the envelope and counted. He took some of the bills out and gave them back to Jason. "We'll go by day rate."

Jason folded it and put it in his shirt pocket. "Any word on Hoffer?"

"I haven't had a chance to check on it."

"What can we do to prevent another kidnapping?"

"Catch them, but the time for that has passed. I don't know how likely another attempt is, but it's possible. Unless you want to volunteer to spend the rest of Donna's childhood watching her, there's not much you can do. And you're not qualified anyway."

"Is there anything you could do?"

"Not without disclosing the previous kidnapping to law enforcement."

"Why's that?"

"Think about it. They have the resources. They have the computers, the contacts, the budgets, the people. With Ms. Court's restrictions, there's very little we can do."

"We should have gone to the police."

"You already knew that."

"It wasn't my decision." Jason shook his head. "Maybe I should have anyway."

"Maybe."

"Maybe. At least she's back."

Swofford nodded. "At least she's back."

Jason opened his door. "Thanks again."

"Call me if you think of anything."

"Yeah."

ason walked home and didn't go in. He got into his truck and drove around for a while before getting onto the Pacific Coast Highway and going north. He turned around past Santa Theresa and headed back to Venice.

He stopped by the canals and sat with the engine going and his foot on the brake for ten minutes before parking and going up the walk to his front door.

It was open a little, and he could hear low conversation inside, and the soft grind of Robert's rain lamp. Familiarity flowed over him, and he was grateful for his living room and the people he could hear in it.

Martin and Robert looked up from the couch as he pushed the door open. Leon was reading a comic book on the carpet.

"I made coffee," Martin said, looking at Jason. He got off the couch and went into the kitchenette. Jason tossed his jacket through the door of his studio and sat on the chair.

"I've had probably a really bad idea," he said as Martin brought in a mug of coffee and sat down. The mug said *Café du Monde* on it. Martin had bought it over the Internet. None of them had ever been there. "Thanks." He sipped and then said, "Swofford said what we were missing by not contacting law enforcement is resources." He toyed with his mug. "Translate 'resources' for me."

"Uh, stuff," Martin said. "Manpower, equipment, you know, contacts . . ."

Robert said, "Money."

Jason nodded. "Money. Money buys stuff. Money is resources. With enough money, you have the manpower, the equipment, the contacts, all that."

"Sure, okay," Martin said. "With money."

"Think someone might find the resources if we offered a reward?"

Robert said, "That would have to be one awfully big reward."

"I was thinking a million dollars."

"Great," Martin said. "Great plan." He tapped his head. "Oh yeah: If we had a million dollars."

"We do have a million dollars." Jason swirled his coffee and looked down into it. "We're just keeping it with the kidnappers right now."

"How would that work?"

"Offer the million to whoever can find it."

"It's clever," Robert admitted, "-ish," he amended. "Cleverish. But it has a fatal flaw: Who but law enforcement or private investigators has the immediate resources to track down kidnappers without being paid up front?"

Jason dragged his gaze up. "That's not a flaw," he said slowly. "That's the whole idea."

he broad, smooth avenue was as he remembered, its trees
vividly correct and green against the blue sky.

The gate, too, with its calcified metal lions, was the same,
breaking the tall, concealing hedge. Jason got out and pressed the
buzzer. In a moment, the heavy gate halves opened.

He drove slowly up the cobblestone drive and parked in front
of a stolid mansion that said "old money" as clearly as Kevin
Washburn's shouted "nouveau riche."

The heliport on the small rise to the east was empty. An
attached carport sheltered a black Bentley and a tan Nissan that
was a few years old. His memory added a Lamborghini, a Vector,
and a restored Karmann Ghia.

A cobblestone path led through an unkempt decay of leath-
ery plants. The last time Jason had walked up the path, two men
had flanked the door. This time, he used the knocker.

A serious-looking girl in her twenties let him into the large
front room. Two red doorways still faced each other across it.
The sculpture of the giant cancerous turkey giblet, or whatever
it was, was still there. The discreetly lighted collection of paint-

ings on the white walls seemed complete, but the Lucite cases that had held small sculptures were empty.

"Uncle is in here," she said. She led him through a dark, paneled hallway, past an open archway on the right that over-looked a broad stairway and a big, empty room. There'd been a grand piano in there. A Steinway C.

At the end of the hallway, she gestured Jason through an open door. He went in.

A slender man sat behind a mahogany desk in the study, his hands in his lap, leaning over a handwritten ledger in the low light of a desk lamp. His combed hair fell in thin strands over his scalp. Bookshelves covered the walls from floor to ceiling, except where interrupted by a cold fireplace. A black leather chair faced the desk. Two rows of prescription bottles stood in formation on a silver tray at the man's elbow.

The girl came in behind him. "Please sit," she said. He put his backpack down next to the leather chair and sat. The girl slipped around and whispered to the man.

"Yes," he said. He continued to study his ledger.

She rested her hands near his head, on what Jason realized were the handles of a wheelchair.

Finally, Pascal closed the ledger and looked up, his pitted skin made worse by the bleak shadows cast by the single light source. In the dimness, his eyes seemed black and hooded. The amiable snake, Jason remembered. The narrow face was skeletal.

The gaze didn't waver. Last time, Jason had made some smart remark or other. This time, he just sat in the leather chair and waited.

When Pascal finally spoke, it was without having moved.

"It is only due to your costing me so little that I did you no harm."

In their last deal, Jason had tricked him. "I may be able to even things a little. Maybe a lot."

"What do you bring me?"

"A child has been kidnapped."

In Pascal's long pause was the implication that Jason's appraisal of the value of this news was inflated.

"A shame."

"She was recovered yesterday. The kidnappers got away with a million dollars. If you find the kidnappers, you find the money. You'd have to find them soon, before their trail is cold and the money is laundered."

The snake eyes showed no interest. "You wish a percentage."

"No."

"What benefit do you derive?"

"I want the kidnappers found."

"You derive vengeance."

"Not quite."

Pascal became less intent. He glanced at the ledger on his desk. A white hand flicked weakly from his lap. "You play games of implication and ambiguity."

"I promised I would make sure the child was safe. Until the kidnappers are found, I have not kept my promise."

"To whom was this foolish promise made?"

Jason shook his head.

"Do you have information to lead me to these men?"

"I have scant information. I don't know whether it can lead you to them."

"I will examine the scant information."

Pascal indicated the edge of his desk with one white finger. He leaned forward, returning to his ledger. The girl stepped out from behind his wheelchair and crossed to the door. Jason stood and took up his backpack, unzipped it, and placed a sealed envelope and a pink can of Almond Roca where directed.

Pascal looked up. "What is this?"

"Only a private joke."

"You were not serious when last we met. You still are not."

"The universe has few constants. Be comforted when you encounter one."

Pascal didn't laugh. The girl showed Jason out.

aybe he shouldn't have dealt Pascal in.

He went home and stared at his studio. He could start his computer and turn on his instruments.

Then there'd be something wrong. An incorrectly connected cable, or a 60-cycle hum in the main outputs, or the computer wouldn't see the keyboards. Always something. Always some obstacle to *sitting down and doing music*.

Some people managed anyway, but . . .

Forget it, he thought. Not today.

Maybe he shouldn't have dealt Pascal in.

He looked through his CD rack. The ones he liked, he didn't want to hear because he knew every note. The ones he didn't like, he didn't like, and he only kept them around in case his tastes changed.

In the living room, he found the bag he'd taken to New York and got the two John Ray Hoffer CDs. In his bedroom studio, he repatched a couple of cables so he could hear them. No sound came out. Once he found the problem and repatched the cables, he sat on his futon and looked at the booklet while he listened to *Mother's Fresh Picked*, idly skimming.

A couple of cuts in, the competent music was doing very little for his impatience. He was about to take out the CD and put in a Chess Blues compilation when his gaze snagged on the credit list.

Promotion: Kevin Washburn

"Wa ha," he heard himself say.

Last time he'd read the list, he hadn't yet known the name. He opened the *Hurricane Warning* jewel case and looked at the other booklet.

Promotion: Kevin Washburn

Well.

HE DIDN'T KNOW what to do, but driving around and thinking had never gotten him in trouble. He took the little pickup through downtown, out the 110. When it ended in Pasadena, he let himself end up on Marengo.

The Manor was boarded up and dead. He parked in his old space behind it, head-in to a block wall.

The long grass behind the peeling back door waved in the late afternoon breeze. He walked around the side of the big old house and tried to look through the dirty screen into his bedroom window. If he stood on tiptoe, he could see a sliver of flat gray carpet between the boards.

He sat on the concrete back steps, picked some of the long grass, and scattered it. A hundred feet in front of him, the gate to the parking structure under the condos winched open to let a car out, a familiar sound that he hadn't heard since moving. The green garden hose he'd found in the Dumpster and duct-taped to near-integrity was still attached to the spigot near where he sat, dripping from the squeeze nozzle. Apparently, the water service hadn't been shut off yet.

He looked at the familiar junk under the flimsy staircase to what had once been Paul Reno's room. The remains of a gas barbecue were scattered on an old blue tarp. Waldo, the gray and white cat who'd belonged to someone in the condos, didn't appear when Jason called.

He picked some more grass and ripped it up idly, tossing it onto the breeze. *Promotion: Kevin Washburn.* A loan shark promoting two Hoffer albums. Dwight calling the same loan shark before heading down the hill on his motorcycle. Dwight needed money for Donna's ransom and called Washburn? Hoffer needed money for his two albums and called Washburn? Had Dwight met Washburn through Hoffer? Had Hoffer met him through Dwight?

He stood and walked to the front of the house and went up Marengo without a destination. The breeze was nice, and he wasn't getting anywhere thinking about Dwight and Hoffer and Washburn. He ended up at a supermarket on Lake, where he bought a can of cat food.

Back at the Manor, he opened the can and put it on the walk up to the back step, then called Waldo again. He waited for a while. No cat appeared.

He went back to his truck. Dwight, Hoffer, Washburn. Washburn, Dwight, Hoffer. Musician, musician, promoter.

It all jangled around and felt obvious, but didn't connect with itself. He backed out of the parking space and angled around to back toward the driveway.

Thirty feet in front of him, a scrawny, dirty cat was crawling surreptitiously from under the house. It moved through the long grass toward the open can, sniffed it, and began to wolf.

Jason left the engine running so as not to spook the cat with sudden silence. It eyed him over the can as he opened the door and got out, but it kept wolfing. Jason went up the walk as naturally as he could until it growled at him through chunks of cat food. At first, he couldn't tell what cat it was.

Waldo was in bad shape. His fur hung in dirty dreadlocks, and the underside of his jaw was grossly swollen on one side. He let Jason approach to about ten feet before shying toward the crawlspace under the house. When Jason withdrew a little and sat on the walk, Waldo crept back toward the cat food and resumed eating, watching him.

When the moment seemed right, Jason put his hand out and got Waldo's attention with a little kissing noise. Waldo watched him but didn't come any nearer.

They looked at each other for a few minutes as Waldo ate all the food.

Jason reached to his left and plucked a dandelion stalk and brushed it back and forth over the long grass. Waldo just watched it for a while, but Jason could see his pupils dilate, and when he finally pounced, Jason snapped him up by the scruff and rushed him toward the truck.

He almost made it.

Halfway there, Waldo suddenly caught on and turned into a furry cloud of furious sharp things.

Jason flung the screaming banshee into the cab, slammed the door, and sucked the bleeding nest of slashes in his forearm. Waldo landed clawfirst and leapt from dash to seatback, yowling.

It had been Jason's plan to lock the cat in the back and then walk to the store for a cat carrier. But Waldo was bouncing around inside the cab with its keys in the ignition and the engine running.

This was not as planned. An analysis of the situation presented itself:

Good

The cat is in the truck.

There is no danger of further injury.

I could go buy a cat carrier.

I could go anyway, and gamble on the integrity of my fellow humans.

At least the fiend can't drive.

Thankfully, no one saw me be an idiot.

Bottom line: The cat has no thumbs and a brain the size of a walnut.

Bad

I am not in the truck.

There is no chance of going home soon.

If I leave the truck with the engine running, it won't be here when I get back.

Even if that worked, the fiend will never submit to being put in a carrier without shredding what's left of my arms.

No down side to this one, far as I can see.

Except the cat, who will remember and use it against me.

Sounds like a guitarist, only less fuzzy.

Jason pressed his stinging slashes. Waldo screamed at him from the cab, an ugly feline with a lousy attitude.

Waldo was pissed.

"This," Jason told him, up close to the window, "is called détente, you scrofulous furball."

Waldo shrieked at him through the glass, ears back, nose to the window. Waldo didn't care about détente. Waldo cared about severing Jason's spinal cord at the neck and dragging his flopping body under the house.

Maybe Jason could slip into the cab if he were quick and sneaky— He chose his moment and cracked open the door. Waldo rammed his head into the crack.

Jason stood with the door barely ajar and a cat snout trying to squeeze out of it.

"Cat— " he began, and didn't finish. Waldo didn't care what he had to say anyway, since Jason was going to die soon.

A sharp flick on the snout, and Waldo pulled back long enough for Jason to close the door. He looked around at the abandoned back yard, the junk under the staircase.

His gaze lit on the garden hose.

He looked back at Waldo.

"All right," he said. "Fine."

hat the heck happened to you?" Martin said as he came in. Robert looked up from a book on the floor.

Jason's clothes and underwear were wet and uncomfortable and his arms were scratched and bleeding. A low moan radiated from the rolled-up tarp he was carrying and built to a muffled shriek.

Martin stared. "—the *hell* is that?"

Leon appeared in the doorway to Robert's room, eyes wide.

"Wolverine," Jason said. "Better close the doors."

Leon jumped into the front room and closed off both bedrooms as Martin shut the front door. Jason put the bundled tarp on the carpet, unfolded it a little, and stepped back. Waldo shot out and halted instantly as he saw the unfamiliar house. His tail flicked angrily and he glared murder at Jason, Leon, Martin, Robert, the room in abstract, humanity in particular, and God, who had failed to consult the cat.

"Whoah!" Robert said. "It's Waldo!"

Martin, too close for Waldo's taste, dodged back from a claw swipe. "And he's pissed."

"Oh, no," Leon said. "Poor little kitty!"

"Give him a little room, bro. Let him get used to the place."

"I found him like this at the Manor," Jason said, looking at his scratches. Around the slashed skin, they were pink and puffy. "We must have been the only people taking any care of him before we left."

Waldo snaked into the kitchen and froze there in the smelling pose.

"I thought he belonged to somebody in the condos," Martin said.

Robert nodded. "He did. He used to have a collar. They must have moved and abandoned him."

Crouched carefully in the kitchenette doorway, Leon looked up at Martin. "They abandoned him?"

"Looks that way, bro. Wow, what's that lump under his jaw?"

Jason said, "Why don't you take a closer look?"

"Oh, yeah, and maybe after that, I'll run a cheese grater over my lips and squeeze my balls in a garlic press."

Robert put his hand out. "Jason, give me your keys. I'll go to the pet store on Pacific before it closes and get cat food and a litterbox while you clean your wounds." He paused, shuddering. "A *garlic* press?"

Leon said, "I want to go."

"Can he go?"

"Can I go? Please? Please?"

Martin said, "Okay, you can go."

"Can we get him a bed?"

Robert took Jason's keys. "If they have one we can afford."

WALDO HOLED UP behind the refrigerator. Jason was all for him staying there forever, but Martin angled the fridge out from the wall and tried to coo him out.

"Hey!" Martin exclaimed, jerking back suddenly at the muffled bang of a small, furry body hurling itself against metal. "Man, poor Waldo."

"Yeah, poor Waldo," Jason said. He had doused his arms in hydrogen peroxide and glopped neosporin ointment on them, and they were bandaged to the elbows and throbbing.

"Poor little guy. That was his head."

"Good."

Robert and Leon came back with cat stuff and set to arranging it. Robert filled the litterbox and stuck it under the hinged table next to the new cat carrier, and Leon carefully surveyed the entire house for a good place for the darling wee cat basket with the plaid cushion and blue ribbon. It ended up in the living room where the little savage would be sure to appreciate it.

Robert was stocking the kitchen cabinet with cans of cat food.

"How much?" Jason asked him.

"You don't want to know."

Jason watched him empty the shopping bags. No two cans were the same color. "You got one of each flavor, didn't you, so he wouldn't get bored."

"Just because you're happy eating the same thing every day, that doesn't mean a more advanced life form would necessarily feel the same."

Jason nodded. "Um . . . you guys got a minute?"

"Sure."

"Martin?"

Martin was angled around the refrigerator again, cooing. He extracted himself. "Yeah?"

"I was looking at the Hoffer CDs Zeb gave me, and I found Kevin Washburn's name, listed as 'promotion.' "

"Okay," Martin said slowly, "so . . . what does that mean?"

"I really don't know."

Robert's gaze disconnected and he stared toward the ceiling. "Huh," he said absently.

"Should we call Swofford?" Martin said.

"Okay," Robert said to himself, not in response to Martin. They ignored him.

Jason said to Martin, "I intend to call Swofford. I just wanted to see what you guys thought about it."

"Okay," Robert said again. They ignored him again.

"I dunno, man. Seems to me like an easy enough thing to explain. Washburn's a loan shark, right? So he backed Hoffer's CDs at some insane interest rate and got a 'promotion' credit for it. When Dwight gets into trouble and needs ransom money, Washburn's the guy he calls."

"Yes, that would seem to make sense."

Robert returned to Earth and said, "What about this. What if Hoffer got the money to produce his CDs from Washburn, so when Dwight needed money to pay Donna's ransom, he called Washburn?"

"Damn," Martin said after a pause. "That's brilliant."

"Oh. I guess you just said that."

Jason said, "My instinct is that it's true. But my other instinct is that we're missing something."

Robert said, "Look at it the other way around. Our theory explains the associations between Hoffer, Washburn, and Dwight, right?"

"Right."

"So what *doesn't* it explain?"

"Everything else. I don't see how this is a useful approach."

"No, take it seriously. What is not explained by this theory?"

"Well . . ." Jason didn't get it. He shook his head. "Things not explained by the theory."

"Like what?"

"Uh . . ." He groped. "Like why there's gravity."

"I can tell you that," Martin said. "Big objects have gravity."

"All objects have gravity," Robert said. "If you're not talking relativistically, anyway. And anyway, that's not *why* there's gravity; it's just *where* there's gravity."

"What do you mean?"

"Well—"

"Forget gravity," Jason said. "I'm sorry I mentioned gravity."

"What I was trying to get at," Robert said, "is that if you have the feeling we're missing something, but all our questions are answered by the theory, we need to look for questions that are not answered by the theory."

"Okay. You start."

"The earliest record we have of Washburn showing up is in Hoffer's old CDs. Where would Hoffer have met him?"

"Anywhere at all. Gosh, that was useful."

"Your turn."

"Uh . . ." Jason thought. "Who met Washburn first, Dwight or Hoffer?"

"I don't see any way of finding that out. My turn. Does Lissa know Washburn?"

"I doubt we can get that answered."

Martin said, "Not that I mind being skipped or anything—"

"Oh, sorry I skipped you," Robert said. "I'd skip Jason, too, if I didn't think it would unambiguously underscore my egocentrism."

"It's okay. Here's my question. How come rock tours get canceled?"

Nobody had an answer. They stood in the kitchenette and looked at each other and felt dumb for not wondering that sooner.

"Maybe they ran out of money," Leon said behind Jason.

Jason moved around to see Leon and they all stared at him.

"It was just a guess," Leon said uncomfortably.

"*Cherchez la lucre*," Jason said. "Or something like that."

HE GOT SWOFFORD'S machine and left a message about Kevin Washburn's name showing up on John Hoffer's CDs. Don't know if this means anything. Call back whenever.

Waldo was still behind the refrigerator. Jason hoped he'd be happy there. Leon was sitting on the floor, talking to the back of the refrigerator, a comic book unread next to him.

Swofford called back that evening.

"I don't get much from the Washburn thing," he said. "Also, no prints on the Bronco or the Falcon, and both VIN numbers came up stolen. I got something else for you, and it's not good."

"Okay."

"The guitarist, Hoffer. He's dead."

Jason rubbed his forehead.

"It gets worse," Swofford said. "The ballistics from the slugs they took out of him match a weapon registered to Dwight Cooper."

"No. Uh-uh. Dwight wouldn't shoot Johnny Ray."

"Hoffer controlled Cooper's money."

"No way—"

"Hoffer bailed him out, looked after him, gave him a place to crash when he needed it. He took care of his money. He's the closest thing Cooper had to family, and family's always the first place you look when there's a murder."

Who takes care of Dwight? Jason had asked Cora.

Mostly Johnny Ray.

"All right." He was suddenly tired. "I just thought he would pull through."

"Everything's a crap shoot. Get some rest."

"Yeah. Thanks."

Swofford hung up.

he telephone woke him. He banged his head on one of his speaker stands when he got up, stubbed his toe on his chair, on the way across the room, and felt all over his studio work surface before finding the phone on the chair.

"Hello."

"Our accounts are balanced."

Pascal.

"You found them."

A weak cough. "You have kept your foolish promise."

Foolish promise . . . what foolish promise?

The promise to ensure Donna's safety.

A little chill shivered through him. Jason hit the start button on his computer, so the screen would cast some light in the room. "What do you mean—"

Silence on the line. Of course Pascal wouldn't say outright on the phone that he'd killed them.

"Um, who were they?"

"That information will be withheld."

"Uh—"

"You tricked me in our previous dealing. I take my compensation now."

"Uh—"

"No conversation," Pascal said. "Goodbye."

The click of the hang-up didn't come. Pascal was waiting, and there was only one thing to say.

"Goodbye," Jason said.

Pascal hung up.

HE SAT ON the edge of his futon in the thin light for about an hour before getting up and going into the living room. A lyrical breeze floated in through the miniblinds in the kitchenette window and connected, somewhere in his memory, with a Lutoslawski violin line.

Robert was sprawled on his stomach on the blue couch, his right arm and leg draped over the edge onto the carpet, his face smushed into the cushion, his pillow bunched atop his lower back.

His eyes opened. "Who was that?"

"I'm going to wake Martin. I'll tell you both about it." Jason went to the door to Robert's room, where he could barely see Martin and Leon lying next to each other.

"Martin," he whispered.

"That doesn't work," Robert said behind him.

Leon shifted in the bed. "What do you want?"

"I have news," Jason said. "Wake your brother up."

Leon said, "Martin, wake up!" very loudly.

"Ung," Martin said, moving.

Jason sighed. "Thanks, Le."

"You told me to."

Martin rolled onto his back. "Wha, wha's goin' on?"

"Wake up," Jason said. "I need to talk to you."

THEY WERE IN the living room. Jason could see into the kitchenette, where the refrigerator was still angled out. A sudden change in breeze direction rattled the miniblinds above the sink, pulling them toward the wall. Leon was in Robert's room with the door closed.

Martin said, "What is it?"

"Pascal found the kidnappers."

"That's great."

"I think he, um . . ."

He stopped. Martin and Robert both got guarded looks on their faces.

"He what," Martin said, slowly.

"Can Leon hear us?"

"He's in there with the door closed."

"Well . . . it's what you think."

They both looked at him and didn't say anything for half a minute. Then Robert said, "This is really very, very weird. I don't think I'm upset."

"Yeah. I know," Jason said. "Me neither. It's a little chilling."

Martin blew air out his pursed lips. "I guess it's what—"

The door to Robert's room opened. Leon stood in the doorway, wide-eyed. "He killed them!?"

Martin stood. "Le, I told you—"

"They're dead?"

Martin seemed to be trying to think of what to say. "Nobody said that," he said.

Leon blinked. His eyes darted, his gaze not settling on anything.

"Donna's okay," Jason said.

"She's safe," Robert said. "You don't have to worry about her anymore."

"No!" Leon whined.

Martin crossed to him. "It's okay, li'l bro."

"No!"

Martin put his arms around Leon. "It's all right, Le. She's—"

Leon struggled out of Martin's embrace. "No, it's not all right!" he said. "You don't understand."

Martin looked helplessly at his little brother.

Robert said, "Oh, no, the kitchen window! I opened it before I went to bed!"

"Where's Waldo?" Leon cried.

Martin reached for Leon again. "I'm more concerned about you."

"No!" Leon yelled. He darted past Martin, wrenched the door open, and leaped down the steps and away. Martin spun to follow, but stopped at the open door.

"Do . . . we go after him?" Robert asked, poised. The front gate clanked.

Martin stood at the front door and looked out, chewing the inside of his cheek, looking worried.

"No," he said uncertainly. "He won't go far. He'll look for Waldo."

"Shouldn't he know you care?"

Martin's face worked as he struggled.

Jason said, "Give him five minutes to calm down a little, then bring out a can opener and some cat food and my flashlight and help him look."

"Good idea," Martin said gratefully.

"Not bad," Robert agreed.

Jason waved it off. "Good ideas are easy when you speak third."

"I'm sorry I said that about the window being open."

Martin remained at the door. He shook his head. "This is gonna be a long five minutes."

THE PHONE RANG just after Martin went out, carrying the can opener and the cat food, Jason's studio penlight sticking out of his back pocket. It was two in the morning. Not an unusual time for Jason to get a phone call, but usually the only two people who knew he'd be up that late were Robert and Martin.

"Cooper's conscious," Swofford's voice said. "I told him Donna's okay, but he won't cooperate with the cops until he hears it from you."

ubes and adhesive fabrics stuck to Dwight where he wasn't bandaged. His head and body were patchy with shaved areas, and the hand that rested atop the thin blue blanket was purple and missing nails. His beard was gone, his face battered and stitched, its skin pale, bruised, and inelastic in the inhuman fluorescent light. The left side of his head was encased in bandages. Only his right eye showed, and the lower right side of his face.

The eye was the weird thing.

It was lucid.

It locked on Jason from the white-sheeted hospital bed and tracked him intently across the room.

"Mr. Cooper here," the cop standing next to the window said, "refused to make a statement until he'd spoken with you."

Jason stopped at the bed.

A man in a brown suit next to the cop said, "As Mr. Cooper's—"

Jason tuned him out. Dwight's half-gaze was intense and searching.

Jason nodded.

Dwight relaxed. The brown eye blinked and welled with tears. "Jason the hero." The whisper was rough and cracked.

"—make any statement which might—"

Jason left the room.

"STAY IN TOWN," Swofford told him in the hospital corridor. "I told Mendelssohn you would."

"A cop named Mendelssohn."

"Cops have names too."

"Anything new on that ballistics thing?"

Swofford shook his head.

"I just can't see it," Jason said. "I just can't."

is certainties dissolved as he drove the 10 toward the ocean in the dark.

Something had his stomach trembling and his breath short, and he started feeling claustrophobic in the cab of his own pickup. He turned off the murmuring radio in the middle of an NPR news segment and said "Uncle" aloud, and exited the freeway. The first open place was a donut shop, yellow on a somber street of closed businesses and desolate parking lots.

Dwight's gun.

He sat at the back, the only customer, and had a bear claw the size of Portugal and a cup of stinky coffee. The air in the shop was warm and sugary.

He didn't know anything.

Hubris, Robert had said. If we get involved in this, it's hubris. Robert was right. Robert was usually right, and . . . he was right. What was Jason doing, making the kinds of decisions he'd been making? Taking Cora's offer—what was that? Who was he to do that? Picking up Leon in San Diego and fighting Frank to do it— what the hell? Watching someone else's daughter. Chasing Lissa

Court away when she'd visited Donna at the field trip—his leg muscles tensed and his stomach clenched in shame as he thought of it.

Everything very justifiable. Everything logically defensible. Nothing to point at and say, "That decision was not supported by the available data."

But why was *he* the one making the perfectly justifiable bad decisions?

Why did he get involved in this?

Why had his getting involved taken so many bad turns?

Every single goddamned move, something that had seemed like the right thing to do, had turned out badly. Helping Martin with Ed had led to Hoffer and Dwight. Watching Donna for Bellweather had turned into chasing her mother away from her and attacking a man in front of a bunch of kids. Picking up Leon in Long Beach had become a fight with Frank, and then Leon's mom had abandoned him to Martin. Watching out for Donna for Cora had turned into a physical attack by Lissa Court.

He found it potentially amusing for later that he liked eating bear claws even when he was having an existential crisis.

(Sarah Fletcher behind the alley doorway: *Maybe not ever.*)

He noticed his breathing becoming tight. Sugar overdose. Either that or he was getting emotional, which would be irritating because he didn't feel emotional.

And once Donna was kidnapped, agreeing not to call the police had led to Dwight bashing himself up—probably going to get ransom money—and Hoffer was dead, and Lissa Court's house was gone, and the kidnappers had gotten away with it, which had sent Jason to Pascal.

Who'd killed the kidnappers.

Every step thought out and reasonable. Every step backfiring and hurting someone. Why?

Why was Dwight an addict?

Why was Hoffer dead?

Why did his solution to Donna's safety result in a very bad man gaining a million dollars?

Why did Jason's sincere efforts turn into awful things?

Tears of frustration refracted his vision, little rainbows jittering around every light source and reflection. He obstinately refused to blink, refusing to release the tears and let them flow.

The side of his left fist banged into the wall. He'd intended to do it softly, just a thinking gesture, but the donut guy looked up, startled, from behind the case and moved closer to a dirty phone mounted on the wall near the cash register. Jason gave him a little wave of apology. The guy lingered near the phone.

Why were things as they were?

Why?

Why?

It wasn't night anymore. The light that pressed against the cold donut shop window was dirty gray.

His forearms throbbed in their bandages. The last line of the story Robert had read to him in the New York bookstore floated through his thoughts: *You should assume it was the explanation.*

Which had nothing to do with—

As he thought that, he saw how wrong the thought was, and the world spun a small fraction of a degree and left him sitting stock-still in a brand-new donut shop, staring at an alien yellow table and the cold crumbs of a bear claw.

"Oh," he said. His eyes were wide open.

The unfinished story wasn't unfinished.

Sometimes, you just don't get to know why.

He ran the moral through his thoughts a few times before crumpling his napkin in his cup and leaving the donut shop, relief throbbing through his body where the ache had been eviscerated.

eroic Fiddling," he said to Robert as he entered the groovy beach pad.

"Flatulent Crocheting," Robert greeted him back from the blue couch. He was lying under his blanket and studying his paperback of conversational Hebrew under a book light that was no longer necessary in the daytime. The book's ripped title page showed where the cover was torn off.

"No, that was the name of the painting."

"The painting?" Robert repeated. His eyebrows shot up. "Oh! The painting in Martin's book. Oh . . . Oh! It was supposed to look like strokes of a bow!"

"Right. Are they still looking for the beast?"

"Yes." Robert turned off his book light. "You figured out the story."

"Yeah."

"Do you want to tell me?"

"Sometimes, you just don't get to know why."

Robert looked crookedly at him. "Is that your take on the story, or your response to my question?"

Jason ran a hand over his face. Scratchy; he should shave. "I spend all my time trying to figure things out. Why's Dwight an addict, what's the proper response to this, the proper response to that, what's best for this person, for that person . . . But you know what? Stuff people do—hell, even stuff you yourself do—sometimes you just don't get to know why."

"This can't be a new thought for you."

"It is, actually. Well, the new part is that not only do I not *get* to know, but I don't *need* to know. Why do I need to know why Dwight's the way he is? Answer: I don't. How's it make any difference to anything? Trying to understand just gets you sucked into it."

"How so?"

"Okay, an example. How'd we get involved in any of this?"

"Celia Weather hired us to watch Donna."

"Why?"

"Because she wouldn't let anyone watch her but The Giant."

"Wrong. That's just what they want us to think!" Jason heard what he'd just said and took the opportunity to pose momentarily as an army major from the movies, pointing at Robert and squinting his eyes. Becoming himself again, he said, "No, the real reason we had to be hired is because her daddy went off on a rock tour instead of being around to be her daddy. Right there, we accepted that he had to be away. We accepted the reality that was presented to us. But was it really reality?"

"Well—"

"Hell no, it wasn't reality. He didn't need to be off on a rock tour. He could have been staying home and living off his royalties. And if for some reason the royalties weren't happening, he could get a job. Take care of his family. Work for a haberdasher."

"I think I'm maybe mostly following you."

"Okay . . . uh . . . Trying to go with the situation as presented is what did us in. We let other people tell us how the world is."

Robert shook his head adamantly against the couch. "No, I don't think that stands up. How could we know differently? We had no available information to suggest the contrary."

"Sure we did," Jason said. "Sure we did. When there's dissonance between intellect and instinct, always go with instinct. I *know* that. But I forgot it. Sometimes logic won't show you a way out even when you're wrong. I didn't see a logical error anywhere, so I kept going. But no matter how far outside the box you try to think, you're always inside a bigger box. That's the box someone like Dwight counts on you being in. So things get weird, and even though it doesn't work, you keep trying to think your way out. "But"—he spread his hands—"you can't think your way out of a paradox. You can't untie a Gordian knot. Once you accept a fatal puzzle on its terms, you're dead. The only way out of a closed system is to stop thinking and start paying attention to your own instincts. That's why you *have* instincts. If intellect were enough, we'd just have that."

"I'm with you," Robert said slowly. "Maybe. Sort of. What do your instincts tell you to do now?"

Jason smiled. The lingering relief was still lovely. "For one thing, they say forget Dwight, forget Hoffer, forget Lissa and Donna. Lissa and Donna have needs—big ones—but we're not the ones who can fill those needs. Trying to help them will hurt us and, for that matter, maybe even them. Forget Pascal, forget kidnappers. Forget why Kevin Washburn's name shows up on both CDs. It doesn't matter. Let it go. Forget it."

"You think you can do that?"

"I'm doing it. But you know mostly what my instinct says? Why I can let the other stuff go so easily?"

Robert shook his head.

"It says Martin. And Leon."

Robert stared at him gravely. Then he nodded.

"Yeah." He shook his head. "Wow, yeah. We got totally sidetracked."

Jason nodded.

Robert looked abashed. "Maybe we haven't been very good friends."

"I intend to be one from here out. So. And, uh, sorry I said 'think outside the box.' "

"It was painful, but—" Robert shrugged under his blanket —"at least it wasn't a sports metaphor."

ROBERT HAD JUST risen from the couch when Martin opened the door, holding the new cat carrier. Leon edged in ahead of him, carrying Waldo.

Everyone was silent and still until Martin had come in and closed the door. Leon stroked the top of Waldo's head gently.

"Well, I'm impressed," Jason said. Waldo looked at him and hissed, beginning to struggle. Leon put him down, and Waldo went straight to the kitchen and slithered in behind the refrigerator. "Where was he?"

"Under the front house," Leon said.

"The food lured him out?"

Martin put the carrier down. "Leon sat on the dirt and talked to him until he just came out and let him pick him up."

Jason looked at Leon. "Very good."

Leon shrugged.

Jason pointed toward the kitchen. "Did you happen to get a look at that bulbous thing under his jaw?"

Leon's carefully hardened expression broke into worry. "Do you think he might die?"

"I doubt it. It's probably just an infected scratch. You can take a look at it in a little bit. But first . . . you got a minute?"

Leon glanced at Martin. "Yeah."

Jason angled his head at the door and got up, wondering whether Leon would follow him. He went down the front steps and leaned against the low chain-link fence.

Leon came out, still looking worried. "What."

"I want to apologize to you."

"For what?"

"For what happened with Frank."

"Okay."

"Maybe I could have figured out something that didn't put you in the position of standing there, watching things get out of hand. If the gun hadn't been there, I probably would have come up with something."

"It's okay."

"Well." Jason nodded once. "That's for you to decide. All I wanted to say was I'm sorry."

"Okay."

Jason put his hand out. Leon shook it and hurried back into the house.

Magic touch with kids, there. Another few meaningful conversations like that and Leon would be asking Jason for girl advice and begging to try on his varsity sweater.

The chain-link rattled as he pushed away from it, grimacing, and went in.

Leon wasn't in the kitchenette, so he was probably in the bedroom. Martin was sitting on the arm of the couch, listening to Robert.

Robert said, "Why am I telling you this? Jason, you tell him. What you told me about your instinct."

"I figured out—" Jason stopped. "I mean, I *realized* that trying to understand things intellectually sometimes isn't a good thing."

"You didn't know that?" Martin said, surprised. "Wow. Naw, man, especially when there's a junkie in the mix. Junkies are smart. They tie the whole world up in a big knot and make you think it's straight. Gut feeling's the only weapon you got against that."

"Well," Jason said. He sighed. "I guess I would've learned that sooner had I been paying more attention to my own friends instead of chasing off after Dwight Cooper's problems."

Martin's head jerked a little, as though a usually smooth motor inside his neck had caught momentarily.

"Whoah." He stared at Jason. "Time out, time out, time out."

Taken aback, Jason paused.

"Gimme a minute."

They stood silently in the living room. After a minute, Martin got up and went out the front door. They heard the gate creak and bang.

"What did I say?" Jason asked.

Mystified, Robert spread his hands.

THE NICE THING about an adult leaving unexpectedly was that there was no conflict about whether to go after him. When he was ready to come back, he would.

Leon was on the floor by the refrigerator. He got up and came to the kitchen door. "Where's Martin?"

Jason said, "He's out for a walk."

"I think Waldo needs to go to the vet."

"The thing under his jaw?"

"It's really swollen. I think it hurts him. I touched it and he made this sound, like . . ." Leon imitated a yowl through clamped teeth. "He wanted to scratch me."

"Do you think you can get him out from behind the fridge and into his carrier?"

"Yes."

"If you can, we'll take him to the vet."

LEON HAD WALDO in the carrier in fifteen minutes. Jason was standing on the front steps, locking the door amid unceasing feline commentary while Robert and Leon waited, when Martin came around from the front.

"You going to the vet?" he asked.

"Yeah," Jason said. "Leon got him into the carrier. There's a twenty-four-hour pet hospital on Lincoln."

"I'll take him." Martin held out his hand. "Borrow your keys?"

Jason twisted the truck key off his ring and passed it over.

"Thanks, chief. Come on, li'l bro."

"They're not going to put him to sleep, are they?"

"No, li'l bro, I don't see why they would."

Leon didn't budge.

"Le, we won't let them put him to sleep."

"You promise?"

"I promise."

Leon's face betrayed deep feeling for an instant.

"You really promise?"

"Yeah, I really promise, so let's go take him to the vet and get him fixed up."

After a hesitation, Leon trudged forward, his hands together in front of him on the handle of the carrier. Martin followed him, his hand lightly on Leon's back as they walked, until the walkway narrowed and made them go single-file between the fence and the front house.

The gate banged.

"Martin decided something," Jason said.

Robert nodded. "Yeah."

"That is one worried and stressed-out kid."

Robert nodded again.

CORA SMITH CALLED and asked to come by. She knocked on the door five minutes later and came in with a flat white cardboard box.

"I knew you would be feeling badly," she said.

Jason took the box awkwardly and struggled with what to say.

Robert said, "You didn't have to do that."

"You boys did your best. That's all anyone can do."

Robert stepped back and looked at Jason. "Would you like to come in?"

"No, thank you, darling. I have to get back."

Jason said, "How is Donna?"

"She wasn't hurt," Cora said. She shook her head in doubtful amazement. "She remembers leaving for school, and then waking up with her mother. It looks as though she will be fine."

"Really?" Jason asked. He'd expected much worse.

"It does look that way."

"I'm very relieved to hear that."

"Yes."

"And Lissa?"

"She is happy to have Donna back, but she is worried about the kidnappers coming back for her. We all are."

There was a long moment of silence.

"Well . . ." Robert said, still looking at Jason.

"I really must go," she said.

"Thank you for the pie," Robert said at Jason.

"Thank you for looking out for my Donna."

She stepped down onto the walk.

Robert, where Cora couldn't see him, bulged his eyes out at Jason and jerked his head toward her, through the wall.

"Mrs. Smith," Jason said reluctantly as she started away.

She turned. "Yes?"

He paused as he tried to think of what he could say, exactly. Her expression was polite as she looked at him and waited.

Finally, he said, "They're not coming back."

He watched for a reaction, and thought he saw a flicker of something within the politeness.

"Thank you, dear," she said softly.

loom was overtaking Venice from the east, darkening the rustling palm trees. Jason imagined it slithering up the canals like smoke, seeping through cracked windows as the imaginary terminator swept across the planet. Mark your doors so that I may pass over you.

He was sitting on his step, watching it, thinking that in some other universe, a Jason Keltner who smoked was gauging the sky and having an evening cigarette. Robert and Martin were inside with Leon, who was sitting with Waldo, who had been tranquilized by the veterinarian. Waldo was cross-eyed and couldn't walk, but the vet was unscathed. Nobody had pushed Martin for an explanation of his behavior earlier, and he hadn't volunteered anything.

The gate banged and Grace Altamirano came up the walk.

She stopped where he was sitting. "I'm here to get my son."

Jason looked at her and said nothing.

"Do I just walk *in*?" she demanded.

In the other universe, the smoking Jason took a long last drag, narrowed his eyes at her, flicked the butt into the dirt.

"Martin," he said into the open door. "Your mom's here."

"I don't need attitude from the likes of you," she said.

Jason watched her.

Martin came to the door and said, "Mom."

"I came to get my son."

Jason looked at his hands.

There was a long, long silence from Martin.

"Did you hear me, Martin? I'm here for my son."

Jason started to get up.

"You can stay," Martin said. He came out, casually took the first step. "Changed your mind, did you, Mom?"

"And what if I did? I'm his mother, and I'm here to get him, so bring him out."

Martin casually took the second step. The hair on the back of Jason's neck began to rise. He started to raise a hand.

"It's all right, chief." Martin took the third step.

The points of Grace's cheekbones reddened. She trembled. "You get him out here right now, Martin Jacob Altamirano, or—"

"Or what, Mom?" Martin's voice was soft. It was the most unyielding sound Jason had ever heard. He looked at his hands again. Grace stopped.

Martin stepped onto the walk. "Or what?"

"Don't you play your games with me, you—"

"Yeah, Mom?"

Her fists were balled at her sides, her mouth tight.

"What were you going to call me, Mom? It was 'little shit' when I was Leon's age, wasn't it, but it looks like he got that hand-me-down."

She slapped him furiously. His head rocked and the sound of the snapping blow ricocheted between the two houses. Fifteen-microsecond pre-delay, that part of Jason's mind guessed; at least a dozen discrete echoes.

Martin said, "You hit me all you want, Mom. You're not taking him from this house."

"You—"

"Don't call me any more names, Mom."

"You—"

"Don't you *call* me any more names."

Jason slid his shoe on the rough step. The sound was stark in the taut moment.

He saw Martin try to relax.

"Here's how it is, Mom. You can either go get the police, or you can go get whatever man drove you here—"

"How dare you—"

"—because that's what it's going to take to budge *my little brother out of this house!*"

Martin's anger showed now, dark and dangerous.

Grace melted.

"Oh, Martin . . ." She shook her head sadly. "This has been so hard on you." She moved close to him. "I've made some mistakes, I know, but I try to be a good mother. We can work everything out. I know we can do better, and he misses his school and his classmates so much—"

Martin said nothing. The muscles of his jaw worked a little.

"Jason," she said, turning. "You can't let him keep a little boy from his mother. Talk to him." She put her hand on his arm.

Jason's breath had stopped at some point, he discovered. He exhaled and pulled his arm away.

She drew back and looked at both of them. "So that's how it is."

"I told you how it is, Mom."

She raised her hand.

"Uh-uh," Martin warned, deadly quiet.

The hand went down obediently. "I will be back." Her voice

was warbly with rage. "You had better believe I will be back. What do you have to say about that, you bastard?" Her voice convulsed, making it impossible for her to yell. "And as for you; we can still press charges for what you did to Frank."

Martin pointed toward the street, a single jab.

She whirled and stalked unsteadily down the walk. A full minute after the ringing clatter of the front gate, a car engine started. Through the gap between the houses, they watched the green Camaro roar away down Ocean.

Martin was very, very still. Jason said nothing and didn't move. The palm trees rustled.

Martin glanced up and looked into the doorway. Jason turned. Leon was standing just inside, cradling Waldo. Robert stood behind him in shadow.

"I love you," Martin said.

47

It was an unusually quiet evening.

Once he was able to stay mostly upright, Waldo had tottered off behind the refrigerator, and Leon sat on the kitchen floor near it, leafing through a comic book. Robert lay on the couch and studied his Hebrew book, sometimes speaking aloud. Martin sat on the floor against the couch and drew in his sketchbook. The door to Robert's room glowed with illumination from the silent rain lamp.

Jason cleaned his studio, untangling tiny dust kitties from under knobs and wiping down dusty top surfaces. He decided to try to back up the settings in his synthesizers onto his computer. That was a very basic thing that everybody else seemed to be able to do.

He was still trying to get the computer to recognize the keyboards when Martin's voice said, "Yo, Jase, gimme a minute of your time, my friend."

He went to the doorframe and leaned in it.

Martin said, "I'ma make this quick."

"Okay."

Martin shook his head. "Every time I think I've got it licked, it just pops right back out somewhere else."

Jason saw Robert trying to understand that too.

". . . what does," Robert said.

"You know what Jason said about how he should've been around for me, but he was off taking care of Dwight, and I said all that about junkies tie it up in knots and make you think it's straight?"

"Yeah?" Jason said.

"Well, look what I did. You can take that same . . . that same . . . that whole same thing and pick it up and just fit it right down on top of how *I* acted. Same bullshit, different junkie. Sure, I'm not running around looking for dope anymore, but do you see how I folded you both all up into my fucked-up family?"

"I think you're whipping yourself unnecessarily," Robert said. "And I don't really understand why. I don't think it's the same thing at all."

"Oh no? Jason said you two should have been here helping me with Leon. That's bullshit. You"—he pointed at Robert—"should have been out getting acting jobs. You had two parts on two TV shows before all this. You had something going. Do you have any roles now?"

Robert looked uncomfortable. "I just have to do more auditions."

"Yeah. And you—I can't remember the last time I ever heard any sounds coming out of all that stuff you got in there."

"Yeah," Jason said, a little ticked. "Well—"

"Don't get me wrong, man. I'm not trying to cut you down, either of you. All I'm saying is, look what happened. You heard Mom yesterday—Frank might press charges."

"All you did was ask for help," Robert said.

"Do you see the mess that created?"

"You can't be attributing that to your past as a drug abuser."

"Look. You guys aren't supposed to have to see addictive behavior coming, not from me. I'm supposed to see it coming from myself and not let it happen, and I didn't. I missed it." Martin shook his head. "I missed it, big time."

Jason's anger sparked. "Yeah, Martin, what an awful person you are. Forget that I've sucked you into my stupid problems too. Forget that you've watched my back way more than I've watched yours. Forget the danger you've gone through for me. No, that doesn't matter. It doesn't matter that maybe I *liked* helping you out and maybe it was *nice* to be on the other side for a change. No, you're right. You're just a jerk. That's how I always think of you: Martin the asshole. How awful you are that you couldn't be perfect when you ask for help." He paused and almost didn't say it: "What a little shit you must be."

Martin's eyes narrowed quickly and Jason saw his temper flare, barely under control. Christ . . . why had he said that?

Martin stared at him. Jason felt awful, but he couldn't think of what to say or do. However Martin responded, he had it coming. He stood and waited, cringing but trying not to let it show.

Martin said, with much feeling, "*Ouch.*"

He turned his head and closed his eyes and raised his eyebrows. "Ouch!"

Jason said in a rush, "I'm sorry. That wasn't mine to say." He looked at Robert. Robert had a braced-for-impact face, his lips pulled back. Jason felt the same expression in the muscles of his own face.

"Oo," Martin said. "That *smarts.*"

"I'm sorry."

"Whew." Martin blew out air.

"Sorry."

Martin didn't answer at first. He was looking at the wall.

"Don't be sorry," he said eventually. He scratched his head.

"No, don't ever be sorry for telling me the truth."

"You're not a junkie," Robert said.

"Robert—we'll argue about it later."

"You're definitely, definitely too hard on yourself."

Jason said, "You know how you said if it was eight-thirteen A.M. when you started doing drugs, it's still eight-thirteen A.M. when you get off them?"

"Yeah, so?"

"You're like, seven A.M. the next day, I think."

"Oh definitely," Robert jumped in, nodding encouragingly. "Seven thirty-five, seven-forty."

Martin snorted a little despite himself and brushed away the comment with his hands. "All right, guys."

"Like, almost a quarter to eight," Robert said.

"I got it, Robert."

"Maybe ten 'til."

"Yeah, thanks, I got it, Robert." Martin got up. "You know what I could really use right now is a big hug from my li'l bro."

Leon, sitting on the kitchen floor, kept reading his comic book. "What if I don't want to give you a hug?"

Martin went to the doorway. "Well, then I'd be very disappointed."

Leon didn't respond.

"You want to talk, Le?"

Leon shook his head.

Martin slid down the doorway to sit with him. "What is it? You've been pretty stressed out over this stuff with Donna, but she's okay. We got her back. She's safe."

Leon stood up. "Here, kitty."

"Le, I'd like to know what's on your mind."

"Kitty kitty . . ."

"Are you worried about Waldo?"

"Come on, kitty . . ."

"Bro, I'm out here. I'm not inside your head. If there's something you want to talk about, you have to tell me, because I can't read your mind. But just guessing, if I were you, I'd want to talk about Mom."

Leon pushed out of the kitchen and through the front room into the bedroom.

Martin spread his hands and looked at Jason and Robert.

"I have no idea," Robert said. Jason shook his head.

Martin stood up to follow Leon. Leon came out of the bedroom with the bag he'd brought his things in from Long Beach and flung it across the room against the door. It was full. He barged by Martin, pulled the cat carrier out from under the table, and knelt by the refrigerator.

"Here, Waldo. Here, kitty."

"If it's because I sent you off with Mrs. Smith, I feel really bad about that, and I want to talk to you about it."

Waldo sneezed behind the refrigerator. Leon pressed against the refrigerator door and tried to reach back.

Martin shook his head. "No, no, don't just give me the silent treatment. Family shouldn't play that. Whatever's eating you, you tell me about it and we take care of it. We fix it."

"Like you fixed—" Leon bit off the rest. He stood up and tried to rock the refrigerator. "Come *on*, kitty!"

"Like I fixed what?"

Leon succeeded in moving the refrigerator a little. Waldo didn't show. "He won't come out!"

"Okay," Martin sighed. He started to get up. "You want to ignore me, I can't do anything about it. You're not a little kid. When you're up to it, you just—"

"Like you fixed the kidnappers?" Leon said, facing the refrigerator.

"Le..."

Leon pointed at Jason. "He said they got killed!"

"No," Jason said after a moment. "I didn't." It was a half-truth. He hadn't said the kidnappers were dead, but he'd meant it.

"You're a liar," Leon accused him, beginning to tremble. "You lie and lie and lie!"

Martin said, "That man's no liar. Understand this."

"I've—" Jason began.

"You lie and lie!" Leon insisted. He was shaking, looking at Martin now. "I don't want to go to prison!"

"Bro—" Martin shook his head. "Why are you talking about prison?"

"You don't know anything! We have to *go*! Come *on*, kitty!"

Martin touched Leon's side. "I'd like you to explain it to me."

Leon squirmed away and ran into the front room. He snatched his bag up off the carpet. "He said I'm an accomplice and I'd go to prison too if he did." His voice was beginning to break.

"Who said this?"

"He said—" Leon's voice broke. "He said anything that happened to him would happen to me too."

"*Who*, bro?"

Leon was crying and holding his stomach now, the bag dangling off his arm. "We have to *go*! I don't want to get *killed*! He won't come *out*!" He doubled over, beginning to retch through his tears.

Shock was on Martin's face as he glanced at Jason and Robert. He went through the front room and got down on his knees to put his arms around his little brother. Leon's face broke into an awful grimace, and without hesitation, he clutched at Martin and cried into his shirt. "I don't want to get killed!" he cried. "I don't want to go to prison!"

"It's all right, little man," Martin said. "It's all right. Whatever it is, we can fix it."

"I don't want to get killed—" Leon's words were so blurred now that they were almost incomprehensible.

"Whoever told you that, they were wrong," Martin said. "You don't have to go to prison. You're not going to get killed. None of that's going to happen to you."

Leon looked past Martin at Jason through a glaze of tears.

Jason said, "Nobody got killed."

"You're a liar!"

Jason opened his mouth to speak but could say nothing. He and Martin looked at each other, helpless.

"You're lying," Leon sobbed, the words distorted by racking gasps.

He was right. They were.

"I'M NOT," ROBERT said suddenly.

Everyone looked at him.

The Giant walked assuredly to Leon and squatted. "Have I ever lied to you, young Leon?"

Still clutching Martin, Leon's tears slowed slightly as he tried to think.

"Ever?" Robert pressed.

Leon shook his head. His face and Martin's shirt were soaked. "I don't, I don't think so."

"Everything will be fine," Robert said. "You can trust me, boy, and I won't lie to you. Is that understood?"

Looking desperately into Robert's eyes, Leon nodded.

"It's all right," Robert said. "Whatever is causing you hurt, we can find a way to take care of it."

"It's okay, li'l bro," Martin said.

"Do you believe me?" Robert said.

Leon nodded.

"Very good!" Robert smiled and tousled Leon's hair. "Now, you have to tell me. Who told you these things?"

"The—the kidnapper."

No one spoke. Outside, some kids were walking on the sidewalk, talking loudly.

Robert said, "You know these kidnappers, do you?"

Leon put his face into Martin's shirt and nodded, very slightly and very slowly.

Martin rubbed Leon's back. "Do you want to tell me who it was?"

Leon shook his head.

"Young Leon," Robert said. Leon pulled his head up very reluctantly and looked at him. "You will not go to prison, and I promise that you are not going to get killed. Do you trust me?"

Leon hesitated, and then nodded, his face still buried in Martin's shoulder.

They all waited.

Martin said, "Do you want to whisper it to me?"

Leon shook his head.

Robert said, "Do you want to write it down?"

Leon nodded. He sat up a little and wiped his eyes.

Jason picked Martin's sketchbook and pencil up off the floor. The sketches on the open page were of Leon sitting by the refrigerator. He turned to a blank page and gave it to Leon.

Leon got up with the sketchbook and went to the hinged kitchen table.

"What should I call it?"

Robert said, "I say you shall call it 'What I Have to Say.' "

WHAT I HAVE TO SAY
BY LEON

I was helping my Moms boyfreind Ed sell drugs, he gave me a cut of the take. He said if you ever tell I go to prison and you do too. I did'nt want to sell drugs. I mean I did at first but, then I did'nt. He said whatever happens to me the same thing happens to you so keep your dam mouth shut Le. I said OK. He said if I go down you go down too.

Hes the one who kid-napped Dona, I could tell because I recognized his voice and when he kid-napped her told me I better keep quite and poked me in the chest. Now hes killed and I dont want to get killed or go to prison either.

The End.

"I HEARD YOU," Leon said to Jason. "You told Martin somebody killed Ed."

Robert finished reading the story and looked up.

"Leon," he said. "Do you still trust me?"

Leon nodded.

Robert gave him his story back and said, "Nobody killed Ed.

He's never coming back to hurt anyone. Nobody is going to kill you. Do you understand?"

"Is he in prison?"

"I can't tell you," Robert said. "Will you trust me?"

Leon stared at Robert. "I don't know."

Martin said, "We can't tell you everything now, but we'll tell you when you're older. I promise."

"I, too, promise," Robert said.

"Are you sure he's not killed?"

"Positive, li'l bro. You don't have to worry about anybody killing you or sending you to prison. I promise I'll do everything I can to be here for you and make a family for you. Will you trust me?"

Leon looked at Robert.

"You are a brave lad," said The Giant. "We trust you. Will you trust us?"

"Yes."

Leon relaxed. *Thanks*, Martin mouthed at Robert, behind Leon's back. Robert nodded very seriously.

WALDO CAME OUT from behind the refrigerator that night, and took possession of his basket.

"I DON'T BELIEVE in lying to children," Robert worried later, lying on the couch in the living room. Martin and Leon had gone out for late-night big brother/little brother ice cream at the Denny's near the Bay City pier. It didn't fix anything, Martin had admitted to Jason before they'd left, but trying to make a few good memories couldn't hurt.

Jason leaned in the doorway to his studio. "It was the best thing there was to do," he said. "The Giant was the only one who could have done it. Your most meaningful role to date. You're a compassionate and generous man. I'm proud to be your friend."

"Yeah." Robert frowned and picked up his Hebrew book. Then he put it down. "Thanks. Do you think maybe Martin's right, and I put my energies in the wrong directions?"

"I don't know."

"I mean, I get all intensely into chess, or bread baking, or whatever—" He shook his head.

Jason said, "Or bar mitzvahs, or learning how to tap three with one hand at the same time as two with the other, or getting involved in your friends' problems when you should be sending out head shots and doing auditions?"

"Yeah." Robert frowned. "Yeah. Or, I hope you don't mind my saying, doing CD-ROM game music instead of composing for real."

"I don't mind. I don't know. Maybe it's possible to do both, but I guess I don't know how."

Robert stared at the wall.

Jason went into his studio and undressed. Exhausted, thankful for the chance to rest, he hung his shirt on his office chair and his jeans on one of his speaker supports, and then slid into his futon and into a wide, wet spot that was soaked through his blanket to the bottom sheet.

Snug in his little basket, Waldo watched Jason carry the trash bag of wet bedding out the door, on its way to the Laundromat.

I t was a huge apartment complex just on the Valley side of the hills. Corporations quartered newly transferred managers there until semi-permanent housing could be found. The well-off newly divorced moved there when they were too depressed to have any other preference. Every three buildings, a swimming pool burnt the air with chlorine. Next to each, enclosed common areas with brown-painted tables and canned soda dispensers went unused.

Apartment J–434 was in the tenth building, on the fourth floor, down a creaky, thin-carpeted corridor of brown doors with mechanical pushbells and hand-lettered name slips on them. The slip under the bell said "Burnout" in black ink. Martin rang.

Dwight's dark blonde beard was on its way back, cut through with a scar that ran down the left side of his head, crossing the strap of his black eyepatch. His good eye was reddened. He wore a black outback hat and a fringed jacket. His hair was short. He didn't seem surprised to see Jason. A man who never showed surprise, Jason realized, was a man who always seemed in control.

Dwight gestured at the patch brusquely with the curve of his cane. "Always wanted one of these." He laughed a little, uncomfortably.

Martin pointed at the name on the door. "Burnout?"

"It's French, man. It's pronounced 'Burnoo.'"

Jason thought that was mildly funny, but Martin said, "You really want that on your door?"

"If the chapeau fits, man."

"You can work on that later. But . . . we're early because Jase wanted to talk to you before we went. We came in separate cars—he's not going to the meeting."

"Jason the hero," Dwight said. "Well, like I said, Dwight Cooper pays his debts. Whatever you want to know."

The inside of the apartment was dry and sober. The carpet was green and the oak entertainment center was scratched. It was no less cheery than any hotel room in purgatory.

"What's up?" Sitting in his leather on the striped, scratchy couch between the throw cushions, Dwight looked like a scorpion in a row of stuffed animals.

Jason said, "I don't need to know why you did anything you did, but I'd like to know what happened. I know you gave your gun to Ed in exchange for drugs, because that was in your statement to the police. But the rest, I'm shaky on."

"That's a lot of story, man."

Martin looked at his watch. "We got thirty minutes."

"You sure you want the whole ugly thing?"

"Yeah."

Dwight's mouth quirked. "I dunno, man. There's stuff I didn't tell the cops, stuff I don't want anyone to know."

Jason nodded. "The only person I'll tell is Robert, because he loves Donna. Besides that, it won't go any further."

"I dunno."

Then he started talking.

Hurricane's Last Gig

I think I'm all cried out right now.

Johnny Ray was my brother. Not by blood, you both understand, but by all the other things.

I remember one time . . . this was one of his favorite stories. We were doing this gig at the Fairway. We were doing "Set It Up." He always said it was "Samantha," but it was definitely "Set It Up." It's time for Johnny Ray's solo, and we come chuggin' out of the turnaround and everything's bookin' along just fine. Now, I'm out front, so I can't see any of this, but I can hear fine, and Johnny Ray's just *got* it. I mean, it's just a fuckin' beautiful solo. The way he tells it, he says, "Man, it was the best tone I ever had, that night, just beautiful, you know, with just that . . . that nice touch of harmonic distortion and ring, and everything's beautiful, so I sorta turn around, you know, to smile at my amp because it's doing such a beautiful job— and I turn around just in time to see it go completely up in smoke and flames, whomp!" And then he'd shake his head and say, "Best tone I ever had."

We always said he should get an endorsement deal for Bic lighters.

. . .

We came up together. We were from the same place. His daddy was a salesman, bought him his first guitar, and we hooked up, you know, just two white boys playing the same places, trying to make it real.

He was more than a brother. Man, we'd play together, we'd drink together, we'd score together . . . drugs, women, everything. I'll never forget the day we got us our first record advance. That's the day he bought me that gun.

I couldn't just fade away. I couldn't let it go. But you know you can't make music without money. There was this guy that came up with money for Johnny Ray's solo albums, so we called him and he put up the funds for the record and the tour and he got to hang around and pretend he was Mr. Big Shot, call himself "executive producer" and all that shit, but he really didn't do shit. We did it all. Shit, man, everybody's self-producing these days. You do it long enough, you know how to do it. Blue Oyster Cult produces all their own stuff now—they been in enough studios, they know how to do it.

You got to have a tour. No tour means no airplay, and no airplay means no sales.

At that point, I'd been clean for four years. Four long, hard-won years, man. Shit. Day of the first gig with the new band, I freak. One of the roadies in Long Beach had this connection nearby. I didn't have any cash, and there was nobody to watch Donna. I stuck her in the car and grabbed that nice old gun out of my guitar case and drove out to see that connection. That little voice was yelling at me the whole way—don't do it! Don't blow it! You got something good going here, man, you know? I knew exactly what I was doing, exactly. It was like watching myself. I told Donna to stay in the car and I found that guy Ed, and traded the gun for a fix. Why? I can't tell you. Nobody knows why a junkie does anything, least alone himself. Nobody should have ever trusted me to take care of her. That was the day you helped Johnny Ray get me into the car for that pre-tour gig. He found out where I was and fired that roadie's ass and came and got me.

You should take this as a lesson. Never trust a junkie less than five years clean.

Man, that tour.

We thought, no problem, Pearl Jam did their own promotion, Zeppelin paid promoters what they wanted to pay. Prince could do it. We're a name act, we'll draw. But man, that tour . . .

No. Skimming wasn't the problem. Everybody will always try to skim, that's a given. There's ways to deal with that, ticket counting and such. No. Our problem was we went out with too much production, way, way too much. We thought we'd make it up on the door. *That* was our big mistake. Three semis and a bus, plus flying the band, plus lights and pyro and sound, and the door sales didn't happen. We're spending a hundred grand a day just like it's water.

We had this backup plan.

It was Johnny Ray's idea. I don't want to seem like I'm putting it all on other people, but man, I didn't want nothing to do with no kidnap scam. But he knew about little Lissa's insurance, and Donna likes him. Liked him, I mean. He said he would just take her off someplace for a few days and we'd cash in on the insurance and bail out the tour and no one would get hurt. Donna would get a few days' vacation and the tour would go on. Everybody happy except the insurance company, and shit, who cares about them? Fuck insurance companies. So, okay, whatever. Johnny Ray's getting off on all the planning and the, like, logistics, you know? and it's not like I ever thought we were ever gonna actually do it.

But all of a sudden, there we are, bleeding money, and it starts looking like maybe we're gonna do it after all. Johnny Ray starts planning this and figuring that. He did it for me, man. It was all for me. He knew how much that tour meant to me. He hired that security lady to make it all look good, but he knew he could snatch Donna anyway. He was on the inside, you know?

Then we had that scare, when Lissa showed up and everybody thought she was kidnapping Donna. That's the moment I realized I couldn't go through with it. I'm no hero, man, but I couldn't let it happen. Even totally wasted, I couldn't do that to my only little girl. Even if she didn't know what was going on. She was the last precious thing to me, the one last true thing. Do you understand? She was the one last true thing.

You probably thought when I said you saved my little girl, I meant you saved her from Lissa. Well, think again.

And that was that. Once you start bouncing paychecks on the road, man, your tour's over. So we said thank you very much and everybody went home.

Me and Johnny Ray didn't talk to each other much after we got home. Maybe we could've got over it with time, but . . .

I always tell my whole life story to dope pushers, man. I know I do it, but I never knew why.

I went to the house to see my little girl. Everything was so empty. I got worried and let myself in. I know where the spare key is. I almost didn't answer the phone when it rang, but I was too worried, man, and too wasted.

When I found the note . . . Man, I freaked. I knew who it was. I knew it was that pusher dude, because I had a bad, bad feeling ever since I told him the plan. I told him the plan, and then when we didn't do the plan, he did the plan. I knew it was him. I could feel it in my bones.

I called Johnny Ray and told him, and Johnny Ray said he'd take care of it. He went to get her.

You know what happened.

With the very gun he bought me out of friendship all those years ago, that I gave away for a fix that day.

He loved little Donna, man. He loved her almost as much as I did.

After you came and left me on the floor at the house, that Ed called again. He said he wanted a mil. I said where's Johnny Ray, Johnny Ray was supposed to talk to you. He said I don't know what you're talking about, get me a mil or Donna's . . . Donna's dead.

I'm so scared, man, I'm scared, I'm freaked, I'm wasted. Where am I going to get a mil? Nobody trusts me like that. The only thing I can think is I call the promoter shark dude who backed the tour and he turns me down. But he's my only hope, you know? So I get on the bike to go see him, and you know the rest.

I hate to say this.

Maybe I shouldn't say it . . .

I should be honest. I got to start being honest again. Today's the first day, right?

Without the Dwight Cooper Band up there in the spotlights and touring and all that shit, there wasn't no Hurricane Hoffer. You ever heard his solo stuff?

What'd you think?

Yeah, so you know what I'm saying.
So maybe it wasn't all for me like I said.

Lord, I miss my bro.

I thought maybe if the tour ... he'd ...

Sorry about that. Guess I wasn't as cried out as I thought, you know?

I found out today, Atomic's re-releasing the whole catalogue. Nothing like death to get the vampires crawling out of their coffins.

N ice shirt," Martin said as he and Leon came in, carrying shopping bags. Jason was sprawled across the arms of the living room chair, reading photocopies that had come in the mail. "What's that?"

"Take a look."

"Hey," Martin said, taking them. "These are custody papers." He flipped through them and looked up suddenly. "Wow, he actually did it."

"Did what?" Leon asked.

Martin gave the papers to Leon. "Recognize this?"

Leon studied them. "They look like those same papers, only with other people's names on them."

Martin pointed. "See this here? Dwight granted custody of Donna to Lissa Court."

"Cora called just a while ago," Jason said. "Donna's settling into Lissa's apartment in New York. Frannie didn't like having a child around, so she moved out. It's just mother and daughter."

"What do you think about that?"

"I don't like Lissa, but I think she'll probably be an excellent mother."

"You know, I kinda have that same feeling. I just wanted to hear you say it. What's Cora going to do, now that Donna's got a mommy?"

"She's not sure, but she couldn't talk too long. She has a date tonight."

"Yeah? Anyone we—" Martin's eyes widened at Jason's grin. "Oh. Oh, no, don't tell me."

"I told him if he doesn't treat her good, I'll put sugar in the gas tank of that nice Caddy."

Leon said, "Linseed oil works better."

They both looked at him.

"I never did it!" he yelled. "I just heard!"

"Let's just back up time," Jason said, "and say Leon didn't just say that, and assume that he understands why putting linseed oil in someone's gas tank is not a good idea, right? Okay? Good. So how was counseling?"

"I think it went pretty well," Martin said. "What do you think, Le?"

"It was okay. We saw Robert." He offered the papers back to Martin, who pointed at Jason instead. "He looked different."

Jason took the photocopies from Leon and slipped them into their torn envelope. "Different how?"

Martin said, "You know that look he gets when he's got something new he never thought about?"

"Oh. Did he say anything?"

"Not really. We said hi, and he said hi, and then he went out and we went in."

"Oh."

"Well, anyway, don't worry, Jase. We just stopped by to drop off Le's new school clothes before we go out again."

"No hurry."

After Leon had petted Waldo and gone into the bathroom, Martin said, "I got something to tell you."

Something went heavy in Jason's chest. "Yeah?"

"Frank, the guy whose nose you broke?"

"Yeah?"

Martin sighed unhappily. "He's married." He shook his head. "I thought he might be. So I wouldn't worry about him pressing charges. He'd have to tell his wife he was with Mom."

"Oh." Jason frowned at the envelope in his hands. "Thanks."

"I know," Martin said. "But at least something good comes of it. And, uh, I hope you don't mind my asking, but where's that gun?"

"I took it apart and dropped the pieces into the canals. I didn't know what else to do with it. I don't know how long they'll take to corrode, but that's salt water."

"Sounds good." Martin nodded. He glanced out the open front door. "What's the trash bag?"

"Waldo peed in my bed again. I'm throwing the sheets away this time."

"We gotta do something about that."

"I know. I had to buy new sheets today. It hasn't gotten through to the mattress yet, so I got this liquid-proof pad thing, too. I'm trying to remember to leave my door closed."

Martin's lips twitched a little. "Sorry, chief. It's just funny that after all this, you have met your match, and it's a cat."

"Yeah," Jason said. "Funny."

ROBERT SHOWED UP after Martin and Leon left. Jason was in the bathroom, shaving, with the door ajar and his shirt hanging on the knob.

"Hey," Robert said, knocking.

"Hey."

Robert nudged the door open. "Guess what I found!" From behind the door, his hand came around and presented a glass bottle with a yellow paper label that said "Manhattan Special."

"Hey, where'd you get that?"

"They have them at the liquor store on Speedway. I never knew what they were. Um, can I show you something else?"

"Sure."

Robert hesitated, and then offered a stack of napkins with black handwriting on them.

Jason dried one hand and took them, leaning against the sink with half a face of shaving cream. The letter had a lot of corrections and cross-outs, and the ink had bled into the napkin fiber. And, then, Robert's handwriting was rarely legible to start with.

Dear Donna,

You were a very special little girl, and I hope you had a nice childhood after I stopped knowing you.

I don't know if you will remember me by the time you read this, but you knew me as The Giant. My real name is Robert Goldstein. If everything goes well between my writing this letter and your receiving it, then yes, I am <u>that</u> Robert Goldstein. I hope you liked my last movie. I hope it wasn't <u>Revenge of the Cannibal Pumpkins</u>.

Anyway, my analyst thought that writing this letter might help both you in the future, and me now. Your mother doesn't want you to see me right now, which makes sense, but Mrs. Smith said she would keep this letter for you until you have grown up more. I want you to know that although you might still be harboring hurt feelings from when you were little, I only wanted to protect you from the terrible dangers I was told you needed protection from. I didn't understand until much later that I had been misled.

I've been told that you do not remember your kidnapping ordeal. I hope that's the case. If you would ever like to get in touch with me, I would love to hear from you. I don't expect to be living in the same place as when you and your mother knew me, but until I have my mansion in Malibu, I have opened a post office box for my acting needs. The address is at the top of this letter.

I hope you are happy. I'm sorry I ever made you cry. I wish I could take it back, but time flows on like a crashing river of rainbow-colored flowers.

Love,
Robert
The Giant

"It's nice, Robert. I think she'll love you for it when she's older."

"What do you think about the river of rainbow flowers?" He bit his lip crookedly and looked sideways at his letter.

Jason studied the napkins with him.

"I say keep it."

"I'm going to copy it over. I thought you might want to write one too."

"I'll think about it."

Robert looked suddenly impish and said, "One more thing." He tapped the three-on-two pattern on the doorframe.

"Keep doing that," Jason said. "Okay, now stop with one hand and keep the other hand going."

"Crap," Robert said as he lost it.

"That's for looking smug."

"Gee, thanks." He tried it again and failed. "Anyway, don't worry. I'm not staying. I'm going to buy writing paper and then go see a movie."

"No problem."

HE WAS TIDYING his studio when he found another editorial from Waldo.

He looked at the onscreen computer clock and swore as he stripped the soaked bedding off the futon and put it into another plastic trash bag. He must have left his door open when he was shaving. Waldo watched from his darling basket in the living room as Jason took the trash bag outside and picked up the earlier one.

After stuffing both bags into the cans behind the house, he came back in and regarded the patchy beast glaring up from his little bed.

What was the most practical response here? Not just a response that would let Jason vent, but one that might alter the behavior? One that was appropriate. His responses hadn't all been so appropriate of late. Make a plan, do the plan.

Can't threaten a cat. Can't talk to him. Can't explain to him. Can't toss him out. How to communicate with a cat?

I'm the alpha male here.

Good plan.

He booted Waldo out of the basket and unzipped.

50

T he soft music floating from his studio into the living room was pierced by the bang of the front gate. Maybe it would be someone visiting the front house.

A knock on the door dashed that hope. He sighed, moved Waldo from his lap, brushed fur off his new shirt and pants, and got up from the couch.

Marisa was on the step, dark hair loose over shoulders lovingly displayed by her strapless dress. Dusk shimmered over the palm trees on Ocean. Past her, he could see the trash cans, the tied bags of ruined sheets, and Waldo's short-lived cat bed.

"Oh, it's dark in there," she said.

Jason said, "You have got to be kidding." Waldo purred and bumped around his ankles.

"Oh, what a nice little kitty." She stooped and petted Waldo. The diamond on her left hand glinted gray in the twilight, next to its matched wedding ring. She smiled. It was pretty. "You look nice when you shave. I forgot you actually know how to dress sometimes."

"Thank you." Jason glanced outside for signs of Jack West.

"May I come in?"

"I don't think—"

"Don't worry, Jack's not around."

"Marisa, why do you keep—"

Sometimes, you just don't get to understand why.

He shut up.

"I know, Jason, but I'd really like to talk to you. I just think I may have made a— Oh." Her gaze went behind him and her eyes widened.

"Marisa," he said, stepping aside. "This is Sarah."

"Oh, you're Marisa!" Sarah said delightedly, moving into the doorway beside him. "I've heard so much about you. Would you like to come in? We're just having a nice glass of wine before we decide not to go to a movie."

"Oh, no thank you." Marisa stepped back politely. "I just stopped by for a moment. Well. It was nice meeting you."

"And it was a pleasure meeting you." Sarah beamed at her. Waldo butted Jason's ankles.

Marisa stopped on the walkway and looked as innocent as a politician.

"He's not very good in bed."

Sarah looked at Jason questioningly.

He spread his hands. "I meant to tell you."

"But that would have left you with only two things."

She smiled at him, momentarily distracting God. Spacetime jarred. Somewhere in Athens, the heads of a dozen old marble statues flew off and rocketed into the sky.